Just Wide Enough for Two

By: Kacey M. Martin

*I spilt the dew -
But took the morn, -
I chose this single star
From out the wide night's numbers -
Sue - forevermore!*

All rights reserved. No portion of this book may be reproduced in any form without permission from the publisher, except as permitted by U.S. copyright law. For permissions contact: KaceyMartinLaw@Gmail.com.

Copyright © 2022 Kacey M. Martin

This book is a work of fiction. Any references to historical events, real people, or real places are used fictitiously. Other names, characters, places and events are products of the author's imagination, and any resemblance to actual events, places or persons, living or dead, is entirely coincidental.

Cover photograph is the intellectual property of Kacey M. Martin. Taken at the Homestead on August 21, 2022, Amherst, Massachusetts. All other photographs contained herein were acquired through use of public domain.

To: Nisha – my dearest friend.

April 1847

It was the scream that woke Susan Gilbert. The loud, high, ear-piercing scream that could only belong to one person – her sister, Mattie. Quickly, she got out of bed and put on her robe. The air in the room was cold as ice and she slid her feet into a pair of slippers and cinched the thick robe around her waist before opening the door to follow the noise. She looked over to her sister's empty bed, the quilt lazily thrown back. As she began to walk down the large front stairs, Susan could hear the shouting coming from the parlor begin to turn into audible words and she stopped for a moment in the hallway to listen.

"You cannot do this!" Her sister shrieked.

But there was only the calm, and demure voice of her Aunt Sophia in response, which was too low for Susan to understand. Not wanting to linger in the shadows any longer, Susan turned the corner and entered the room.

Across the large parlor, their Aunt Sophia sat in a tall, wing-backed chair. The fireplace was roaring and the wet, grey sky of the spring morning seemed to make the bright glow of the flames the only light in the room. It bounced and swirled off of her aunt's cold, grey eyes making them look more menacing and relentless than ever. Behind their aunt, their uncle stood with his hands folded behind his back, silently staring out into the greyness of the morning.

After their parents died a few years back, Susan and her sister, Mattie, had been forced to move from their family home in Deerfield, Massachusetts to Geneva, New York to live with their aunt and uncle. When they first moved to New York, the family would travel frequently between New York and Massachusetts as part of her uncle's business affairs, of which Susan knew very little. Unfortunately, they now spent most of their days in New York and Susan had not returned to Massachusetts in over two years.

Their aunt's house was very grand with all the trappings and furnishings a young lady could ask for. It was a modern house, or what some were calling a "Victorian style" house, after the young Queen of England. At the house, their uncle employed a maid, a butler, and a cook. She and her sister shared a room, but only because they chose to do so when they first arrived out of fear and loneliness following the death of their parents. There was a parlor with a beautiful piano, a dining room, and a wide porch that stretched around the front of the house. A large turret rested on the front corner of the house which made it unique from its bulky, box-like colonial style neighbors.

It was all very elaborate compared to the simple home Susan and her siblings lived in with her parents back in Massachusetts and Susan had no real reason to complain about her current situation. She was well cared for, well-nourished, and even had a private tutor to further her education. Her Aunt Sophia, though not a particularly warm or kind woman, was not in any way cruel to her and her sister, and her uncle, on the rare occasion when he was present, always brought them sweets or complimented their dresses. And yet, even with all this, Susan Gilbert was unhappy with her life in New York.

She was over the moon with joy when she learned just last month that she and her sister would be moving back to Massachusetts to begin the fall semester at Amherst Academy. Massachusetts always felt like her home, even though she had not lived there for several years. It was where she was raised, where her parents lived before they died, and where she had some of her happiest memories. She was already counting the days until she could return to the place she called home and escape this beautiful prison.

Near the sofa, her sister stood holding a crumpled piece of paper, her eyes swollen and red, her hair a mess of blonde knots and undone curls.

"I am sorry my dear, but the arrangements are made," Sophia continued, folding wrinkled hands across her thin lap.

"Susan, stop her. Make her see reason!" Mattie came rushing towards Susan, throwing her arms around her theatrically.

"What on Earth has happened?" Susan asked, petting her sister's tussled hair and looking over her shoulder towards their aunt who, as usual, remained both unmoved and unphased by Mattie's dramatics.

Mattie handed her the crumpled piece of paper she was clutching.

"Your brother, Dwight, and I have been in communications regarding your sister's recent . . . behavior." Sophia paused intentionally on the word before continuing, "and we have reached a mutually agreeable conclusion that your sister should receive her formal education at a more . . . remote institution."

With the last word, Sophia raised a single eyebrow towards Mattie, her long, pale fingers gripping the end of the armchair tighter. Susan furrowed her eyebrows, confused at the connotation. Mattie stopped sobbing into her neck and stood up straight.

"She's sending me off to Michigan. Michigan!" Mattie proclaimed. "I suppose I can be friends with the copper miners and marry an Indian while I'm at it!"

Mattie walked over to the sofa and threw herself down dramatically, covering her face and weeping uncontrollably. Susan shook her head trying to process the new information and remained silent. Sophia returned her steely gaze and full attention to Mattie once more.

"Perhaps you should be less concerned with marrying Indians and more concerned with finding a suitable man who *will* accept you, especially after your insidious romance with the town guttersnipe."

Their uncle cleared his throat and Susan watched as he shot a warning look down at his wife. Sophia pretended to ignore his gaze and pursed her lips in defiance.

So that's what this is all about, Susan thought to herself.

Edward Johnson was the local blacksmith's apprentice, with whom Mattie was a tryst for the last several months. Susan had been a cover and alibi for her sister's frequent evening disappearances, even going so far as to lie to her aunt directly about her sister's whereabouts several times. But now, it appeared that their little secret was out and the consequences would be severe.

Ever being the peacemaker, Susan cleared her throat.

"Aunt," she began, stepping closer towards her sister. "I understand your intentions with all this, truly I do, but is there not a less . . . extreme measure to be taken? Could she not still accompany me to Amherst in the summer? Surely there are new opportunities for her there?"

Her aunt curled her lip and snorted. "And have you covering for her just like you have here? Absolutely not. She should have had a man looking after her all along. You both should have. Besides you two clearly cannot be trusted to maintain each other's virtues, so you shall be split up at once. Your sister will go to live with your brother, Dwight, and his wife in Michigan and you shall live with your sister, Harriett and her husband, Willaim Cutler in Amherst."

Sophia unfolded her hands and rang a silver bell that rested on her side table. A few seconds later, their maid, Abigail, entered the room.

"You called, ma'am?"

"Yes," Sophia replied, "kindly pack Mattie's things at once. She will be taking the train to Detroit first thing in the morning."

"In the morning?" Mattie shrieked, standing up and planting her foot firmly into the wooden floor. "I won't even have time to say goodbye to -"

"That is precisely the point." Sophia cut her off.

Susan interjected. "Surely, she could bid farewell to her friends in town, Aunt? You would not have her leaving them without a scrap of news, would you? What would they say at weekly Meeting? Or down at the mercantile? It would reflect poorly on the whole family - her sudden, unexplained absence."

Susan knew just what to say to give her aunt pause. The family's reputation is what caused this in the first place. She would certainly reconsider her decision to preserve its dignity now.

Sophia contemplated this a moment. "I will allow her to say her goodbyes to her friends right here, in this room. We shall both be present for the pleasantries, to ensure nothing dishonorable is said about the family by this ungrateful snipe." Sophia shot Mattie a hateful look.

Mattie began to protest once more but Susan looked at her shaking her head as if to say, "take what you can get."

"Fine," Mattie replied, "but how will I even invite my friends to come to see me on such short notice?"

Susan jumped in at once. "Make me a list of whom you would like to see and I shall go now myself and invite them to come by tonight."

They both watched in silence as Sophia contemplated any potential negative impact such a setup may have. Satisfied with the decision, she obliged with a quick nod of her head. As the two of them left the room, Susan could overhear the deep, low voice of her uncle.

"Sophia, must you really send them away? If Mattie is the problem, why must Susan also go?"

She stopped in the hallway to hear her aunt's reply. "You know as well as I do that Susan is complicit in all of this. Besides, it is also for Harriett's benefit that we are sending Susan to her. Not just Susan's."

The sound of her aunt's chair squeaking meant that Sophia was standing and would soon be around the corner. Susan quickly turned and raced up the steps.

She threw open the door to her and Mattie's bedroom to see a whirlwind of dresses, lace, gloves, and carpet bags. Poor Abigail was in the middle of the tornado trying to delicately fold the fine clothes, but as soon as she would get one folded, Mattie would be right behind her throwing more into her face. Mattie began to curse their aunt under her breath.

"Mattie," Susan begged, grabbing her sister by the arms. "Please see reason here. Make your list and I will go and find your friends for you." Susan handed her a sheet of paper and a pencil. "And for heaven's sake, stop making so much work for poor Abigail. This is not her fault."

Mattie stopped crying and looked at the mound of dresses the maid was attempting to sort through and felt instant remorse.

"Oh, Abigail," Mattie said, flinging her arms around the large woman's thick, dark neck.

Abigail hugged Mattie back whispering, "shhh," quietly into her ear as she rocked her back and forth.

"Michigan ain't all that bad, you know," Abigail continued. "I hear there are lots of new things to do out there. Besides, I hear they got a lot of gentlemen passing through on their way out west. Big, strong, horseback riding gentleman," she said, pulling back and looking at Mattie with a flirtatious glimmer in her eye.

Mattie began to laugh through the tears. "Oh, Abigail," she said, hugging her once more. "What will I ever do without you?"

"Oh, you're gonna be just fine. Now, you listen to your sister and make that list quick, you hear?"

"But, what about Mr. Johnson?" Mattie said, turning to Susan.

Susan and Abigail exchanged a glance. Susan turned around a pulled out a second sheet of paper, shoving it in Mattie's direction. She was annoyed that after all of this chaos, the only thing Mattie could think about was her childish beau.

"Write to him and I will make sure he gets it," Susan stated curtly.

Abigail looked down and continued folding Mattie's clothes, a brief smile growing on her face. Mattie threw her arms around her sister and hugged her so tightly that it made even her corset feel loose.

"You really are the best sister in the world." She leaned over and kissed Susan on the cheek.

It was the kindest thing Mattie had ever said to her and a small tear dripped down Susan's face as she realized for the first time what all of this truly meant. Susan was losing a sister tomorrow. She would be all alone here until she left for Amherst in a few months, and even then, she would be without Mattie. She was worried for Mattie, being so far away in Michigan. Although Mattie was a year older, Susan had always been the mother goose between the two of them. She defended Mattie to their father as small children, covered for her with their aunt, cleaned her wounds when she was injured and read her stories long into the night.

Susan felt an emptiness begin to grow inside her at the thought of losing her sister. She wiped the tear and cleared her throat.

"Just write the letter," she said firmly.

"What will happen to you when I'm gone?" Mattie said, her eyes now bloodshot and almost swollen shut with puffy tears.

"You heard our aunt. I will still return to Amherst this summer and live with Harriet and William. They have me enrolled to attend classes at the Amherst Academy. I'm sure they will have you enrolled at an institution in Michigan soon enough."

Mattie snorted. "And what will they teach me in that forsaken wasteland? How to tan buffalo hides?"

Susan rolled her eyes but let out a small smirk and her sister smiled back, relaxing for a brief moment.

Mattie adjusted herself in her seat and raised an eyebrow.

"Amherst . . . isn't that where that Dickinson girl lives?"

Susan's face flushed scarlet uncontrollably at the reference, but she continued to look down at the dress she was folding.

She cleared her throat. "Yes, I believe it is."

Mattie bit her cheek looking up at the ceiling. "I wonder if she is still. . ."

"Still what?" Susan interjected, her voice sounding more defensive than intended.

Mattie smirked in the direction of her sister.

"Odd."

June 1847

    Emily Dickinson hung swinging upside down from the large oak tree that grew in the front yard of her house. Her long, auburn hair hung freely from her head, nearly touching the ground. Her light blue dress was tucked roughly beneath her knees to prevent her undergarments from being exposed to the people passing by. She felt the blood rushing to her head and her vision began to blur slightly but still, she stayed there, slowly swinging back and forth.

    As she tilted her head to the side, she could just see the outline of the house's roof peeking out from beneath the tree. It was a fine house to be sure, this Mansion she and her family had been living in for the last five years. She and her two siblings had taken to formally calling it the Mansion when they first moved in, and it had stuck in the family ever since.

    It was a solid, sturdy, white, two-story home with a traditional chimney rising from its high roof. A matching white, picket fence lined its perimeter with two separate openings carved into its long, low stretching frame - one for foot traffic and one for carriages. The house sat on two acres of land, of which Emily was particularly fond. She could often be found reading beneath one of the large trees that were planted around the back of the house or picking blossoms from the cherry tree on the side of the house in the spring. She was even more fond of slipping out of scurrying into the woods that abutted the back of large house, a habit which her father, Edward, always intentionally chose to ignore.

    In addition to its grand architectural features, there was a small grove of pine trees that her older brother, Austin, planted when they first moved into the house back in 1840. A garden which Emily primarily tended was also nestled in the back of the house and there was a small apple orchard just along the edge of the parameter of the woods, which she and her sister, Lavinia, or Vinnie as everyone called her, would pick dry in the autumn season.

The second-floor rear windows, including the one in Emily's bedroom, overlooked the treeless Amherst burial ground which the local minister described as "forbidding and repulsive" on one of his many visits to the home. Emily, however, spoke fondly of the view and even named the ghosts she allegedly saw walking up from the graveyard to her window at night.

Finally, the pressure in Emily's head was too much and she swung down from the thick branch, landing somewhat gracefully on both feet before dropping immediately to the ground. Instead of trying to stand up, she lay there feeling the swishing and swirling of the blood leaving her head. She dropped her hand to her side and began to stroke the grass, letting each blade slide between her fingers one by one. She picked up a piece and lifted it slowly to her lips, chewing gently on it. The taste of earth fill her mouth and nose and she paused for a moment to savor its freshness before discarding the grass back to the ground beside her.

"Excuse me," she heard a male voice speak from behind her.

She shot up, quickly, the blood now draining from her head entirely, rendering her dizzy as she attempted to stand. She had been so lost in thought that she did not even heard the man approach. How long was standing there? Did he see her hanging upside down from the tree?

"I didn't mean to frighten you," the man said politely, half smiling.

"Not at all," Emily responded, standing up and straightening her dress, tossing one strand of her loose hair behind her shoulder.

A leaf fell to the ground as she did and Emily looked back at the man, ignoring it but secretly wondering how many more leaves, twigs, and flowers were still nestled in her hair.

"I was wondering if you could help me? I am looking for Mr. Edward Dickinson. I was told this is his home, is that correct?"

Emily paused, taking notice of the man's full appearance for the first time. He was young but older than her, perhaps in his mid-twenties. He appeared to be taller than her father, maybe even over six feet, though she could not tell from this distance; however, even from where she stood now, she could see his soft, bright blue eyes. He wore a thick, wool, navy blue suit with gold buttons and a deep red cravat.

He must be burning up in this weather, Emily thought to herself, though she must admit he did look very fine in the ensemble and showed no sign of sweat or perspiration.

Emily had never been attracted to a man before. Through her years of puberty, she watched as her friends began to sneak off one by one with boys during their lunchtime at school. They would come back all rosy-cheeked and smitten, the boys walking with a new air of confidence. But Emily was never intrigued by the idea. She preferred to eat her lunch alone in the garden or reading under a tree. Sometimes she thought that something was wrong with her. After all, she was 17 years old. Shouldn't she be interested in young men by now? Her sister, Vinnie, was about three years younger than her and she was certainly interested enough for both of them. But Emily found men to be dull and predictable. Perhaps that was the reason she never had a desire to sneak off anywhere with them.

In fact, the only person Emily ever wanted to sneak off with was – *no*. Emily shook her head clearing the memory from her mind. *Don't think about that. Don't think about her.* She focused her attention back on tall man standing before her.

"Yes, sir. This is his house. What is your business with him?" Emily replied frankly.

The man placed his hat under his arm and laughed, taken aback by both the precociousness and forwardness of the young woman standing before him.

"You are quite inquisitive, madam," the man replied, still smiling.

Emily noticed a small dimple in his cheeks as he did and a slight chip in one of his front teeth which made him somehow more handsome to her. There was something intriguing to Emily about the tall, blonde man standing before her. It was not an attraction *per se*, but more curiosity than she had ever felt for a man before. There was something about him – a glimmer behind his eyes perhaps – that drew her in.

"And you sir, are quite presumptuous to assume I would just tell you where my father is, without first knowing who you are or why it is you seek him," Emily quipped back, crossing her arms.

"That seems fair enough," the man replied, stepping forward and extending his hand. "My name is Benjamin Newton. Your father has hired me to be his new law clerk."

Emily reached out quickly and shook the man's hand.

"Nice to meet you, Mr. Newton," she said firmly.

"Would you care to escort me inside? I would hate to knock at the door unannounced." He gave her a kind, gentle look as he held out his arm, motioning towards the front door.

She hesitated for just a moment before continuing. "Yes, of course."

As she turned to open the door, a small green book with a worn, golden insignia on the cover in the man's hand caught her eye. She did not notice it before since she was too distracted by his unseasonably warm outfit and his paradoxically cool blue eyes, but now it stuck out to her like a lighthouse in a stormy sea.

"What are you reading, Benjamin Newton?" She asked, one eyebrow raising slightly.

Benjamin smiled looking down at her. He was so tall compared to her she barely reached his chest line and the closer he stood the more their height difference became apparent.

"Ralph Waldo Emerson. Have you heard of him?"

"No, Emily replied, "who is he?"

Benjamin's smile widened. "He's a man living in Concord who has written some very interesting, and in my opinion, beautiful things about nature, religion, and philosophy. His poems are particularly moving to me."

Emily contemplated this a moment.

"I've always had an interest in writing poetry," she said. "But I don't expect I would be much good at it."

Benjamin shook his head. "You never know. A man like Emerson may change that for you. Here," he said extending the book out to her. "Why don't you borrow this for a little while and let me know what you think of it?"

Emily hesitantly took the small book from the man's hand, turning it over as she examined it.

"I suppose it's worth a try." Emily tucked the book under her arm and pushed open the large white front door and escorted Benjamin inside the house.

Inside, her father sat in the library, a pipe hanging in his mouth as he mulled over a large book. Edward Dickinson was a man of average height and build, though what he lacked in physical stature he made up for in intellect. A graduate of Northampton Law School, Edward ran his own, very successful law practice. On top of that, he sat as Treasurer for Amherst College and had recently been dipping his toe in the sea of politics and he currently sat as a member of the Massachusetts Governor's Council.

He had a head of thick, dark auburn tinted hair that stretched down to the bottom of his jaw in thick, bushy sideburns. His forehead held a permanent line down its center from the perpetual frown he seemed to harness. He was not an angry man by any means, and his children, particularly his eldest daughter, Emily, was spoiled as a child by all accounts. But he was a stern disciplinarian over his family and his word was tantamount to law amongst them all – even his beloved wife, Emily Norcross Dickinson for whom his daughter Emily was named.

The library was Emily's favorite place in the house and she often joined her father as they read together on winter days when she could not go outdoors. Sometimes he would let his only son, Austin in with them as well, though he always grew annoyed with his persistent questions and need for attention. Emily was content to quietly sit and read. When she grew bored, she would simply stand and leave the room - a quality which Edward most appreciated during his work hours. His other daughter, Vinnie, on the other hand was forbidden to enter the room while Edward was working, as she was too impatient for reading books. She would sneak in while he was gone some days and look at the books anyways, though she would rarely sit long enough to read one of them.

The room was comprised of wooden bookshelves that were built into the wall itself. There was a great fireplace with a marble hearth sided by two black sconces. Edward's high, wing-backed chair rested in the front of the fireplace across from a smaller chair which was originally intended to be for Mrs. Dickinson. It eventually became known as "Emily's chair" as Mrs. Dickinson much preferred the confines of cooking and cleaning than that of relaxation and leisure.

A family portrait of the three children hung over the mantle and Emily cringed every time she looked at it. All of the children hated it. They looked ridiculous in it and they were all convinced that is not how they looked as young children. Emily and Austin threatened to throw it into the fire one day at breakfast, only in jest of course, but their mother made such a shriek and fuss at even the mention of it, that their father forbade them to bring up anything to do with the painting again.

"Father," Emily said entering the room, "Mr. Benjamin Newton is here to see you."

Edward slammed his book shut and removed his pipe at once.

"Mr. Newton? Why yes, of course! Do show him in, don't let him linger on the stoop in this heat, he'll melt down to his skivvies."

"Wait until you see what he's wearing," Emily said chuckling under her breath.

Before she could finish composing herself, she turned to leave the room and ran directly into the broad chest of Benjamin Newton. He looked down at her and smiled briefly before turning towards her father.

"Good morning, Mr. Dickinson. I hope I have not arrived too early in the day. My carriage from Northampton arrived this morning and rather than linger in town, I simply came through."

"Not at all, my good man," Edward continued. "Emily, be a good girl and fetch us some tea and biscuits, would you?"

"Oh, really, sir, I don't want to be a bother," Benjamin protested.

"It's no bother," Emily interjected.

Emily went down the stairs to the kitchen, where her mother greeted her, hunched over the long wooden table in the center of the room, kneading a large mound of dough.

Mrs. Dickinson was a slender woman with sandy blonde hair that hung perpetually in front of her face as she was cooking. She was constantly tucking it behind her ears and complaining about how it would turn brown with the grease from her hands. She had blue eyes, unlike Edward's which were the color of mud, and in the right light, a hint of green could be spotted in them — or so she swore. She was a hard-working woman who married for love and in exchange found a life not only filled with love but also one of financial success. It was that same dream that she held for both of her daughters - to find a man they loved, but more importantly, a man who would support them, as their father had done all these years. It was not a dream her eldest daughter, Emily, shared, unfortunately. A fact that created a growing crevice between the two women.

Edward was the head of the Dickinson house, there was no doubt, but Mrs. Dickinson was the neck that turned him. She ruled the house with an iron fist, but at certain times that fist would open, revealing a sweet biscuit inside it. Those were the moments Emily cherished. When she could catch a brief sight of the young, playful bride that still lived deep inside her mother. Not the stern housewife who had long since taken her place.

"Do we have any fresh biscuits?" Emily asked briskly.

"Right over there, of course," Mrs. Dickinson answered, nodding her head in a general direction, still kneading the dough mechanically.

Emily's younger sister, Vinnie sat beside their mother, picking rosemary off the stem and tossing the herbs into the mortar to be ground. Vinnie was the only member of the family to inherit their mother's blonde locks and light-colored eyes. In fact, the two of them were the most alike in every way. Vinnie wanted nothing more in life than to find a man who would whisk her away to some far-off destination like a princess in a fairy tale. She even had a sharp, angled face, much like her mother and she was constantly helping Mrs. Dickinson with chores in an effort to become, "a better lady."

"Where have you been? We need your help in here preparing supper," Mrs. Dickinson inquired. "I'm making your father's favorite, rosemary potato bread."

"Father only likes *my* bread," Emily replied smugly. "And besides, I can't," she said, moving the kettle over the fire to boil water. "I am to serve father and his new apprentice tea and biscuits."

Vinnie looked over rolling her eyes and Emily quickly stuck out her tongue before their mother could notice.

"Why don't I get to serve the tea and biscuits?" Vinnie asked with a low whine to her tone.

"Because you, my dear sister, are covered in flour," Emily replied, touching the tip of her sister's nose playfully and sauntering over to the table where the biscuits sat.

"That's not fair, you're only doing it so you can eavesdrop! You don't even like playing the housewife!" Vinnie protested, but she knew it was no use.

Their mother was so desperate to break Emily of her wild ways that any time Emily showed the least bit of interest in any form of domestic duties, she allowed her to do it. Emily figured out this game several months ago and now used it to listen in on their father's conversations with politicians, lawyers, councilmen, and anyone else of importance who paid a visit. This visit was no exception.

"Mr. Newton is here?" Mrs. Dickinson exclaimed. "He was not scheduled to arrive until this afternoon! Good heavens, quick girls, we must make sure the house is in top shape. Emily, you serve him the tea and biscuits and fix your hair before you go back in there." She shook her head pulling out a rogue twig from the back of Emily's hair. "Vinnie, go to the sitting room and make sure the fireplace is cleaned out. We don't want last season's ashes getting onto any pants. I'll go upstairs and change so I can look presentable when I meet him."

"If that fireplace still hasn't been cleaned since spring, we have bigger issues in this house," Emily smirked shaking her head.

Her mother ignored her daughter's obvious jest and raced up the stairs, leaving the two girls alone in the kitchen.

Before Emily could leave the room, her sister spoke up again.

"I take it you haven't heard the news yet, then?"

Emily paused. She won the upper hand with her sister already and she knew all Vinnie was trying to do was get a rise out of her, but she couldn't stand not knowing something.

"What news?"

Vinnie grinned, satisfied that her sister had taken the bait. "Susan Gilbert is moving back to Amherst."

Emily's face flushed red and she looked down, pretending to hide the obvious impact the news had on her She didn't want her sister to know her excitement, or feel how fast her heart was beating at the mention of Susan Gilbert's name.

"When?" Emily replied, attempting to remain aloof.

Vinnie smirked. "Soon."

August 1847

The carriage pulled up to the small, wooden house on Main Street around 4:00 that day. Susan Gilbert stepped out and was greeted by her sister, Harriet, and her brother-in-law, William Cutler. Harriet held both arms open wide and Susan was immediately struck by how much older than Susan she looked. She knew they were just less than a decade apart in age, but her sister looked worn and tired.

Perhaps it has just been so long since we have seen each other, Susan thought, leaning in to hug her eldest sister. Hariett's once round, porcelain face was replaced by one that looked sunken in and weathered. There were deep hollows beneath her eyes that she clearly tried to hide with rouge. Her once thick hair was now moused brown and hanging down in thin streaks around her face.

William did not look all that different from what she remembered, though to be fair she had only met him once, and that was at her sister's wedding. He was a short man, barely taller than Harriet, and had a head of thick light brown hair that constantly looked messy even after he brushed it. It hung down and covered his eyes no matter how hard he tried to groom it back. "A bad cow lick", Harriet once wrote in a letter to Susan discussing the problem. He had a five o'clock shadow covering his sharp jaw and his bulky fingers nearly engulfed Susan's hand as he took it and shook it firmly.

Once inside, Susan looked around slowly. It was a modest house, much smaller than what she grew accustomed to at her Aunt Sophia's, but she would have her own bedroom and she was promised total privacy. The house came with a barn and a small garden in the back of the fenced-in yard and was centrally located in the town, so her recent arrival was certain to attract many visitors.

Harriet told her to settle in and unpack her things first and that supper would be ready by 5:00. William set down the large trunk by the foot of her small bed, nodded, and left closing the door behind him. Susan was alone at last. Alone and tired.

The trip from New York took three full days of travel and the jostling of the carriage on the bumpy road had exhausted her. She wanted nothing more than to undo her corset and lie down. But she knew her sister would be disappointed if they missed their first evening meal together, and she was sure Harriet had plenty of local gossip to fill her in on. So, Susan simply sighed, bent over the trunk, and began going through her things.

Her room was small, possessing a simple wooden chest of drawers with three drawers for her to place her belongings and a single coat rack in the corner. Susan frowned wondering whether her dresses would all fit. A slim, long mirror sat propped in the corner of the room and a wooden nightstand with a single drawer rested beside her small bed which was pushed against the wall, to make the room seem larger. The chamber pot was already placed beneath the bed and a washbasin had been placed on the nightstand. Sitting down on the lumpy mattress, Susan quickly learned that her bed was even smaller than anticipated.

When Mattie left for Michigan, one thing Susan found she hadn't missed was sharing a room with her sister. She grew to enjoy the peaceful mornings of silence as the sun was rising, without the sound of her sister's snoring to wake her up first. She did not miss Mattie sneaking out the window late at night, going to see her latest suitor, and lying-in bed, covered in anxiety, just praying no one would hear her leave. She missed her sister very much, but admittedly she did not miss the drama that seemed to constantly orbit her sister.

Perhaps it was for that reason that Susan was so grateful to her oldest sister, Harriet, for taking her in. Truth be told, she was looking forward to a change of pace. But most of all, she was happy to be back in Amherst. Happy to be back to the place she considered home.

Mattie was in Michigan and from the letters she sent, was actually doing quite well. She already met a "handsome young farmer named Mark," who was settling a patch of land just west of Detroit. The fact that Mattie had only been in Michigan a few months and had already found a new beau did not surprise her.

She heard a knock on her door and without waiting for her reply, her sister entered.

"I'm so happy you've come," Harriet said holding out her hands towards Susan. Susan grabbed them in response and pulled her closer, smiling.

"Thank you so much for having me, Harriet," Susan replied, "things were getting a bit stuffy at Aunt Sophia's house . . . if you know what I mean."

Harriet chuckled, "oh yes, I believe I do."

Harriet squeezed her hands and began again, "well, supper is almost ready, though I could use your help with a few things around the kitchen if you don't mind? We've recently let go of the cook, I'm afraid. And the maid as well. William only has his stable boy now, so it's up to us to keep things tidy around the house. You won't mind helping out will you, Susan?"

Her sister's face looked drawn and desperate as she finished the sentence, though her voice remained intentionally upbeat and sprightly. Susan paused for a moment. Certainly, she knew she would be required to pull her weight around the house, but her sister and brother-in-law always took great pride in maintaining a fully staffed house, even if it was a small one. She was surprised to hear they were so short-handed.

"Of course not," Susan replied, dutifully.

"Good, good." Harriet patted her sister's hands and kissed both of them before turning back towards the door. "See you down in the kitchen in a moment then," she said before leaving the room.

Susan removed a beige-colored apron from her belongings and tied it around her waist taking a moment to look at herself in the long mirror in her room before heading down to the kitchen.

She decided she would go for a walk later this week once she was settled. There was somewhere – someone she wanted to see. If Susan was honest, it was the thing she had been looking forward to most about her return to Amherst. Because one could not think of the town of Amherst and not think of the Dickinsons. And Susan could not think about the Dickinsons and not think of Emily.

She and Emily were close friends throughout most of their childhood. Deerfield was only a few towns over and her family would often travel to Amherst for supplies, fabrics, and special deliveries. Whenever they visited, they always made a call to the Dickinson house. Back then, the Dickinsons lived in a large house they called "The Homestead" over on Main Street, but for reasons Susan never fully understood, they sold the house and moved to a large white house that Emily called, "the Mansion," on West Street about five years ago

The last time Susan had seen Emily was two years ago when she was 15 on one of her uncle's business trips to Amherst. She asked to accompany her uncle for the sole purpose of seeing Emily and he happily obliged as he always did. That day, he gave her permission to go and visit Emily alone while he attended various meetings around town.

Susan could remember it like it was yesterday. Emily grabbed her by the hand and told her that she had something to show her. She remembered the slight shiver that shot down her spine at the touch of Emily's hand in hers as she grabbed her and led her away from the big white house. They raced off down a winding path leading from the backyard of the Mansion and deep into the woods. It was so narrow in places they were bumping into one another as they ran but Susan didn't care. All she could focus on was the feel of Emily's hand gripping hers as they ran through the thick forest, their bodies playfully colliding into one another as little sparks flew back and forth in the small space between them. Finally, they reached a little clearing where there was a large maple tree swinging down perfectly over a flowing stream.

"This is my new favorite place," Emily said, her brown eyes shining bright like the sun with excitement, "and I wanted to share it with my favorite person."

Emily's was still holding her hand, even though they stopped running. Susan remembered how Emily gulped slightly as she looked down at Emily's hand and then back at her. She remembered the feeling of warmth and excitement that surged into her chest at the slight movement of Emily's finger as it gently stroked the back of her hand. She remembered looking briefly at Emily's lips and then into her dark brown eyes and then before she knew it, her lips were pressed on Emily's.

Susan didn't know what had come over her in that moment, but much to Susan's surprise, Emily kissed her back. It wasn't just the sort of kiss that young girls shared with playmates or even the sort that older girls did when they were "practicing for boys." It was a long, deep, passionate kiss that made Susan's toes curl in her leather boots. After a few seconds, the first kiss ended and they both exchanged a brief glance and smiled.

Before Susan knew it, Emily's hand was behind her neck pulling her closer, kissing her again. They stayed there for what felt like both an eternity and a blip of time all at once, kissing until finally a raven cawed over their head startling them both.

Emily stepped back and covered her mouth, looking shocked and taken aback. Susan apologized, embarrassed at the outburst of emotion. They walked back to Emily's house silent and apart. They had never spoken about it since and their correspondence in recent years was formal and casual, speaking mostly of the weather and their studies. But when Susan found out she was returning to Amherst, the only thing she could think about was seeing Emily again. And the only thing she could hope was that Emily would be happy to see her too.

October 1847

Susan cinched the bonnet tight around her neck and smoothed her dress one more time with her palms. She grabbed a shawl and threw it around her arms for added warmth. There was a crisp chill in the air on this autumn morning and even though October had just begun, everyone knew they were in for a cold winter ahead.

She tucked a loose strand of brown hair beneath her bonnet with the flick of a finger. She was not sure why she cared so much about her appearance. After all, she was just going to see her friend – nothing more.

It had been two weeks since Susan arrived in Amherst, and she had yet to visit Emily. Her sister Harriet kept her incredibly busy with house chores. In fact, Susan began to wonder how the family had functioned at all without her there to cook, clean, and launder. She had been forward to seeing Emily Dickinson again for months, but now that she was only a short walk away the idea of seeing her paralyzed her with fear. What if Emily was mad at her for what happened in the woods years ago? What if she no longer wanted to be Susan's friend? What if she changed since they last spoke? What if she told everyone about their kiss and the entire Dickinson family thought she was a freak?

Susan ran through a million hypotheticals a day over the past several weeks, but finally, she decided to put an end to the torture and simply walk over and see her. A part of her hoped to run into Emily in town, or even at the Sunday Meeting, but she had not been so fortunate.

When they were little girls, Emily and Susan often attended Meeting on Sundays together with their families.

They would sit in the back pew with Vinnie and Mattie. Emily would scribble notes on little scraps of papers she tucked into her gloves and Mattie and Vinnie would play games with twisted strings. But Emily was not at church the past two Sundays, though she did see Mr. and Mrs. Dickinson there both weeks so news of Susan's return was sure to have reached Emily's ears.

Susan placed her hands on her hips and gave herself a reassuring nod in the mirror before turning and leaving her bedroom.

"Just do it," she said aloud.

Once outside, the cold hair filled her nostrils and made her feel invigorated. She knew she made the right decision. The leaves were just now beginning to reveal a dim orange, and most still clung to their green hues. The sun was shining with just a few specks of clouds in the sky and birds were busy making their morning songs.

As she walked, she found herself wondering what Emily would look like. Would her freckles have faded? Would her hair still have the hint of red it once did? What type of dress would she be wearing? How would she do her hair? Does she still bite her cheek when she reads? Would she be taller or did she stop growing at 15 like Susan?

Her mind raced and raced and she found her pace beginning to quicken with each new thought. Her heart was beginning to race faster too now, and as she rounded the corner and saw the big white house on West Street, she paused to catch her breath.

She slowly approached the house, placing each foot down intently and delicately on the front steps before raising a gloved hand and knocking. She listened for a moment, expecting to hear Emily's wild and familiar footsteps approaching the door. Instead, she heard a slow, steady, march, like the beat of a drum. She held her breath as the door handle jiggled and when the door opened, she came face to face with -

"Vinnie?" Susan asked, perplexed.

A tall, slender girl of 14 stood before her, her blonde, long hair pulled half back so the glowing manes tumbled freely down the middle of her back. Her deep blue eyes looked Susan up and down suspiciously.

"Yes?" Vinnie replied.

"I'm so sorry, it's just that I have not seen you since you were just a little girl. My name is Susan Gilbert, I'm a friend of your sister's. Do you remember me?"

Vinnie's eyes lit up with realization and a slight sense of mischief, "Susan Huntington Gilbert," Vinnie said, a fast smile spreading over her face, "of course, I know who you are. As if Emily would have ever let us forget you."

Susan breathed a sigh of relief. So, Emily missed her too.

"Do come in," Vinnie said, opening the door wide for Susan to enter. "Can I get you some tea?"

"Tea would be lovely, thank you," Susan continued, removing her bonnet and taking a seat in the parlor near the piano.

She smiled looking around. It was just as she remembered it. The portraits of Mr. and Mrs. Dickinson both hung over the fireplace with candelabras resting elegantly beside them. The deep blue sofa still sat beneath the large front window. The two, hunter green wing backed chairs still flagged the fireplace on both sides. She recalled many a time when she and Emily would play in this very room – only in winter of course when it was too cold to be outside. They would play marbles and jacks and all kinds of games. Vinnie would always be whining to play with them but they would never allow it. They would, however, on the rare occasion allow -

"Susan Gilbert?" She heard a male voice speak up from behind her, breaking her from her reverie.

"Austin Dickinson?" She exclaimed standing up to greet the boy she once knew well enough to be her own brother.

Austin Dickinson was the eldest of the three Dickinson children, and he wore the title with pride. As the sole male heir, the entire Dickinson estate, including his two sisters, would one day fall under his care and control, a responsibility he took seriously and at times with chagrin. He was taller than his father, his shoulders wider, his jaw narrower and sharper like his mother's. He had a head of shiny, brown hair that curled at the tips of his ears. His eyes were a deep brown like his father's and his skin was pale and free of lines which gave him a boyish charm, even though he was now well into manhood. He was known to be an ambitious but kind man who had two goals in life – to impress his father and to carry on the name of Dickinson.

Austin straightened his shoulders and smiled. "How are you, Susan?" He asked attempting to make his voice sound deeper than it was.

His onyx eyebrows covered his chocolate eyes which were filled with the remnants of childish charm and mischief.

Susan smiled, "I'm well, thank you. I've just moved back to Amherst. How are you?"

"Yes, of course, we have all been eagerly awaiting your return around here. I'm finishing up my schooling at the college," he replied, taking a seat across the room from her and crossing his leg across his lap. "Then after that, it's off to law school, but I'd like to teach a little bit before then I think. Father has asked me to join the family business, you know."

Susan smiled politely. "That's wonderful, Austin. I'm sure your family must be proud."

"They will be," he replied, one eyebrow raising slightly.

Vinnie returned to the room with a tray of tea.

"Austin," she remarked, "I didn't know you'd be joining us; I'd have brought another cup."

Austin looked over at Susan. "Well, if you ladies would allow me to join you, I'd be most pleased for the company." He winked at Susan before turning back to Vinnie.

Susan smiled and tried to conceal a laugh at his boldness. She knew this boy when he was just a child. There was no doubt he was a full-grown man now, but Susan struggled to see him as anything but that gangly teenager riding his horse around town, throwing sticks into neighbors' fields, and pulling her pigtails as she played with his sister.

Not wanting to offend his ego, she obliged. "I would be delighted. But it seems that we are still missing one cup and one sibling. Where is Emily?" Susan asked.

"Emily?" Austin answered. "Has she not told you? I thought you too corresponded all the time."

Susan felt a twinge of pain in her heart as he continued.

"She's gone to complete her studies at the South Hadley Female Seminary in Holyoke. She won't be back until at least the spring, although based on what the headmistress has been writing to father, she may not be so lucky."

Susan felt a weight drop from her chest into her stomach. She waited too long. She knew she should have written to Emily; she knew she should have come to see her sooner.

"What do you mean, she may not be so lucky?" Susan asked.

"Oh, you know how strict they are out in Holyoke. If you bat your eyelashes down there, you'll be swatted on the hand. And we both know Emily isn't a big fan of compliance with the masses. I wouldn't be surprised if they made her stay on for a second term."

"Sugar?" She heard Vinnie say from across the room.

"Beg your pardon?" Susan looked at Vinnie, still reeling with shock at the new development.

"For your tea," Vinnie replied, "would you like sugar?"

Susan snapped back to reality. "Yes, yes please."

Susan couldn't believe her ears. She waited two years for this moment. To see Emily. To feel her back in her arms. Perhaps if she came over sooner? But she knew that logic was futile. Her coming wouldn't have stopped Emily from leaving. She was certain even Emily had little say in the matter. Seminary was not a place she could ever imagine Emily Dickinson wanting to go. Even now the idea of it made Susan want to laugh and cry all at once. It was like picturing a wild eagle being housed in a small cage. She only hoped Emily didn't forget how to fly, so she could come back soon.

November 1847

Dearest Emily,

How can I ever begin to express my regret for not writing to you sooner? I know I have been a dreadful friend and I write now to beg your forgiveness. I went by your house just the other day and was most dismayed to learn that you were gone away to school. Your brother and sister were kind enough to host me for the afternoon, but there was a specter haunting the shadows that day, which I know to be you. Please write to me at your earliest convenience. I hope to see you when you return to Amherst.

Your faithful friend,

Suzie

Emily set down the letter and scratched at the collar of her heavy, wool, black dress - a requirement for the women of the seminary. She hated the color black. She missed her brightly colored dresses at home. She missed her family. She missed the big trees in her yard. She missed baking bread for her father. She missed her new friend, Benjamin Newton. And now, most of all, she missed her old friend, Susan Gilbert. It pained Emily to know that she was back in Amherst, in her own home while she sat here, twiddling her thumbs at this institution.

She had spent years trying not to think about Susan Gilbert. The last time she saw Susan was that day when they were alone in the woods. Emily didn't know why it was so important that she take her down that small, winding path into the woods that day. It was just instinct. As if every bone in her body was telling her to get Susan alone, to drag her and pull her away to that secret place by the creek. So, that's what she did – grabbed Susan and ran. She continued to hold Susan's hand after their arrival at the tree, which was not uncommon for two girls their age to do. What was uncommon however was the hundreds of butterflies that began to spread their wings inside her chest and flutter throughout her veins as she looked into Susan's eyes. Emily barely had time to process the new feeling when Susan kissed her.

She was so flooded with emotions at the feel of Susan's lips on hers she did the only thing she could think to do at the time – she kept kissing her. But then that stupid bird brought them back to reality and Susan apologized for it. She looked so ashamed and embarrassed. Perhaps that meant she regretted doing it? Emily never knew. Susan stopped writing to her as much after that and their friendship went from close to casual. When she heard that Susan was moving back to Amherst a few months ago, she hoped Susan would visit her. But after a few weeks, she still hadn't.

But now, here she was emerging from the past like the fresh dew of the morning. Emily traced her fingers over the outline of the ink on the paper, thinking about what Susan's hands must have looked like as she wrote it., the long, full veins rolling back long her slim fingers. The scratching of the quill as it slowly traced the neat letters onto the page.

Quickly she shook her head and refocused her attention on her dark, bleak surroundings. She was not alone in the woods with Susan. She was not in her room watching Susan write a letter. She was not even in Amherst. She was here in this . . . infirmary.

The curriculum at South Hadley Female Seminary was somewhat challenging for Emily. As a young girl, her father read Shakespeare and Aristotle to her. He taught her to challenge her mind and always think for herself. He read to her in Latin, Greek and German. She attending Amherst Academy and received private tutoring at home. As such, she was well prepared for the academic challenges of the school. The religious challenges, however, were another matter.

Emily considered herself a Christian, to an extent, but she did not enjoy endless sermons preaching of the doom of mankind. She'd much rather be outside enjoying the wonders of God's creation than stuffed in a dark classroom reading the translations of others and the proper role of women for hours.

Aside from the religious rigors of the school, Emily did admit she enjoyed most of her other classes. The curriculum included English grammar, Latin, history, music, algebra, philosophy, and logic. Although the subject in which she had taken a particular interest was botany. She could not get enough of plants and their intricacies.

She had written to Austin about the subject several times, but he, admittedly, was not nearly as interested in it as she was. Within her first week at the school, Emily was placed in the advanced courses. She found the exams to be challenging and attempted to compensate for her misery of constant preaching and condemnation with the intellectual stimulation that the seminary was providing her.

Much to Emily's chagrin, all students were required to help maintain the seminary by participating in some form of domestic work. Emily's job was to carry, wash and dry knives at every meal table, morning, noon and night. She hated the monotony of the task. The blatant attempt at crafting the women into perfect little housewives to one day serve their husbands as they now were taught to serve the Lord.

Perhaps the most revolting aspect of the school was the fact that students were categorized into one of three groups: those who professed to know the Lord, those who hoped to know the Lord, and those who were said to be "without hope." Emily was among eighty women in the "without hope" category when she began attending the seminary. To date, she remained in that category, though the group was quickly dwindling around her. It seemed like every day in convocation, another girl would stand up and profess her faith in the Lord, making Emily feel more and more alone. A feeling which made her miss her life back in Amherst more than ever.

Emily looked down at the letter once more. She could no longer ignore Susan Gilbert in her mind. She had missed her company for too long. To have her so close now and continue to ignore her felt wrong. She immediately pulled out a sheet of paper and began to write.

Dear Suzie,

I could not remain cross with you for all the world's pearls. It is true, that I was disheartened when you stopped writing as often to me. But to have you back in Amherst, at last, brings me great joy. For the time being, I must remain at school. My father feels my education is not yet at an end, though I do long to be home. I intend to come back to Amherst in the spring and to never return to this place again. Give Austin and Vinnie love from me.

Your constant friend,

Emilee

Emily folded the paper and addressed it to Susan. Then, without a moment's break, she pulled out a second sheet of paper and began writing again.

Newton,

I cannot believe you have read something so small of mine and found it so grand. It was my first attempt at poetry but you were right – I do find it to be quite cathartic, especially in such a place as this. Though I know I am no Emerson or Byron, it gives me great pleasure to consider myself even somewhat in their company. Pray, tell me what edits you would have to my last work, so that I may glean all I can from your wealth of knowledge on the subject.

Faithfully,

Emilee

Emily smiled. Here she was staring at two correspondences from two friends she held most dear. Susan Gibert – one of her oldest friends now returned from a sabbatical of sorts and Benjamin Newton – or Newton as she called him - her newest and most intriguing friend who had given her the idea and the courage to begin writing poetry as a means of self-expression and art. He had been right about the impact Mr. Emerson's writings would have on her.

Even though she had only known him a few months, she found Newton to be refreshing, like a gust of crisp wind on an autumn morning. He found his way into the sealed halls of the Mansion on West Street and eventually found his way into a special corner of Emily's heart. Often it was Newton's writings and Newton's alone that pulled her from the darkest corners of loneliness and melancholy these past few months. Her sister would write, and Austin wrote almost as often as Newton. But Newton's words calmed her and worked to soothe her weathered and dried soul in this horrid place more than anyone else's.

Perhaps there was no better friend in the world to her right now, than Mr. Benjamin Newton. She could not wait to introduce him to Susan in the spring. She imagined the long walks they would all share, the discussions of poetry, art, literature, and philosophy.

Sitting back, she smiled, imagining returning to her life in Amherst. Newton, Susan, Austin, Vinnie, and herself. Life would be so grand then. If only it were spring. She closed both letters and tucked them into her dress apron for later postage. Rubbing the back of her neck, she opened her textbook and began to study for next week's examinations.

Suddenly, she heard a loud knock at her door. "Emily, it is time for convocation."

Emily cringed inwardly thinking of the sermon that awaited her in the chapel next door. She hated being so far away, alone in this dreary place. She hoped her father would let her return home in the spring as promised.

February 1848

Emily did not return home in the spring. Susan looked out the window of her small bedroom and pulled the shawl around her shoulders to hide the chill that crept down her spine. She set down the letter that came from Emily that morning informing her that she would not be coming home as planned. The news made Susan feel colder inside than the brisk winter air and she picked up the letter once more to convince herself that it was true.

It felt as if she and Emily were destined to be nothing more than correspondents for the rest of their days. First, she moved away to New York. Then when she finally returned, Emily was gone away to school. Now her time away had been extended even more and even Emily did not even know when she would be able to return home.

Susan sighed and tucked the letter into the top drawer of her chest of drawer, along with the rest of Emily's letters. She also saved letters from Mattie, though they were arriving less often each month now, and she continued to write and receive letters from Abigail back at Aunt Sophia's house, though it was hard to make out her spelling sometimes.

For the first time in a long time, Susan felt lonely. Perhaps it was the lingering winter that was contributing to her melancholy. Or perhaps it was that her friends all felt so far away. Whatever the reason, she could not shake it no matter how hard she tried.

She stood and began to get dressed for the day. Sitting inside would not make the chores go any faster and she needed to be at work at the seamstresses within the hour. She got dressed quickly to reduce the chill that wafted through her fireless bedroom and went downstairs hoping to be able to sit by the fireplace and warm herself before leaving for her duties.

Once she got downstairs, however, it became clear that there was no place for her at the hearth, as William was gathered with several other men in the room. They were leaning over and speaking in low whispers. When she came around the corner, they all stopped talking and greeted her politely and waited for her to leave before turning and resuming their chatter.

Her sister, Harriett, was in the kitchen, cooking oats over the fire and warming the kettle.

"Harriett," Susan inquired, "who are all those men upstairs with William?"

Harriet shook her head. "You know better than to ask about a man's affairs, Susan."

Susan pressed on. "But surely you must have some idea of who they are, after all this is your house too."

"Hush now," Harriett interjected. "You just run along to work and mind your business, you understand?"

Her tone was harsh and it took Susan aback slightly. Seeing the hurt in her sister's face, Harriet walked over to Susan and placed her hand on her cheek, rubbing it softly.

"Bundle up, it's cold out there," she said gently.

Susan left through the kitchen door, being sure to close it tightly behind her. She wrapped the wool cloak around her neck as the wind cut into her bare cheeks. Once she left the yard, she turned east and began the short walk down Main Street to the seamstress's house on Merchant Row. She was originally told that her work at the seamstress' was only temporary, to get Harriet and William back on their feet. But lately, she had been working such long hours she barely had time for her studies. She didn't mind working for the old woman who ran the shop, Miss Mavis. A spinster, by every definition of the word, she was a kind woman who took a quick liking to Susan. She was always giving Susan scraps of leftover fabric for Susan to sew herself new garments or bonnets and she made sure that any tip that was given by a happy customer was shared evenly with Susan.

Susan was almost to the small house that operated as Miss Mavis' shop when she heard a familiar voice pipe up across the street. She looked over and saw that Austin Dickinson was running across the road towards her.

"How are you, Susan?" He said between breaths once he finally reached her.

His cheeks were flushed red from the cold and he wore a fine, black, wool coat with a high collar that covered most of his neck. His dark, curly hair stuck out from beneath a beaver skin hat and he quickly reached up to remove it out of formality.

"Please, Austin, keep your hat on, you'll catch a chill out here without it."

Austin smiled and placed the hat back on top of his head. "You're probably right."

Susan shifted her weight attempting to stay warm as they stood in silence.

Austin cleared his throat. "Are you off to work then?"

"Yes, it's just down there," Susan replied motioning towards the general direction of the house on the corner.

"Allow me to escort you," Austin remarked, holding out his arm for her to grab onto.

Susan looked around for a moment, contemplating the decision. What harm could it do, being escorted by a friendly face to work, especially in such cold and dreary weather? She nodded silently and looped her arm into his. She watched as a large smile spread across his face as they walked. She hoped he would not read too much into such a simple gesture, but knowing Austin, it was too late.

"How is Emily?" Susan asked once they walked a few feet, unable to keep the conversation away from the only Dickinson that occupied her mind.

"Oh, she's Emily. Still rebelling against the system as usual. I wish sometimes she would just be more obedient and . . ." Austin paused.

"More what?"

Austin took a deep breath before finishing the sentence. "More normal," he finally said, "you know, like my mother, or Vinnie, or even you, Susan."

They reached the house and Susan could see Miss Mavis looking out the window at them. She looked down to avoid direct eye contact with Austin.

"How do you mean, more normal? She wears dresses and bakes, and she is attending seminary. What more do you want her to be?" Susan was unable to hide the slight defensiveness of her tone.

Austin shook his head. "I know but it's just, I don't know. Father still lets her behave like a child, and mother is beginning to be concerned that even the seminary will not break her of that habit. She continues to shirk her religious duties and refuses to be seen by any male suitors. Don't you think it's a bit . . ."

"A bit what?"

"Odd?" He finished.

Susan stopped and looked back at the house. Miss Mavis disappeared from the window and Susan knew she was expected to be inside.

"I have to go inside," she replied.

Susan chose to ignore Austin's remarks. She had not seen Emily in years, so who was she to opine on her behavior? But she had to admit, it made Susan smile to think that the girl she knew as a child had not changed that much. Maybe she was odd compared to the rest of society, but Susan would rather have that as a companion than just another society girl, or someone like Mattie whose only concerns were of her latest beau.

"Thank you for allowing me to escort you," Austin said, returning to his formal manner of speaking. He knelt down and kissed her hand and she pulled away before he could stand upright.

"Bye, Austin," she said quickly before turning to head up the stairs to the shop.

Once inside, Susan removed her cloak and watched as the seamstress, Miss Mavis, smirked and pretended to work.

"Was that Austin Dickinson, I saw you with out there?" The elderly woman said finally after realizing Susan would not be inviting conversation herself.

"It was," Susan replied simply.

"You're a very lucky woman," the old lady continued. "His family is said to be one of the wealthiest in Amherst."

Susan cringed at the implication and sat down at the large desk where a garment was waiting for her.

"I don't care about all that nonsense," Susan stated firmly.

The woman nodded and continued working. "Not now, you don't. But someday, you will."

Susan ignored her. She had no interest in Austin Dickinson and she never would. Of that, she was certain. There was only one Dickinson she cared for, and she was trapped in Holyoke for the time being.

July 1848

Emily ran through the house letting her thick, woven robe fly open behind her.

"Father, guess what I am?" She inquired, flapping her arms beside her as she circled his armchair.

The smell of smoke from his pipe flooded her nose as she took her final swoop and she began to cough.

Edward chuckled. "A dying bird?"

Emily caught her breath and then grabbed at her neck, falling dramatically onto the floor in front of him.

"Caw, caw!" She sputtered before hanging her tongue out of her mouth pretending to be dead.

Her father shook his head. "When will you outgrow this wild imagination of yours?"

"Never!" Emily replied, jumping up from the floor and plopping on the sofa across the room from him.

"Well, it's 12:15 in the afternoon. So, *whatever* species you are, I think it is time you get dressed."

She couldn't argue with that. Her father was exceptionally lenient with her conduct, especially since her return from the seminary, but he still commanded a sense of order and formality in his house. She stood up from the sofa and walked over, grabbing his hand and kissing his ring.

"As you wish, my lord," she said in her best effort at an English accent. She turned and began to march as a soldier would out of the room and up the stairs.

Emily Dickinson could not be happier to be home from school and she was already petitioning her father to not make her go back in a month for the next term. The past year at seminary had been one of the most unpleasant experiences of her life. She had been afforded no return to home in the spring as she had originally been promised, a cruel trick that only served to grow her distaste for the entire institution.

Her family was told by the headmistress that her, "immortal soul needed constant prayer," as she continued to show defiance to the liturgy of the school. In a rare and unsurpassed moment, her father defied Emily's wishes and forced her to remain boarded at the school throughout the entire winter and into the summer. By the time the year ended, Emily was practically clawing at the walls to get back to Amherst.

How could eleven miles feel so far away? She asked herself, one cold, winter morning staring out of the frosty window of her dormitory. She took the time to feed her new love of poetry, however, and she sent Newton at least one poem a month for the past year. He would return them to her with marks, edits, notes in the margins, and thoughts.

Susan Gilbert also remained a constant correspondent for that very long year, but sadly, Emily began to see her as nothing more than mere pencil and paper. It had now been three years since they last laid eyes on one another.

Regardless, that was all about to end now as Susan promised to visit Emily the moment she returned from the seminary. Newton was off visiting family in some other part of the state, so their mutual introduction would have to wait. Emily was satisfied with this arrangement, convinced that she needed all of the moments she could gather with each of them alone, but especially Susan.

Emily began to walk upstairs to get dressed when Austin stopped her halfway.

"Is Susan coming by today?" He asked, unable to hide the hopeful tone of his voice.

"Why?"

"Because," Austin replied, "I'd like to see her. We've been corresponding quite frequently, you know," Austin added as if intentionally waiting to cause some stir in Emily.

By "frequently" Emily knew he probably meant he wrote her a few letters here and there that she likely only responded to out of politeness.

"Of course, I know," Emily lied, "but no, she is not coming here today."

The second part was not technically a lie - Susan was not coming to the Mansion but was instead meeting her at a spot in the woods – *their* spot. Austin's face looked disappointed and he continued down the stairs. He stopped at the bottom step looking up at Emily.

"Do you expect she'll be around anytime soon?"

Emily furrowed her brow. "Probably not," she said, again lying.

She was not sure why the idea of Austin and Susan being together offended her. Perhaps it was because she was jealous that he got to spend so much time with her this last year while she was away at school. Perhaps she was ready to have her friend back and all to herself. Or perhaps it was something more - something to do with their last meeting in the woods. Emily could not be sure, but all she knew was that she didn't want to have to share Susan Gilbert with her brother, or even Benjamin Newton for that matter.

Emily continued up the stairs, leaving Austin dumbstruck and disappointed as he walked out the front door.

Once in her room, Emily found herself going through almost every dress she owned before finally landing on one. It was a lavender dress that hung just off the ends of her narrow shoulders. The waist was cinched tight around her corset and she had to call in Vinnie to fasten it up from the back. The dress reminded her of springtime and wildflowers and more importantly, it was a stark contrast with her black uniform at the seminary. She stood observing herself in the mirror, feeling happy for the first time in over a year. She then began running her fingers over the top of her hair and smoothing out the slight imperfections in her dress over and over again. She was unable to conceal her nerves. She was about to see Susan for the first time in three years. For the first time since they kissed. For the first time . . .

The sound of the grandfather clock downstairs alerted her to the time and she realized just how long it took her to get ready. She grabbed her bonnet and raced down the stairs.

"Where on Earth are you running off to?" Her mother inquired, standing by the front door, a feather duster in her hand.

"Out," was all Emily replied before slamming the door behind her.

As she ran, she felt her knees and calves begin to burn. Her mind began to race as fast as her legs with images, memories, and curiosities of Susan Gilbert. Would she look the same? Would her hair still smell of lilac and bergamot? Would her skin still feel soft to the touch? Would she still even *want* to touch Emily? Perhaps she had a beau. Perhaps she hadn't even thought about their kiss since it happened. Perhaps it was just an experiment of some sort.

She let her mind get lost in itself until she was no longer paying attention to where she was running or for how long she had been running.

Suddenly, she ran crashing into something that felt like a brick wall. Emily saw spots in her eyes as she soon realized she had struck someone in all her haste. Feeling horribly embarrassed, she began to stand up.

"I'm so sorry ma'am I -"

"Emily?" She heard a voice say.

The voice was familiar, yet somehow new. She looked the young woman she just plowed into up and down, taking note of the curve of her hips, the lines of her shoulders, and her long, thin neck. The features were unfamiliar to her, but she knew that the warm, brown eyes staring back at her could only belong to one person.

"Suzie!" Emily said, throwing her arms around her before either of them finished standing.

Back down to the ground they both fell with Emily landing on top of her. The two remained there for a second, hugging and laughing until Emily began to stand, pulling Susan up behind her. They both looked down at each other's dresses, now covered in dirt and leaves.

"Oh heavens," Susan said, looking Emily up and down. "What will your mother say?"

"What will my mother say!" Emily replied, smiling wide. "After three years is that all you have to say?" Emily laughed.

Susan shook her head and cleared her throat, focusing on steadying the rapid beat of her heart. Emily looked the same but somehow changed. She matured since their last meeting here. Her lips were fuller, her cheeks, rosier, her hair thicker and longer and her breast now swelled under her dress
considerably which Susan was now intentionally trying to avoid looking at.

Susan looked down smiling and composed herself. "How have you been?"

Just relax, she told herself steadying her breath.

"I am fine now," Emily smiled, casually. She gave off no heir of nervousness or tension which made Susan feel silly for even putting so much stock into their meeting.

"I hear Austin has been pestering you," Emily continued. "I love my brother dearly, but I do hope he hasn't been too much trouble. That school was just awful Suzie; you'd never believe it. They had me reciting scripture like I was a Puritan. Oh, tell me about Mattie? How is she? Does she still enjoy Michigan? Is she married to some cowboy yet? How is your old aunt, Sophia? Still alive and making children miserable? How is your sister, Harriet? What is William like? I hear he's short. Nobody ever sees him at Meeting on Sundays. Do you like living with them? How is the Academy?"

Emily spouted off question after question and Susan laughed and smiled knowing it would be some time before she finally got to speak. Even when they were small children, Emily always had enough energy and vivaciousness for both of them. "That Dickinson girl is wild," the people in town would always say. But everyone agreed that she was simply an excited child who would soon grow into appropriate womanhood.

Seeing her now at the age of 18 confirmed for Susan that the entire town had been wrong. Emily Dickinson would always be wild.

"I've missed you, Emily Dickinson," Susan said when Emily finally stopped talking long enough to catch her breath.

A warm, slow smile spread across Susan's face and she took Emily's arm in hers as they began to walk in the woods as if no time had passed at all.

As they walked, Emily focused on ignoring the jolt of electricity that shot through her at the touch of Susan's arm looped in hers.

November 1848

Benjamin Newton adjusted his cravat and approached the front door more slowly than usual. He was not sure why there was such formal timidity in him now. After all, he had been working for Edward Dickinson for a year and this house was almost synonymous with his own.

He came to Amherst hoping to work with Mr. Dickinson for a few years and eventually open his own practice. Edward Dickinson was said to be a pillar of western Massachusetts and an even stronger attorney. For a man of 26 with his social status, Benjamin Newton had been given an incredible opportunity by working with Edward. Indeed, an experience like this was something Benjamin never dreamed of as a boy growing up on a farm in Berlin, Massachusetts.

Benjamin expected to gain great knowledge, experience, and an improved reputation while working for Edward Dickinson. What he did not expect, was to find someone who intrigued him quite as much as his eldest daughter, Emily did. They corresponded frequently this past year while she was away at school in Holyoke, or as Emily called it, "her confinement."

He chuckled inwardly at the dramatics when he had read the letter describing in detail the darkness of the hallways, the smell of the food which she alleged to be, "of no flavor or particularly good taste whatsoever." He laughed most of all when she spoke of the headmistress whom she declared, "would rather see her locked away in irons than in the front of her assembly each morning."

If there was one thing he learned this past year about Emily Dickinson it was that conformity was not her *forte*. He could only imagine what a handful she was to an institution such as the Female Seminary. And perhaps that is what he liked the most about her. Her lack of conformity, that fire that burned inside her that he knew would never be extinguished. He suggested she take that passion and direct it towards her writing. He was surprised she actually took his advice, and even more surprised that the poems she sent him were quite good. It was clear she was new at the art, and her vocabulary could use some expansion, but he could see great potential in the wily, 18-year-old girl from Amherst and he had taken a particular interest in not only getting to know more of her, but also in educating her in the art of poetry.

Clearing his throat, Benjamin raised his hand to knock firmly on the large, white, wooden door to the Mansion. Before his hand could make contact, the door swung open and a familiar face smiled back at him.

"Newton!" Emily said, throwing her arms around his neck. He smiled, letting his arms surround her small waist lifting her off the ground for a brief moment before remembering his composure.

"Get back inside," he said gently, "you'll catch a chill out here."

Emily complied and they both entered the house together.

"Just wait until you see all the food we have." Emily continued as she took his hat and coat and hung them on the hooks by the door. "It's a good thing father has invited so many people this Thanksgiving, or we'd have to unbutton our trousers and loosen our corsets by the end of the day!"

Benjamin laughed as Emily stuck out her thin stomach dramatically.

"Benjamin, my good man, welcome, welcome," Edward said, sticking out his hand and shaking Benjamin's firmly.

"Thank you for having me, sir, I hope it's not an imposition."

"Nonsense!" Edward continued. "With as much as these Dickinson women have fixed, I expect we shall need you to come around tomorrow for leftovers!"

Benjamin smiled at the idea. "Well, I am always happy to serve the Dickinson household." His eyes shifted over Edward's shoulder for just a moment towards Emily. "In whatever manner I can."

Edward left the two of them alone in the parlor where the conversation shifted to the unspoken, pending topic of Emily's experience at school.

"Oh, don't be daft, Newton, you know exactly how my experience at the asylum was. I will never go back there, just you wait and see," she said resolutely.

Benjamin nodded. "What does your father say about all that?"

"Not to worry there," Emily continued. "It's my mother who needs convincing and I've been demonstrating my 'fine womanly skills in the kitchen' these past few weeks," she said making air quotes. "I plan on making her so dependent on me that the idea of me leaving for another term is simply too much to bear."

Benjamin threw his head back in astonishment. "What a clever girl you are, Emily Dickinson."

"Well, I don't know about all that. I am a *woman* now, or have you not heard?" Emily replied, raising one eyebrow. "I was very upset you forgot my birthday this year, Newton."

"But this is only the first year I've known you!" He replied, protesting his innocence.

"Exactly. And now it can never be undone! But no matter, I'm, sure you have a wonderful present to make up for it. An original poem by Benjamin Newton, perhaps?"

Benjamin waved his hand. "Never. I am a patron of poetry, not a poet. I am, however, intrigued to read more of your work, Miss Dickinson."

Emily raised an eyebrow. "Patience, Newton. I have not yet acquired a full understanding of poetry. Perhaps I require more of your tutelage?" she replied in a flirtatious tone.

"As I said," he remarked, "I am always happy to be of service to the great Dickinson household."

Emily smirked and turned to see her sister, Vinnie, approaching her. She enjoyed flirting with Newton. Their banter was one of the things she enjoyed most about his company. And there was a part of her that knew that that's all it was – harmless flirting and an exchanging of wits. It made her feel excited and safe all at once and it was something she never experienced with anyone before.

"Mother needs you back down in the kitchen," Vinnie said in little more than a whisper and smiled at Benjamin.

"Very well," Emily said, "please excuse us, Newton."

"Yes, do excuse us, Mr. Newton," Vinnie said batting her eyelashes and attempting to curtsy as Emily pushed her out of the room.

As she turned back towards the front room, she could see Austin approaching Newton and shaking hands. The two would likely end up discussing politics or recent legal cases. She was certain her father would be joining them too, and soon her uncle. She wished she had some biscuits to deliver to overhear *that* conversation.

Once they were downstairs in the kitchen, Vinnie began.

"He is so handsome!" She proclaimed, her blue eyes sparkling in the candlelight.

"Who?" Mrs. Dickinson chimed in, rolling out a large piece of dough.

"Mr. Newton, of course," Vinnie continued.

Emily rolled her eyes and shook her head but remained silent.

"What?" Vinnie continued noticing her sister's reaction. "*You* certainly must have noticed he is handsome, especially as much as he dotes on you."

With that Mrs. Dickinson's eyes shot up and she stopped her furious rolling. "What's all this now?"

Since her return from school, Mrs. Dickinson made it clear of her intention to marry Emily off to the first amiable suitor. She already had her brother's friend from school, Joseph Lyman, poking his head around in the mornings for tea, a ploy which Emily saw through like lace.

"Vinnie is just spreading gossip again, mother," Emily said flatly, shooting her sister a dirty look.

"I am not!" Vinnie replied defensively. "He lights up like one of those Chinese firecrackers when you're around. I see you two sneaking off into the library and chatting on and on about poetry."

Emily looked betrayed. She and Newton's meetings and discussions were sacrosanct to Emily. The idea of her little sister eavesdropping on their deep, meaningful talks was more offensive than if she had caught them making love in the barn.

"You watch your tongue, Lavinia Dickinson!" Emily snapped, slamming her hand down on the large wooden table, causing a puff of flour from the dough to fly up in the air.

"Enough!" Mrs. Dickinson said firmly. Both girls froze and looked at their mother.

"If Mr. Newton has intentions with Emily, he should make them known. If he does not, you two should not be spending time alone. It's not becoming for a young lady."

"Well, if he had any interest in Vinnie, he would have already made it known," Emily snipped. "Besides, I don't care what his interest is in me, I have none in him. Not in *that* capacity anyways," she clarified.

There was a heavy pause that hung in the kitchen and it was not until the final remains of flour settled back onto the long, wooden table that Vinnie finally spoke.

"But why not?" She asked. Her voice was sincere and not prying as it was before. "He *is* handsome and you two do seem to get along quite well."

Emily looked at her mother who had by then commenced with braiding the large pile of dough on the table.

She looked back at her sister. "I'm just not interested."

Emily knew she had no logical reason for *not* wanting to marry Benjamin Newton. But for some reason, the idea simply did not appeal to her. In fact, she couldn't imagine herself marrying any man at all. The entire notion felt unnatural to her, just as it had in the days of her youth. She shrugged and returned to her duties. Maybe the right person would come along and change her mind one day. But then again, maybe not.

***

Harriet Cutler shouted as she dropped the large cast-iron pot, boiling water spilling over onto the dusty floor of the kitchen. The fire hissed as it trickled into the flames. Susan ran over and picked up the pot with a covered hand, placing it on the table as her sister intended, and knelt by Harriet.

"Is your hand alright?" Susan attempted to lift her sister's hand to inspect the burn, but Harriet refused, insisting it was nothing.

"My own clumsiness," Harriet replied, feigning a smile.

Susan stood up and ripped the edge of her apron, making a slim wrap that she used to cover her sister's burned hand.

"Susan! Your apron!" Her sister protested.

"Nonsense," Susan continued, "I can mend it tomorrow. You need to put some butter on that hand for the pain."

Harriet stood, gently touching the fabric. "What a waste of fine butter that would be. Besides, I'm afraid we have no butter in the house."

"Oh Harriet, surely you can afford a bit of butter for the holiday?"

"We would have plenty of butter, had William not sold off the cow last week. Said we needed it to buy the goose and make repairs to the roof in spring."

Susan could not believe her sister was in such a state. Harriet always wanted the finest things when they were little girls. She could remember one Christmas when they all got straw dolls but Harriet got one with a porcelain face. Mattie was furious of course, but Harriet agreed to let her play with it as a compromise. Susan couldn't have bothered to even care about dolls at the time, so the sentiment had been lost on her entirely. But now, here she was, on a dirty floor, with no maid, no cook, and not even a cow to provide butter or milk.

"But Harriet," Susan continued. "If things are so bad, why not sell this house? Move somewhere farther outside of town? Somewhere where you could both raise livestock or grow vegetables? Somewhere more manageable for both of you?"

Harriet guffawed at the idea. "What, and become a farmer's wife? Spend long days on my knees milking cows and chasing chickens through the yard? Feeding the pigs Sunday mornings instead of attending Meeting like a proper lady? Absolutely not. It's one thing for a family to keep a cow and a few chickens, it's another thing entirely to make it a livelihood."

Susan brushed off her hands and returned to mash the potatoes she had been preparing. She did not expect such a harsh reaction from her sister, but neither had she expected such harsh conditions when she came to live here.

Since her return last year, Susan had been forced to drop out of the Academy after just one term. Her brother-in-law, William, insisted she get a job as a seamstress to make money, which she loathed. That job, which started as only a temporary, part-time position, was now her full-time career, much to her dismay. Susan longed to use her mind, to exercise her intelligence, to teach, to learn. But her family insisted she pull her weight and make money. Now it seemed like all of her hard work didn't even matter since they couldn't even afford butter for Thanksgiving Day.

"Harriet." Susan pressed down the boiled potatoes until they smoothed. "Where has all the money gone that I have been paying to William each week?"

Harriet was silent so Susan continued, "I don't mean to offend you, Harriett, but it seems as if I am paying almost my full wages to him, and yet there are no improvements around the house. If anything, things seem to have gotten worse."

"Well, having you here is an expense you know? There is more food, more milk, more . . . everything!"

Susan nodded quietly and Harriet continued slowly, "but, as you know, gentleman all have their vices."

Harriet paused a moment as if to listen to the creeks of the wood upstairs and make sure they were truly alone before speaking further. "Well, Susan you see, William has gotten himself into a bit of debt with some local men here and . . . your money has been going to pay off that debt."

Susan stopped and turned to her sister. "You mean he's a gambler?"

Harriet shushed her sister and waved a hand in front of her face motioning for her to lower her voice.

Susan could not believe this was happening. She dropped out of school and was working her fingers to a bloody pulp for this? She worked so often that she had not visited Emily in weeks. She even declined an invitation to spend Thanksgiving with her and her family just to be here to help Harriet.

Harriet approached Susan. "He's going to stop. He's sworn he's going to stop."

Susan wiped off her hands on her apron, the fringed marks where she tore it for her sister now coming further and further undone.

"And what if he doesn't? Am I to simply stay here, single-handedly supporting his habit?" Susan asked, her voice sharp and curt.

Harriet looked down at her hands. They were wrinkled and worn. She was embarrassed for herself and her husband. Her sister was right, she knew she was. But how could she explain how all of this had happened when she did not fully understand it herself?

"I don't know what to say," Harriet finally spoke.

"Say that you won't tolerate it anymore," Susan replied.

"How can I make such a promise? He is my husband. He is the man of this house. I have no right to speak on matters of finance."

Susan continued to shake her head, "I don't know what to say either then."

Harriet stepped closer and grabbed her sister's hands, pulling them close to her chest. She looked Susan deep in the eyes before speaking.

"Promise me, dear sister. Promise me you'll marry a good man. A man with reputable character, and most importantly . . ." Harriet leaned even closer to Susan lowering her voice to almost a whisper. "A man with money."

May 1849

Susan,

Would you do me the honor of accompanying me on a picnic this coming Saturday? I believe the weather will be fine for a walk and your company would bring me much joy on such a pretty, sunny day. Please reply at your earliest convenience so I can make the arrangements.

Regards,

W.A. Dickinson

Austin,

It would be a sin to keep such a lovely day all to ourselves. I have written a letter to your sisters inviting them to join along as well, and I shall invite Harriett and William, of course. Do invite whomever you think would enjoy the weather with us.

Sincerely,

Susan H. Gilbert

"Hurry up, we're going to be late!" Austin chirped, checking his gold pocket watch for the tenth time in thirty seconds.

"You cannot be late to a picnic, dear brother," Emily replied, reaching out and tucking his pocket watch back into his vest gently before prancing over to the mirror to tie her bonnet.

"We told the Cutlers and Benjamin that we would be meeting them at noon. It is now 11:56 am," he proclaimed, pulling out his pocket watch yet again.

"Then we have four minutes to spare," Emily said calmly, winking at her brother and retying her bonnet for the second time.

Vinnie raced into the room, adjusting the shawl over her pale, thin shoulders. "How do I look?"

Austin and Emily both stopped to look at their sister. A young woman of 17, Lavinia had truly blossomed over the past few years. Her long, blonde hair had continued to grow and she now tied it up in stockings at night that caused it to fall down the middle of her back in large ringlets during the day. Her eyes continued to shine so blue that Emily swore she could see straight through to the other side of her head if she stared at them long enough. She wore a baby blue dress that was stitched with lace daisy's coming up from the bottom hem and her fair shoulders jutted out from the top portion of the garment.

Emily smiled. "You look perfect, Vinnie. The bees will love your daisies."

Vinnie smiled and rolled her eyes. "Leave it to you to think of the bees."

"Well, someone certainly has to," Emily replied, her brown eyes soft and warm in the late morning light.

Austin checked his watch once more and huffed loudly at his two sisters who now seemed intent on making them late for this outing. They had spent the entire day prior preparing a large basket of cheeses and fruits and Emily had baked enough fresh bread to feed a small militia. At the mention of a picnic, Emily had raced upstairs to write a letter inviting Benjamin Newton to join them and Vinnie had immediately begun going through every dress she owned to find the right one for the occasion.

As promised, Susan had invited her sister Harriet though William was unable to attend due to, "prior engagements." Austin could not be certain what engagements a man had on a Saturday that would prevent him from joining a picnic, but he paid it no mind. Austin saw this day as an opportunity to "get in good" with Susan's family, though why their opinion mattered so much to him, he hardly understood. He was a Dickinson after all. She should be lucky to be with a man of his stature and reputation. But Susan Gilbert had seemed anything but thrilled at Austin's flirtations as of late, and he was beginning to wonder if there was something wrong with her or if there was something wrong with him that repulsed her.

"That's it!" Austin proclaimed, sticking out his chest and straightening his vest. "I am leaving!"

"Calm down, dear Oliver," Emily replied using her favorite pet name for him since childhood. "You'll be all flushed for the picnic."

And with that, both girls pranced out the front door gracefully, leaving Austin standing in the foyer still clutching his pocket watch.

The weather was superb, especially for late May, and Emily skipped ahead of them as they walked together down West Street. She could not help but feel a rush of excitement. The idea of seeing Susan on such a beautiful day made her spirits soar. Austin tipped his hat and greeted passersby politely, as a gentleman of Amherst should, and Vinnie gently nodded and smiled quietly, as every young lady ought. Emily, however, paid no mind to any passing humans and only managed to say "good morning, sir," to an Irish Setter who trotted by, accompanied on a leather leash by his master.

"I wish we would get a dog," Emily said a few moments later as they walked quietly.

"Father would never allow it," Vinnie remarked. "He hates how they smell."

"Says you," Emily retorted, with a small smirk.

"I'd much rather have a cat," Vinnie replied mostly to herself.

Within a few more moments they arrived at a large, green expanse of land overlooking a dark, black pond. The wind from the late spring air made the water choppy and the trees blew loudly in the breeze all around them. Across the field, Emily saw Susan and her sister walking toward them.

Emily took off in a sprint with Austin yelling after her to "behave like a lady." Emily jumped into Susan's arms so hard the two almost fell over on top of each other as they had during their first reunion in the woods. Susan laughed, picking up Emily briefly, her arms now strong from months of work.

A few months ago, Susan and Emily walked through the woods together, even though the ground was still thick with snow. Emily insisted there was still life to be observed out there even in the dead of winter and Susan complied, only for the chance to spend time alone with Emily. As they walked, their hands grazed casually, swaying with their uniformed steps. They stopped to rest on a fallen tree, when Emily grabbed Susan's hand and removed her glove, alleging she could see the future by tracing the lines on one's palms.

"Trust me," Emily said, "it's science."

Susan chuckled and allowed her glove to be removed but when Emily turned her hand over to look at her palm, she jerked back instinctively.

Emily reached out again asking to see her palms, and that time Susan did not resist. They were not the hands of a lady. They were hard, calloused, and worn. Her fingernails were short and brittle and her knuckles swollen, the tips of her fingers numb from needle pricks and sewing.

With just the gaze of Emily's brown eyes, Susan burst into tears and told Emily all about William's gambling debts and the long hours of washing dishes, cooking, sewing, and mending. On top of that, she said she was now tutoring for a local family, the Boltwoods, to make extra money, all of which of course was going directly to fund William's gambling habit.

Emily did not say a word. Instead, she simply rested her arm around Susan and pulled her close. They sat there like that for a while, neither of them speaking and Susan softly crying and breathing into Emily's chest. Emily pulled her closer, smelling the faint trace of bergamot and lilac lingering in Susan's hair. Then, eventually, Emily wiped a tear from Susan's cheek, bent down, and kissed Susan's hand on her rough palm before sliding it back into the small glove. To Susan, that brief moment felt every bit as intimate as when their lips first connected years prior.

Like their prior kiss, the two had not spoken of their winter time in the woods since, but there was an unsaid vow taken that day between the ice-covered trees that had bonded the two young women, even more than they were connected before. Susan now wrote to Emily every other day when she was not calling on her and the two had become even more inseparable ever since that winter.

"Emily!" Susan said, slapping her playfully away. "You'll send us both down into the mud."

Emily stood straight and smiled, extending an arm to the woman who now approached them from behind Susan.

"You must be Harriet."

The woman's face was pale and sunken in. Dark circles rested permanently beneath her cloud grey eyes.

She extended a hand that proved to be as cold as her eyes upon contact and Emily tried to contain the shiver that ran down her spine when their skin touched. It was hard to believe that this was Susan's sister. Susan had always been so full of life and warm-hearted. To imagine her sharing blood with such a cold, idle soul puzzled Emily.

As Emily was attempting to look away from the woman whose steely gaze she could not break, a soft and familiar voice made her jump.

"You must be Susan Gilbert." She heard over her left shoulder before looking and seeing the large hand of Benjamin Newton reach past her towards Susan. "Emily has talked about you so often. It's a shame we have not had a chance to meet until now."

His voice operated like a flame in a dark room and Emily watched as he shook hands with both Susan and Harriet, his warm demeanor quickly melting Harriet's cold exterior.

"A pleasure to meet you, Mr. Newton," Harriet replied politely, a simple smile spreading across her face.

"How dare you sneak up on us, Newton!" Emily said teasingly.

"Did I sneak? Or do you simply lack spatial awareness?" He remarked, winking at Emily.

"What a typical man to blame a woman for being sneaked upon!" Emily retorted.

Susan laughed politely and watched as the two continued to exchange banter and remarks, teasing each other with backhanded compliments and exchanging flirtatious glances. Austin and Vinnie were finally catching up to the group now and Susan nodded and extended a hand to Austin who knelt to kiss it, lingering longer than she preferred. She pulled her gloved hand back and adjusted her dress.

"Shall we sit?" Susan said abruptly.

The group looked up as Emily and Benjamin finally stopped flirting. Austin and Benjamin spread the large quilt the Dickinsons brought on a patch of thick green grass that was nestled a few hundred yards away from the large pond. The chosen picnic site had no trees nearby giving the party the opportunity to soak up as much rays of sunshine as possible.

Emily and Benjamin sat next to each other across from Susan, who claimed a seat between Vinnie and Harriet, leaving Austin to complete the circle next to Benjamin. Vinnie began to unpack the cheese and fruit while Emily bragged about spending all day the day before baking the bread, looking intensely at Benjamin when she spoke.

"Well, then I am sure it tastes delicious," Benjamin replied, a flirtatious smirk plastered across his face.

At that moment, Susan decided she did *not* like Benjamin Newton. *Why is he looking at Emily like that?* She thought, her inner voice unable to contain the annoyance. *Why is she looking at him like that? Like he hangs the moon and stars. He is handsome, but not so handsome as to capture Emily's heart, surely.*

Susan clenched her jaw and breathed in slowly, focusing on the sounds of the birds chirping off in the distant trees, the ripple of the water in the pond, and the slight rustle of wind as it blew through the trees that were just beginning to show their leaves. She turned to her sister to attempt to strike a new conversation in an effort to distract her from the constant sound of Benjamin Newton's voice, but it was to no avail. At every word he muttered the sound of Emily's high, perfect laugh pierced through her eardrums like hot needles. Finally, Susan gave up.

"It is a marvel we have not yet met, Mr. Newton," Susan said curtly, interrupting Benjamin mid-sentence.

"After all, it appears that you are around the Dickinson house even more than I am."

Emily could not be sure, but she thought detected a slight tone of hostility in Susan's voice. She cocked her head slightly sideways to her friend, who ignored her.

"Indeed, Miss. Gilbert," Benjamin continued. "But I am afraid Mr. Dickinson keeps me locked away in his office most days. I have been fortunate enough to see you and Emily sitting in the yard on a few occasions, but unfortunately, I can only watch from afar during the work week."

His polite response made her angry and she worked hard to contain her emotion as she sank her teeth into a warm strawberry feeling the juice exploding in her mouth. She hated the way he looked, so handsome and genuine and good. She hated those piercing blue eyes that stared back at her with nothing but integrity and honesty. She hated his silk cravat that was tied absolutely perfectly beneath his thick, wool jacket. And she hated the way he looked at Emily and more than that she hated the way she looked at him.

"Suzie and I will have to create a device to rescue you one day!" Emily chimed in, in an attempt to ease the now growing tension. "Perhaps you can climb to the window and we can beg you to let down your long hair," she said, laughing.

Benjamin laughed and tossed his head allowing his blonde locks to wave back and forth like a shaggy dog.

The conversation went on for what felt like an eternity. With Susan staring at Emily, Emily staring at Newton, Austin staring at Susan, and Vinnie staring at Newton. Round and round it went until Susan felt her head spinning from the unspoken tension. The only person who seemed to be oblivious to the swirling dynamic was Emily. It was as if she was lost in a trance, hanging on every word Newton said. When he pulled out his book of Emerson's essays and poems to begin reading, Susan thought she may burst inside her corset watching how Emily swooned and hung on his every word.

"Susan," Austin began from across the blanket, "I wonder if you might join me for a walk down by the pond for a moment?"

Susan looked over to Emily who, at the mention of Susan's name, had quickly returned her full attention to her for the first time since the arrival of Benjamin. She looked at Emily for a lingered moment before replying.

"I would love to."

Susan stood from the blanket and brushed her hands off on her dress before reaching over and taking Austin's arm.

Emily watched over her shoulder as Susan and her brother walked side by side away from the group in the direction of the pond. She saw their arms graze gently against one another, saw their hands touch for brief seconds as she and Susan's had in the woods last winter. She imagined Austin removing Susan's glove and kissing her hand as Emily had. The thought was enough to make her skin hot to touch and she began to burn inwardly. It was almost like having an itch in the center of your back. It seemed to be the only thing she could think about but the one thing she could not reach or satisfy.

Did Susan leave with Austin because she actually wanted to? Or because she had been jealous of her flirting with Newton? Emily did not do it on purpose, but she could not deny that the idea of causing some emotional reaction in Susan crossed her mind briefly as she grabbed Newton's arm once or twice. Emily puzzled at Susan's reaction for a few more seconds, then she quickly turned around and asked Newton to read everyone another poem and as usual, she listened intently as he spoke. But even the beautiful words of Ralph Waldo Emerson coming from the mouth of Benjamin Newton could not contain this new storm that now grew inside her. She knew what this feeling was, of course, she read about it before. *"Beware the green-eyed monster,"* she thought to herself, recalling her favorite Shakespeare play. But she had never experienced it herself. For the first time in her life, Emily Dickinson was jealous.

December 1849

Vinnie bounced down the front stairs, her loose, blonde curls falling down in front of her face. She had not even paused to drape a shawl over her shoulders, a decision which she already grew to regret as the cold, Massachusetts wind cut straight through the single pane windows and down the halls of the large house. The fire places were lit so she knew her parents were awake but the front parlor stood empty. She peeked into the library discovering that it too sat still. She peeked into the breakfast room and while there was another fire ablaze, there was no one occupying the room.

Vinnie shrugged and walked back into the parlor to wait. In the corner of the large room, sat an eight-foot-tall Douglas Fir, its thick green branches sagging slightly from the weight of the homemade decorations that hung from them. Strands of popcorn flowed around the tree like the layers of one of Vinnie's finest dresses and paper cornucopias filled with sweets, fruit and nuts rested precariously on the limbs of the large tree.

Overhead she heard the loud footsteps of her sister and Vinnie knew her hopes of sharing a few moments alone with her father were vanquished. Once Emily was awake his entire attention would be turned towards her, especially today.

"Merry Christmas!" Emily pronounced as she shot around the corner and raced towards her sister.

Emily dove onto the sofa directly on top of Vinnie who squealed and began to laugh. Emily began to kiss her sister's cheek ferociously and Vinnie continued to giggle and push her away. The two sisters sat up. They were both red-faced and still laughing when their brother rounded the corner.

"God bless us, everyone!" Austin said, making his best Tiny Tim impersonation and smiling. He walked over and hugged each of them.

"Oh! Can we please read that today? You know it's one of my favorites," Emily begged.

"Certainly," he replied gleefully. "Vinnie where in Heaven's name is your robe? You'll catch a chill," Austin asked protectively looking at his youngest sibling who sat trying to contain a shiver.

"I left it upstairs," Vinnie replied, lowering her head slightly.

"I'll get it!" Emily jumped up and placed both of her hands on her hips. "Austin, you time me. Ready?"

Austin barely caught the words she was saying before Emily shot out of the room, rounded the corner, and could be heard pounding across the floor upstairs towards Vinnie's room. The two left downstairs exchanged a glance and shook their heads. Their sister was always an eccentric one. Antics like this no longer shocked them.

Soon the footsteps returned and Emily could be heard panting and scrambling down the steps. She flew around the corner and nearly knocked over the tree before tossing the garment to Vinnie.

"Time!" She hollered.

Austin laughed before pronouncing, "17 seconds!"

Emily wiped fake sweat from her brow and panted exaggeratively.

Suddenly, a new set of footsteps could be heard, this one coming from down the hall. The three siblings all looked at one another before turning their heads to see their mother enter the room.

"What in God's Creation is all of this ruckus I hear?" Her hands and arms had remnants of flour on them and she had not even taken her apron off which contained stains of fruits, a clear sign she had been busy preparing pies for the evening meal.

"Happy Christmas, mother!" Emily proclaimed as she rushed towards her and flung her arms around her. Austin and Vinnie followed and the three of them engulfed their mother with hugs before she had time to protest.

Mrs. Dickinson was not known for being an affectionate woman, but her children admittedly were her weak spot and she could not refuse them a hug or kiss every so often. This, however, was the most affection they exchanged since the children were very small and she allowed her steely reserve to break for just a moment before snapping back to her traditional role.

"Alright, that's quite enough now," she said firmly but kindly.

A small smile crept across her face, without her permission and she turned now to conceal it.

"Where is father?" Emily asked.

"Oh, he'll be along," Mrs. Dickinson replied. "Emily and Vinnie, why don't you come help me in the kitchen? Austin, you just relax and your sisters will bring you some tea."

Emily rolled her eyes. The sole fact that her brother had the fortune of being born a boy was enough to make her resent him when they were children. But now that he was a full-grown man, the domestic roles had become even more apparent in the Dickinson house. Austin was constantly invited into their father's office to discuss legal matters with Newton and her father while she and Vinnie were now called upon to serve all of them. Emily did not mind it most days, and she was still using her old role as an eavesdropper to her advantage. But lately, the role had been forced upon her more frequently, and even the scraps of conversation she was gleaning were not enough to remove the bitter taste of domesticity that clung to her palate.

She also knew deep down she only had herself to blame, as her ploy to remain away from seminary worked. She had not been forced to return to the awful place, but her mother now expected her to help with household tasks for most of the day.

A monster of my own making, she thought.

Austin sat in the chair by the fire and laid his slippered feet close to it, raising his arms behind his head and letting out a deep sigh. Emily forced herself to look away before thinking hateful thoughts about the brother she loved so much.

Once they were in the kitchen, Emily set to plucking the large goose that was strung up by the fire. She hated the task, but it needed to be done and Vinnie did it for Thanksgiving this year so it was only fair she assumed the duty for Christmas. As she plucked the dead bird, she let out a low sigh, looking over at her sister peeling potatoes and her mother, rolling out dough.

"Mother," she began. "Why do we not have a maid?"

Her mother did not stop what she was doing before answering, though Vinnie's eyebrows shot up.

"Don't be silly, Emily. Why in the world would we need a maid? Your father has three able-bodied women in his household, does he not? It is our job to keep this house clean, wash the clothes, mend what needs mending, and provide a hearty meal for your father and your brother especially once he is a college graduate in a few months."

"What will Austin do when he completes his schooling?" Vinnie chimed in curiously.

"He will attend law school, of course, and then return here to join your father at his business."

Vinnie nodded silently but soon spoke again, "but what if he doesn't want to go to law school?"

Her question was asked in innocence as it came from a girl of 17, but the subject was one of heated debate in the Dickinson house. Austin expressed a few times that he may not want to be a lawyer like his father and his grandfather before him. That he may choose to pursue other careers and he even briefly mentioned the idea of leaving Amherst and heading out west to work with one of his friends from school. Each time it was brought up, both parents were there to squash the matter like an ant at a picnic.

"Your brother will be an attorney and he will take over this father's business one day. That is settled," Mrs. Dickinson said, in a matter-of-fact tone.

Emily shot a look at Vinnie as if to say, "just drop it," and Vinnie quickly resumed her peeling.

After about half an hour of working in silence, they heard the sound of the front door open and a loud male voice they knew all too well. Their father was home. The two girls looked to their mother who glanced back with a knowing look.

"Well, go on then," she said, lifting off her apron as she waved them upstairs.

The girls took off up the kitchen steps and raced down the hall. Edward stood in the doorway carrying a large basket in his hand. He did not even have time to remove his topcoat and hat before the girls surrounded him.

Austin, who had fallen asleep by the fire, was now standing up and yawning and Mrs. Dickinson was coming down the hall from the kitchen.

"Alright, alright," Edward said, "you girls are behaving like bears on honey. Why don't you go sit down? Both of you." His voice had a low snap to it and they quickly obeyed.

As soon as they were seated, they noticed the struggle he was having with the large basket, and their curiosity only began to mount. It looked as if the basket was moving in his hands.

Emily scooted to the edge of her seat on the sofa and looked at the basket as if she could see right through it by staring more intensely. Edward and his wife exchanged a glance and Edward stepped forward, setting the basket on the ground. He lifted the lid slowly as he said, "Merry Christmas, children."

As he did, a small furry brown and white head popped out of the basket and let out a low whine.

"A puppy!" Emily shrieked so loud that Vinnie had to cover her ears.

She slid down to the floor and watched as the small, tri-colored animal clumsily fell out of the basket. It had big paws and long, floppy ears and he soon began bouncing playfully around the large room. He was so small that his efforts of walking in a straight line proved futile and he could only take a few small steps before collapsing either from exhaustion or tripping over his own ears. Austin joined Emily on the floor and began to play with the small creature. Vinnie remained on the sofa but smiled slightly as the young pup bounced back and forth between her siblings.

"What kind of a dog is it father?" Austin asked.

"He's a Newfoundland. Pure bred, of course," Edward remarked with an air of pride in his voice.

It came as no surprise to Vinnie that Emily got her dog. Ever since their picnic last spring, she chimed on and on about how much she wanted one. She knew it was only a matter of time before their father gave in to her desires. Plus, the fact that Emily's birthday was earlier that month and she had only received a set of pencils and new stationery guaranteed a larger Christmas gift for their father's favorite child.

"Vinnie, dear," Mrs. Dickinson spoke quietly, "I think there is something else in there as well."

Everyone paused, except for the puppy who continued to dance in an imaginary circle, as Vinnie slid over towards the basket and lifted the lid. Inside, curled up into a tiny ball, was a small, grey kitten. It was no bigger than the size of Vinnie's palm and it opened its mouth and made a soft squeaking noise as Vinnie gently stuck her hand in the basket and scooped it up.

"Oh, Father!" Vinnie said, bringing the fragile kitten to her bosom and holding it close.

Mr. Dickinson shook his head. "All thanks should be to your mother. I was firmly against the idea of any pets, as you well know. But your mother informed me of how much help you both have been to her around the house this year and well . . . let's just say she convinced me such good behavior deserved a good reward."

Mrs. Dickinson looked down and smiled softly at her youngest child. She could see the immense happiness that had taken over her at that moment and it brought her a great amount of happiness as well.

After a few moments of debating names for the pets and watching the two attempt to play with one another, Vinnie placed the kitten back into the safety of the basket to sleep while she resumed her duties in her kitchen with her mother. Emily on the other hand took her dog upstairs to "introduce him to her room," and to write letters to Susan and Newton. Austin and his father shared a spot by the fire while the meal was prepared, reading the morning Christmas edition of the paper and, much to Austin's chagrin, discussing the current political issues facing the Whig party.

The Dickinson household truly was alive with the Christmas spirit all day that day and Emily could not recall a time when the entire family had ever been so happy together. Later that afternoon, Vinnie played with her new kitten for hours on end, watching as it pounced on a single thread of yarn until there was nothing left but frayed edges of string. Likewise, Emily played with her new puppy as he chased his tail and yapped innocently at Vinnie's small cat. Austin took a few moments to try and teach the young dog to sit but he simply wagged his tale in response, and Austin soon gave up.

Once the children were tired of watching the pets run in circles, they all sang carols while they each took turns playing the piano. Following a huge Christmas supper, each of the children gathered and ate sweets from the cornucopias in the Christmas tree. They ended the day of festivities by reading *A Christmas Carol*. Ever since its publication five years ago, Emily insisted it be a part of the family tradition each year. Of course, Emily also always insisted on reading the chapter where Ebeneezer Scrooge sees his death and visits his own grave, which Vinnie found to be morbid, but not surprising for her peculiar sister.

That night, as Emily lay in bed, she pulled her new puppy closer to her as he snored curled up against her in her small bed.

"Goodnight, Carlo," she whispered into his long, floppy ear. She took the name from one of her favorite books, *Jane Eyre*.

Emily fell asleep dreaming of her and Carlo, walking through the orange and red woods of autumn, and racing through wide, green fields of spring. She dreamt of snowball fights and summer breezes. She dreamt of many Christmas mornings to come and many days of warmth, smelling flowers, and writing poems. And she dreamt that Susan Gilbert was with them for all of it.

June 1850

Winter made its annual exit from Massachusetts around March but the spring hung heavy with cold, thick clouds and rain that year. The streets were filled with mud, which made walking less and less pleasant. The air remained cooler for longer than usual and even by May, Susan still found the weather too cold to go without gloves on her short walk to work at the seamstress's house on Merchant Row.

Much to the delight of the town, a circus came to town that spring, and visitors could pay one penny to see the bearded lady, a pair of Siamese twins, and a strong man at the freak show. One could pay a nickel to sit under the big top and watch as a man in a red jacket and a black top hat shouted and waved his arms around while a woman in a white, sparkled suit with a diamond tiara rode standing up on the backs of two grey horses around the ring.

It all sounded spectacular to Susan, but the price was more than she could afford to spend, though she was certain William would be attending and waging bets with her hard-earned money. Emily was forbidden to go by both of her parents and even Austin stated he would not be attending as he found its contents to be, "unsuitable for ladies and gentlemen in a civilized society."

And so, for Emily and Susan, the spring went on just as many of the springs in Amherst had gone on before it. Wet, cold, and uneventful. It was not until the end of June that the sun finally began to make its presence more permanent. By that time, Susan was so anxious to get outside and walk around that she would have accepted almost any invitation that made its way to her doorstep.

She was pleasantly surprised, when the invitation that did come for her that warm, summer morning, was from none other than Emily Dickinson.

Susan looked down at the letter once more before tucking it gently away in her apron pocket. Emily wrote her less and less these days but happily that meant she was visiting her more and more. The latest letter was now a week old, and it was perhaps the longest she had gone without seeing Emily in several months.

She pulled it out one more time and read it.

Dearest Suzie,

Mr. Carlo Waldo Dickinson and Miss Emily Elizabeth Dickinson request the honor of your presence on a stroll through the town of Amherst this Saturday, June 29, 1850. Carlo tells me he misses your sweet smile and the smell of your warm perfumes in the summer heat. I told him to mind his manners and to be a proper gentleman, but you know how dogs can be. Looking ever so forward to your company.

Yours entirely,

E.E.D.

Susan chuckled at Emily's personification of her dog. Ever since Christmas, she spent more time with that dog than even Susan, which only made Susan fonder of her. The fact that she would rather spend her days in the company of a dog than in people, was one of the unique characteristics she loved in Emily Dickinson.

Unfortunately, her moments with Emily were the only happy ones she had as of late. Her brother-in-law's gambling habits continued to drain the entire family of all finances and Susan was working harder than ever as a seamstress, tutor, and *de facto* housewife and maid for the family. Her fingers and back ached at the end of each day and she often found herself missing the days of her youth at her Aunt Sophia's.

Her sister, Mattie, wrote her a letter last month informing her of a marriage proposal she received. The man, Stephen, was a minister of all professions and Susan laughed heartily at the idea of her wild, rambunctious sister leading the tame life of a minister's wife. But Mattie said that she loved the man, and how could Susan be anything but happy for her sister? Of course, Mattie inquired as to Susan's own love affairs - or lack thereof - just as Harriett had almost every week for the last year.

"That Austin Dickinson fancies you, you know," Harriet said like a grandfather clock chiming each hour on the hour after their picnic last year.

"Don't be obtuse," was all Susan would reply.

But Harriet was relentless and she was constantly chiming on about how much money the Dickinsons had and how handsome a man Austin was. How it would make a smart match and how she should not be a fool like she was.

"Harriet, I do not love the man," Susan finally snapped one day.

Her sister frowned. "I married for love. Look where it got me."

Susan refused to contribute any further to the delusion of her and Austin Dickinson from that day forward. The truth was the only Dickinson she wanted to spend time with, was Emily.

There was a sudden knock at the kitchen door and Susan tossed off her apron and tucked a strand of hair with a licked finger down over her ear. She picked up the tin tray she was cleaning to check her appearance and pinched her cheeks before racing to the kitchen door.

Emily knew that using the front door was a waste of time by now. She would be greeted by Harriet and kept in the front room and forced to make pleasantries for an hour before she would finally get to see Susan. Plus, Harriet refused to let Carlo in the main rooms of the house and so she and the dog now made their entrances through the kitchen door most days.

Susan flung open the small, wooden door and smiled as Emily and Carlo stood side by side on the other side of it.

Emily raised one arm into the air and proclaimed, "we've come to rescue you, fair maiden! Here, climb aboard my noble steed with me, and let's be off!" She motioned to Carlo who scratched an ear in response.

The dog had grown quickly since Christmas but he still had the look of a puppy about him. His paws were far too big for his still-growing legs and his ears hung low on his face. His fur remained long and shaggy, with mixes of brown, white, and black spread all across his back and body. He obeyed every command Emily taught him, and he followed her nearly everywhere she went these days, even out for errands in town. He was seen so frequently by Emily's side that the dog had become almost as infamous as the entire Dickinson family for his clear devotion to the middle Dickinson child.

Susan laughed and looked behind her before quickly shutting the door to the kitchen, practically ushering Emily and Carlo out of the doorway. She didn't want Emily to see the state the house was in. Since Emily's last visit, things had become even worse financially as they were forced to sell the last of their real silverware and exchange it for tin ones. She trusted her friend intrinsically with all secrets of her life, but she was ashamed of the state her family was in and she didn't want to be seen as a charity project.

Emily pretended to ignore the obvious effort to keep them from entering the house and leaned in to hug Susan instead. They stayed like that for a moment, and Susan could feel the warm skin of Emily's bare arm as it wrapped around her neck. It gave her goosebumps that even the June heat couldn't conceal. Susan pulled back, gently pushing Emily away and smiling.

"Shall we?" Emily said, extending an arm for Susan to grab, as a gentleman would when escorting a lady.

The three of them proceeded to walk down Main Street, slowly, while Emily tipped an invisible top hat to those passing by. The queer looks from the townsfolk they passed made Susan blush. She was feeling very self-conscious today, though she was not sure why. Emily was always an oddity, talking to animals, collecting leaves, and hugging trees. The looks they got from the townsfolk today were no different than the same looks they had gotten a hundred times before. Yet, for some reason, today Susan found herself recoiling from Emily each time she heard a snicker or saw a raised eyebrow. Emily, as usual, remained unphased.

"It was lovely to see you in Meeting last week, Miss Gilbert," Emily said, continuing her gentlemanly ruse.

The sound of Emily's playful voice broke her from her inward turmoil momentarily and made her shoulders drop slightly as she released the tension from her neck.

"The blessing was all mine, good sir," Susan said, playfully bumping into Emily as she went along with the game.

"I say, is that a new dress you are wearing today madam?" Emily said, pausing and looking Susan up and down slowly.

Susan blushed as Emily's eyes made their way down her chest and to her hips. While she knew it was all in fun, she could not help but feel like it *was* a man who was looking at her in such a way. She also could not help but feel the immediate response that was rising quickly in her chest and running straight down between her legs at the site of Emily looking at her like that.

Susan cleared her throat. "Why no, dear sir, I am afraid this has been worn many days before."

Emily reached over and grabbed Susan's hand in hers before bending down and kissing it gently. Susan looked around and jerked her hand back. It was instinct, nothing more. Most days Susan would kill to have Emily kiss her hand, her cheek, any part of her. But today, now, exposed in front of half the town, Susan felt ashamed of the act. Ashamed that she wanted it – and more - to happen.

"What's wrong?" Emily asked, her voice now resuming its normal tone, proving that their little game was over.

"You can't do that," Susan said sharply, again looking around.

"Why not? It's just make-believe, Suzie," Emily replied her brown eyes looking innocently at Susan.

"I know . . ." Susan said, pausing. "Just, don't. It's not normal."

Her voice was harsher than she intended and she could see the look of hurt take over Emily's face. It was as if someone placed a jar over a flame, and she watched as the light that was once been behind her warm eyes began to fade.

"It won't happen again," Emily turned from Susan and knelt to pat Carlo as a way to distract herself from the hurt that the words had just caused.

His long tail swung back and forth at the gentle contact and he leaned into her as she scratched behind his ear.

Emily Dickinson had always known she was not normal. She wasn't blind or impervious to the stares and whispers of the people in Amherst. But she never cared about any of that. Because to those who mattered she was normal. To Austin, she was normal. To Vinnie, she was normal. To Newton she was normal. To her father she was normal. And she thought, at least until this moment, that to Susan she was normal. She thought Susan saw her differently than the rest of the mindless drones of Amherst. But now, all she felt was alone and foolish for even thinking such a thing. As she patted Carlo, she focused all of her efforts on not crying. Nothing would embarrass her more right now than to be the crazy Dickinson girl crying in the middle of the street.

"Perhaps we should just keep walking?" Susan said, attempting to lighten the mood and divert the conversation to an easier topic.

She felt horrible for having said that and she had no idea why she said it in the first place. As soon as the words left her mouth, she instantly regretted it. But it was too late.

"Emily, I didn't mean to . . . what I mean is . . ."

Emily stood up straight and cleared her throat.

"Yes, let's walk," Emily said, her voice cold and monotone.

It was the first time she could remember ever seeing Emily behave this way. Emily was always perky and bubbly and bouncy, even on the hardest days. But she could see now the full impact of her words. She had wounded her, deflated her, injured her. And she felt sick about it.

The two walked in awkward silence for a few moments, and Emily ignored everyone they passed while Susan nodded politely. Carlo trotted beside them obediently, never barking or pulling at his leash, a true homage to the time Emily spent training him the past six months.

Susan was looking down counting the cobblestones when she heard Emily's voice perk up.

"Newton!" Emily shouted.

Susan lifted her head and looked across the street. Benjamin Newton was waving back at them and beginning to cross the street in their direction. Susan felt her spine tighten. Ever since their picnic last spring, there was little more Emily could speak of. Every time they were together it was, "Newton told me the best story the other day," and, "Newton had very good advice about this." Susan knew she had no legitimate reason to dislike the man, but she didn't see why Emily was so fascinated by him.

Benjamin was nearly at them now and he removed his hat as he walked up.

"Good morning, ladies," he said politely, "you're looking lovely today, Miss Gilbert."

Susan bowed her head in gratitude and thanked him for the compliment. Part of her wondered if he was being sarcastic. She knew the dress she was wearing was worn and not at all fair, however, his voice and demeanor seemed sincere, so she didn't question it further.

"You're looking dashing today yourself, Newton," Emily chimed in. "Is that a new cravat I, see?"

Newton laughed. "Always one to notice the details, Emily. Indeed, I just picked this up in North Hampton last week."

Something about the way he said Emily's name made Susan cringe silently.

"We should be getting on with our walk," Susan said abruptly.

Emily looked back at Susan for a moment before turning to Newton again.

"Oh! Newton, you must join us! It's too fine a day to be walking alone and besides, we are just two poor, helpless females who need the protection and accompaniment of a fine and upstanding gentleman such as yourself."

Newton laughed as Emily continued her dramatic presentation of the situation and Susan remained silent.

"Besides," she continued, "it wouldn't be *normal* for us to be out here all alone."

Emily shot a look out of the corner of her eye toward Susan as she finished her sentence.

The message was quickly received and Susan ached inwardly knowing it was directed toward no one but her. Newton smiled widely at the obvious jest she made regarding their need for male companionship, and he looked at Susan briefly before saying, "well, I don't know about being *normal*, but I would love to accompany you."

Susan writhed inside. She wanted to spend the day with Emily alone, but then she went and hurt her feelings over something incredibly silly and now she would be forced to share her time with this man she barely tolerated.

And then, as if Susan could not feel any worse about the entire situation, she watched as Emily looped her arm into Newton's and handed Carlo's leash to the man. Now Emily was walking with Newton just as she had been walking with Emily only moments ago.

The three of them walked in silence for a few moments, before reaching the edge of the town where there was a small cemetery on a hillside. A thick patch of dark clouds had gathered directly over their heads and the sun was now blocked, making the cemetery look even eerier than it usually did. A crow bellowed somewhere in the distance sending a chill down Susan's spine. They all paused along the edge of the black, wrought iron gates and looked out over the rounded, grey heads of those long gone. Emily finally broke the silence.

"There is another sky, ever serene and fair, and there is another sunshine, though it be darkness there."

Emily sighed as she finished the last word and Newton stepped back and began to applaud.

"Well done, Emily. Tell me, when did you pen this new verse?"

Emily blushed at the praise. "Just last week. I wrote it in a letter to Austin actually. He said it was quite good. I was going to send it to you, Newton, only you encouraged me to share my poetry with new audiences and so I figured Austin was as good an audience as any."

Susan's jaw clenched slightly. "I didn't know you wrote poems, Emily," she said, now with a slight tone of hurt in her own voice.

Emily turned to Susan. "I wouldn't consider them poems, just scribbles on a page really."

"Nonsense," Benjamin interjected, "Emily has been sending me her poems for a few years now, and I have seen the marked progress she has made. She is becoming a fine poet and one day, you will read her work in books."

Emily turned and swatted at Newton to silence his proclamations, but smiled.

"For a few years now?" Susan stated, unable to hide the surprise and betrayal in her voice.

She told Emily all about her family's financial issues, she confided in her about her darkest struggles and thoughts. And now she just learned that apparently, her friend had been sharing something so intimate with another person but not with her.

"It's not as significant as Newton is making it, Suzie," Emily remarked blankly.

"Don't be silly, Emily," Susan replied, adjusting her tone to hide her hurt. "Mr. Newton says you are a great poet. And I am sure he's right. After all, he is a well-educated gentleman who knows of such things."

Newton, oblivious to the inward tension between the two women continued. "She truly is remarkable. I think she should try to get something published in the Springfield Republican soon. What do you think Miss Gilbert?" Newton inquired genuinely.

"I agree." Was all Susan would say.

July 1850

Dear Suzie,

I am sorry for having offended you with my childish antics. I miss you.

Your friend,

Emily

Emily kissed the bottom of the letter before folding it neatly. She had not seen Susan since their walk with Newton last month, and things felt incredibly tense between them for the first time in their long friendship.

The more Emily thought of Susan Gilbert, the more she realized that she did miss her, but not as one usually missed a friend. Not in the way she missed her when they were separated as children. The way she missed her now felt much more intense. It felt like one of her lungs had been removed and she was unable to inhale fully without it. She could not explain this feeling that continued to grow inside her since their walk with Newton, but she could no longer ignore it either.

Emily watched as the wax poured down over the edges of the letter, dripping slowly and flowing like thick, red blood. She was being mesmerized by it when she heard a knock on the door.

"Come in," she said, removing the dripping wax and quickly pressing the large "E" seal into it. She watched as the hot wax squeezed out of the edges of the seal and pressed down firmly before removing it altogether.

Her brother stood in the doorway, hat in hand. "I'm going to call on Susan Gilbert."

The words caused Emily to whip around in her seat and nearly drop the letter to the floor.

"What do you mean you are going to *call* on her?"

Austin rolled his eyes. "You know what I mean, Emily. I am going to pay a visit to her home and spend time with her family. I would like to foster that relationship."

Emily felt as if her insides were on fire. To call on her meant that he was seeking to make what was a friendly, casual relationship a romantic, formal one. She loved Austin more than most sisters could love a brother and he had been her confidante these many years. As a young man of 21 and a recent graduate of Amherst College, it was only natural that he would begin the process of selecting a future bride. But the idea of Susan and Austin being man and wife was enough to make her insides burn. It was not just the idea of losing Susan as a friend that made Emily writhe, it was the mental image of them . . . acting as man and wife . . . in bed. Emily shook her head at the thought and shivered.

Austin raised an eyebrow, observing his sister's visceral response to the news.

"Okay . . . well mother thought you may have a letter or flowers or tree branch or something for me to take to Susan?"

Emily jerked back to the present reality and clutched the letter tightly in her hand.

"I have a better idea," she replied, "why don't I join you?"

"Join me?" Austin remarked. "As I call on Susan? That would be highly irregular, Emily."

"Nonsense," Emily said, standing and walking towards her bedroom door. "In fact, I find it to be just the opposite. Susan is *my* friend. It would be far less conspicuous than if you went alone. Besides, Harriett and William know me by now and I could act as a sort of intermediary between you and them. I would be an asset to you, dear Oliver."

It was at least partially true. Emily spent more time with Harriett than Austin, though she would hardly classify them as friends. However, William was never at home when Emily passed through to pick up Susan, a detail which she intentionally omitted from her tale.

Austin frowned and stroked his chin as he thought. His sister did raise interesting points. He only met Harriet at the picnic and she had barely spoken two words. He knew little of her husband, William, and he and Susan had not had a substantial conversation since the picnic last spring. Their letters since then had not progressed beyond mere pleasantries and he had hit an impenetrable wall with his efforts of reaching Susan Gilbert. Perhaps having Emily there to ease the tension would play to his advantage.

"Alright, fine," Austin said, but Emily was already down the hall and heading towards the stairs.

"Vinnie!" Emily yelled.

Vinnie exited her room, her large cat lazily draped in her arms.

Much like Carlo, Vinnie's cat had also grown since Christmas. Her face was now a flattened pancake of grey fur with two beady green eyes that shot from side to side at anyone who passed her. Her entire body was covered in long, grey fur that was soft to touch when one was fortunate enough to actually pet the beast without being swatted at. Her favorite past time was hunting and pouncing on poor Carlo, who knew better than to bite the smaller creature but lived in constant fear of the cat hiding around a corner and assaulting him. Vinnie was the only person who managed to stay in her good graces, and everyone assumed it was only because she was the one who fed her twice a day.

"What is it?" Vinnie replied soundly slightly annoyed.

"We're going to visit Suzie. Join us!"

"Wait, what?" Austin said trailing behind her.

But it was too late. Vinnie had already disappeared back into her room; the mere mention of a social call was enough to grant her immediate excitement. She reemerged seconds later this time without a bonnet in her hand instead of a cat.

"I'm ready!" Vinnie proclaimed, her blue eyes shining in the summer light.

Austin shook his head. *I should have never told her I was going to see Susan,* he thought as the three Dickinsons made their way to the wooden house on Main Street.

When they arrived, Austin felt himself getting more nervous than he originally anticipated. He stood in front of the door and cleared his throat, adjusting his cravat. He could hear a slight chuckle from his youngest sister who stood behind him and he shot her a brief look of reproach from the corner of his eyes. Slowly he raised his hand to the door and knocked before taking a step back, bumping into Emily who was standing so close they shared the same breathing space.

Harriet answered the door, a look of surprise coming over her. She quickly wiped her hands on her apron ashamedly and began to fix her hair.

"Why, Mr. Dickinson, what a pleasant surprise. And I see you've brought your lovely sisters. Please come in, come in."

Austin removed his hat graciously and entered first with Emily and Vinnie following closely behind. Collectively, they made their way into the front room. It was a modest room, not finely furnished like their Mansion on Pleasant Street, but it was sufficiently furnished nonetheless. It had a small fireplace, a single winged back chair propped near the hearth, and a long sofa in front of the front window, which was handsomely upholstered, Austin assumed by Susan. Austin took the seat near the fireplace which now sat dormant due to the summer heat and Emily and Vinnie sat together on the sofa across the room. The room had two windows, both of which were open to allow the breeze to make its way into the stale room and Austin noticed that the tables were all well dusted and kept.

Emily looked to Harriet. "I suppose Susan is upstairs and William is not here?"

Harriet paused for a moment taken aback by the girl's forwardness.

"You are correct on one account, Miss Emily, but my husband should be home any time now."

Emily knew it was a lie. It was more likely that William would not be home until after midnight when he would come in smelling of booze and regret. At least that is how Susan recounted it to her over the past year.

"Excellent," Emily replied, standing up abruptly. "I shall go and fetch her then."

Before Harriet had time to interject, Emily was gone, up the stairs and out of sight.

Austin adjusted himself nervously in his chair and fidgeted with his hat which had not yet been taken and hung. Harriet noticed the inadvertent impropriety and jumped to his side.

"Please, Mr. Dickinson, let me take your hat. I apologize I was so taken aback by your visit . . . I should have taken it from you sooner."

"Nonsense," Austin replied politely to reassure the frantic woman. "It is I who have intruded today. Forgive me for simply calling unannounced like this."

Austin's efforts were proving fruitful as Harriet began to relax slightly.

"You are most welcome here anytime, Mr. Dickinson, as are you, Miss Lavinia," she said in Vinnie's general direction, Emily's name being intentionally omitted from the standing invitation.

An awkward silence hung in the room and soon Harriet began speaking again to fill the space.

"I hear you are a graduate now, Mr. Dickinson, do tell me about your plans if you don't mind?"

Vinnie sighed heavily and looked up to the ceiling. She hoped the visit would be livelier than this. She had heard the story of Austin's triumphs with the education system of Amherst more times than she could count.

"Austin Dickinson, top ten in his class at Amherst College."

"Austin Dickinson, the next best esquire of Amherst."

"Austin Dickinson, Edward's only son."

"Austin Dickinson, Austin Dickinson, Austin Dickinson."

The accolades played like a loop in her mind over and over most days. The last thing she wanted to hear was her brother rattle on about his endless list of accomplishments, while she seemed to have none of her own. But she adjusted herself upright and braced herself for the long retelling once more.

Meanwhile, upstairs, Emily stood in front of Susan's bedroom door as nervous as Austin had been just moments ago. She looked down at her dress and wished she had changed into something nicer, though she was not sure why. Susan had seen her covered head to toe in mud. They bathed together as children and bled together as teenagers. There could be no state in which Susan Gilbert had not seen Emily Dickinson. And yet, now, standing outside her bedroom door, she wished she looked prettier.

Shaking the insecurities from her head she raised a hand and knocked gently.

"Enter," she heard the familiar voice echo from the other side.

Obediently, Emily turned the knob and opened the door.

Inside, Susan was seated at a small wooden desk near the window. She was leaning over, intently writing something, and hardly noticed as Emily entered her room.

"What are you writing?" Emily asked.

At the sound of Emily's voice, Susan shot around in her seat and looked immediately towards the door.

Emily stood in her doorway, her long auburn hair parted down the middle and tucked tightly over the tops of her ears in a low bun. She wore a deep blue dress with long sleeves that belled out around her frail wrists. The dress covered the top of her clavicle and had a simple, white collar attached to it. She could not remember a time when Emily looked more lovely, but she felt that way almost every time she saw her, no matter how often or what she was wearing.

Susan, feeling her eyes lingering for too long, looked back down at the paper on her desk and cleared her throat nervously.

"It's a letter to you."

Emily took a step into the room and closed the door behind her. It was the first time Emily had been in Susan's bedroom with the door closed and their growing proximity made Susan's heart race. The room was small enough when just Susan occupied it but now with both her and Emily, it seemed that the air was growing thinner between them as Emily approached her.

"I wrote you a letter too," Emily said, holding out her letter to Susan.

Susan stood from her small wooden chair and walked closer to Emily. She reached out and took the letter, her fingers gently grazing the tips of Emily's as she removed the paper from her hand.

Emily felt a jolt of electricity speed through her entire body at the touch and she jumped slightly, unable to hide the reaction. Susan stepped closer.

"I'm sorry for embarrassing you," Emily began.

Susan lifted a finger and pressed it to Emily's lips.

"No," Susan said. "I'm sorry for behaving the way I did. You did nothing wrong, Emily."

"But I must have because . . ."

Before Emily could finish speaking, Susan grabbed both of Emily's hands and stepped even closer to her, the letter from Emily tumbling uselessly to the wooden floor beneath their feet. There were only inches between them now. Emily could feel the air catch inside her chest as Susan's warm, sweet breath invaded her parted lips.

"Emily," Susan said, quietly, slowly leaning in closer to Emily's mouth.

Emily began to feel her body being pulled closer and closer to Susan's. Their eyes were locked now and she could feel Susan's hands in hers, pulling her nearer with each second, the little remaining distance between them quickly closing in. Emily felt the room begin to spin and she could no longer think of anything other than her lips touching Susan's.

"Emily, the truth is I . . ."

She was close now. So close she could almost taste the wetness of her lips. Emily inhaled deeply and began to close her eyes, leaning in to fill the remaining space between them. She was just about to touch her lips to Susan's when all of a sudden, there was a knock at the door. Susan dropped Emily's hands and walked quickly back across the room, sitting down at her desk. Emily instinctively took a step back and cleared her throat. After a few seconds, Emily heard her sister's voice on the other side of the door.

"Emily? Austin asked me to come to see what is taking you so long."

"We'll be right down, Vinnie," Emily replied, her voice shaking uncontrollably as she placed one hand protectively on the door.

Emily listened as she heard the footsteps walk back down the stairs, leaving her and Susan alone at last.

"Austin?" Susan inquired, her voice raised and slightly breathless.

Emily almost forgot all about her brother's presence in the room directly beneath them and shook her head to clear the fog that now consumed her.

"Yes," Emily began, stuttering slightly. "He. . . he's come to call on you."

Susan stood up and adjusted her dress, smoothing out any wrinkles. Her dress, plain and maroon, was not nearly as fine as Emily's, but it would suffice for the occasion. Susan began to walk across the room and towards the door, but Emily stopped her, grabbing both of her hands attempting to recapture the intimacy that was robbed from them.

"Sue," Emily said, gently stroking the back of her hands.

It was the first time Emily had ever called her that. Throughout their entire lives together, she had always been "Suzie" to Emily. But the new name seemed to fit the shift that just took place in their friendship and Susan admittedly liked the sound of it escaping Emily's lips.

Susan looked at Emily, a forced coldness in her eyes now.

"Yes?" She replied.

"Tell me what you were going to say before," Emily begged, trying to pull Susan back into the moment they shared.

But for Susan, that moment was gone now. There was a man downstairs calling on her. A man that she was expected to be attracted to. A man her sister had been pushing on her for years. A man who should not be kept waiting. She did not have time for these foolish emotions, no matter how deeply it pained her.

"It doesn't matter," she replied, slowly letting her hand slide out of Emily's.

Emily stood aside, allowing Susan to leave the room. She looked over towards the desk and saw the dried, black ink of lines written on a page. *A letter for me*, she thought. But she would never get to read it now. Emily bent over and picked up the letter she brought for Susan and tucked it back into her dress. There was no point in leaving it for her.

Emily heard Susan downstairs as she greeted Austin. She slowly closed the door to Susan's room, taking a long, lingering look at her bed.

September 1850

Emily knelt down and let the cold water flow through her fingertips. The air was crisp, typical for this time of year, and the sky was heavy with thick, grey clouds. She thought back to her first time in the woods with Susan years ago when they were 15. They kissed back then. They kissed more than once that day. On the mouth, likes boys and girls. Like lovers. That moment had been so passionate it nearly consumed Emily and it was all she could do not to think about that day for years after.

But she was a child then, though she felt very much grown up at the time. In a few months, she would turn 20 and her teenage youth would be behind her. She knew that meant that her mother would become more insistent on her finding a husband and the word "spinster" would begin to creep into the daily vernacular. She knew that her brother and father too would begin to pressure her into marriage. Over the last year, even Vinnie made making comments about how it was unfair that she could not be courted until her eldest sister was first married off.

And yet, with all of that pressure, there was only one thing that consumed Emily's thoughts, and it was certainly not marrying a man. It was Susan Gilbert.

She wrote to Susan, asking her to meet her here today. They had not spoken since a month ago in Susan's bedroom. Emily replayed the scene over and over in her mind, especially when she was alone with her thoughts at night.

She remembered how Susan's hands felt in hers, warm and soft. She remembered the jolt of electricity that raced through her hands, up her arms, and directly into her heart as Susan inched closer and closer to her. She remembered her lips parting instinctively as she felt Susan's breath trickle across them.

Just thinking about it now was enough to make Emily's entire body feel warm and her heart race. Everything felt different between them now. At that moment, Emily wanted to kiss Susan again and she believed that Susan wanted to kiss her too. But she needed to know the truth. She needed to know if this feeling she had been wrestling with for years was as one-sided as she assumed it to be.

The thoughts sent Emily into a deep spiral over the last several weeks and she spent every waking moment trying to forget the memories. But with every chirping bird or blowing leaf, she was reminded of Susan. She could not get her out of her mind no matter how hard she tried. And so, finally, Emily wrote Susan a letter.

She delivered it herself this morning, leaving it with Harriett at the front door. Harriett had been polite enough to invite her in for tea and scones, but Emily knew the financial burden such a simple visit would place on the household and she did not want to see Susan in front of her sister anyways. They spent enough time around prying eyes. Emily needed to see Susan alone. She knew that Susan would know what the note meant and that Susan would know exactly where to go.

But she delivered the letter five hours ago and still, there was no Susan. Emily looked up. She could see through a hole in the trees that the sun was just reaching the 3:00 marker and she wondered if she should not return home soon.

Suddenly, she heard the sound of a branch breaking behind her. She spun around and saw Susan staring back at her. She wore a simple, brown plaid dress with golden patchwork woven into it. She wore a crocheted shawl over her shoulders and a dark brown bonnet, which was a different shade than her dress. Emily knew she must have made the dress herself with spare fabric at the seamstress's house but she could not help but think that Susan Gilbert looked like the best dressed woman in all of Amherst standing before her.

"You came," Emily said.

"Of course, I did," Susan replied.

Her voice was soft, causing Emily to smile uncontrollably. Emily took a few steps toward Susan and looked down at her feet. The idea of looking Susan directly in the eyes felt like trying to stare into the sun, and Emily was certain she would be blinded if she tried.

"How are you?" Emily began, uncertain of what else to say.

"I'm fine," Susan continued taking another small step toward Emily.

"Emily, I . . ." Susan continued, but Emily stepped closer and raised her hand, cutting Susan off.

"Please," Emily said, "let me go first?"

Susan nodded silently and bit down on her bottom lip. Emily looked down again and tried to look at anything but Susan's soft lips that now bent slightly at the pressing of her front tooth.

She cleared her throat. "It's just that I . . ."

Emily had practiced what she wanted to say countless times today. She recited it line by line for at least a dozen flowers, for the apple trees in the back yard, for Carlos. Even Vinnie's fluffy, pancaked face cat received an abridged version of the speech as she lurked around the doorway to Emily's bedroom that morning. But now that Susan was here, living and breathing and staring back at her, the words seemed to catch in her throat and not want to leave.

"I can't stop thinking about you!" The statement came sputtering out uncontrollably and she furrowed her brows, embarrassed, as she lifted her eyes to Susan.

Susan smiled slightly. "I would be lying if I said that I've thought about anything but you since that day in my room."

Emily let out a slight sigh of relief at the realization that she was not going mad. That Susan felt the same way she did. That these feelings were, at least in some way, reciprocated.

"But," Susan continued, her voice now lower than before. "Emily, these feelings are nothing more than . . . than a childish, school girl crush. Simply our female emotions getting the best of us. It doesn't mean anything."

Emily looked into Susan's eyes now, but it was Susan who looked away. Emily remained silent, hearing the words repeat in her head as she felt her heart sink.

It doesn't mean anything. She heard the words echo again and again until she had to shake her head to stop them from repeating. She was not sure how long she had stood there, entranced by Susan's rejecting words.

"Are you alright?" Susan asked, placing her hand on Emily's.

Emily looked up at Susan, the familiar bolt of electricity shooting through her again at the simple touch of Susan's hand.

"I don't believe you," Emily said, boldly staring straight into Susan's eyes, her chin jutting forward slightly in defiance.

Susan dropped her hand and continued to look at the trees behind Emily's shoulder, the dirt that now crawled up her boot, anything, anywhere but at Emily.

"Sue," Emily said, her voice just above a whisper.

Susan smiled and looked down. "I like that you call me that now."

"Sue, look at me," Emily said, a mixture of firmness and desperation in her voice.

Susan looked up. Staring back at her were the fierce, warm, brown eyes of Emily Dickinson. She inhaled slightly to catch her breath, but it was no use. Her heart raced in her chest so fast she couldn't breathe. She knew looking at her too long would cause this response, that's why she had worked so hard to avoid all eye contact. But there was no going back now and Susan began to feel uncontrollably drawn into Emily's arms.

"Yes?" Susan said but her voice cracked halfway through the word.

Emily, sensing the slight trepidation in Susan's voice grabbed both of her hands.

"Tell me again that it means nothing," Emily said, slowly closing in the space between them.

They were so close now that Susan could smell the sweet aroma of fruit lingering on Emily's breath and the soft smell of roses and lavender wafted down from her hair.

Susan opened her mouth but no words came out, only a faint weak croak from the back of her throat as she attempted to speak. She shook her head and tried to look down again, but Emily's hand was there to cup the bottom of her chin and lift it gently back up to her eye line.

"Sue . . ." Emily began, but before she could utter another word, Susan felt her entire body lean forward and plant her lips firmly onto Emily's.

Electricity shot through Emily as she pulled Susan closer, feeling her entire body pressed against her breasts and stomach. She lifted her hand to the back of Susan's neck and pulled her face further into hers, their lips moving in a quick and hungry rhythm.

Susan tugged at Emily's dress and she pushed Emily against a tree and slid her hands down to her waist, pulling her hips into her. Emily threw her head back as Susan began kissing the hallow of her neck.

Neither of them had ever felt this way before. It was as if the entire world around them became a dark blur and all that existed was their two bodies, desperate and thirsty for one another. It was so much more this time than it had been five years ago in this same spot. They were adults now. They both knew this wasn't a phase and they certainly knew they weren't practicing for any boys. As their bodies began to move against one another beneath the dark green leaves of the September sky, it became clear to both women that this is what they wanted all along.

Emily was about to wrap her leg around Susan when a loud noise broke their spell and they both jumped before turning to see a large deer leaping off into the forest behind them. They both looked at one another before starting to laugh. Emily leaned her head against Susan's and Susan lifted her hand to Emily's cheek, stroking it gently as she smiled.

"Well, if that isn't déjà vu," Susan said, letting her hand slide down and rest on Emily's thin, pale neck.

"I was wondering if you remembered that first kiss." Emily smiled before kissing Susan again, this time slowly and softly.

"Remember it?" Susan said, removing her lips briefly from Emily's. "Emily, it's the only thing I've been able to think about ever since I came back to Amherst. I thought about it even before moving back here. thought about you every single day I was gone."

Emily paused for a moment, pulling back to look deeply into Susan's eyes, her hand lingering playfully on the back of her neck.

"I thought about you too, Sue. More often than I'd like to admit." She stroked her cheek gently and leaned in, kissing her again.

A few moments later, still soaking in the tenderness of their kisses; they felt the first drop of rain. They began laughing again and Emily stepped back holding up her hands and spinning around.

"Isn't it gorgeous?" She hollered as the rain fell harder and harder.

Susan shouted. "I don't know if that's the word I would use, but we need to get inside, we'll get ill!"

Emily kept spinning for a moment before conceding. The last thing she wanted was to make Susan sick. They walked back to the Mansion, just like when they were 15 years old, only this time they walked back hand in hand.

After about a fifteen-minute walk, they reached the front door of the Mansion and ducked beneath its awning just as the sky fully opened up before them. The rain was now so thick they could not see to the gate of the house. Emily frowned and turned to Susan, smoke billowing from her mouth as she spoke, shivering.

"You can't walk home in this." Emily started shaking her head.

"I'll be fine," Susan protested her teeth chattering as she rubbed her hands on her arms.

"Nope," Emily said firmly, "you are joining us for supper."

Susan peered down the street. It was raining too hard to ask to borrow their carriage. Even the horses would have a hard time seeing in these conditions.

She sighed heavily and conceded. "As you wish, Miss Dickinson."

Emily smiled proudly at having won the battle. She opened the door to the Mansion, ushered Susan safely inside and then called out to her mother. A few seconds later, Mrs. Dickinson rounded the corner and gasped when she saw the girls' appearance. Carlo was soon at the front door with them, sitting beside Emily, sniffing and licking her wet feet.

Emily could only laugh as she began to shake her entire body like a dog. Carlo jumped up and down and barking in excitement. Susan covered her face and giggled and Mrs. Dickinson backed away to avoid the splash.

"Emily Dickinson!" She scolded. "Both of you get upstairs this instant and dry off! Susan, you may borrow one of Emily's dresses while I hang yours to dry. Please stay and join us for supper, no sense in walking home in this downpour."

Susan thanked Mrs. Dickinson and she and Emily exchanged a glance before scurrying up the stairs. Carlo remained at the bottom of the steps, and let out a long yawn before trotting back to the library where Mr. Dickinson was no doubt awaiting his return.

They rounded the corner at the top of the stairs and continued laughing and bumping into one another loudly. It was as if they were drunk. Drunk on kisses and rain and love. Vinnie stuck her head out of her bedroom door and shushed them both, her flat-faced cat also peaking her round head out to lay judgment on the two soaking wet girls before scurrying back inside. Before the door to Emily's room could finish closing, Susan was behind her, kissing at her neck and down her arms.

"Wait!" She said suddenly.

Susan jumped back. "What's wrong?"

"I need to write something down," Emily said, racing over to the simple, brown desk by her window and pulling out the middle drawer.

She sat down at the small chair and knelt over, fiercely scribbling, not stopping to look up and barely breathing. Her fingers flew so intensely over the page that Susan did not dare interrupt her. It was clear that whatever words she was putting down had now consumed her, even more than Susan's touch had moments prior. Susan cleared her throat from the other side of the room.

"What are you writing?"

"A poem," Emily replied without looking up.

"Oh," Susan continued, a slight tone of disappointment escaping her lips. "For Mr. Newton, I assume?"

Emily stopped and turned briefly to face Susan, locking eyes with her. There was something different about her at that moment. It was as if someone had thrown dry kindling onto a pile of embers. Something had awakened in Emily Dickinson. A passion burning deep within her had been unleashed, and Susan could feel it staring back at her from across the room now.

"It's a poem for you, Sue."

December 1850

The autumn of 1850 was exceptionally warm and the farms in the surrounding countryside reaped a bountiful harvest. Corn, pumpkins, squash, Brussels sprout, and cabbage were in plentiful supply which made for a grand and luxurious Thanksgiving Day for even the poorest of houses. Children could be seen playing in the streets long into November and ladies wore only their shawls and bonnets to Sunday Meeting with no need of heavy, wool capes.

But eventually, as with any other year, the last amber leaf fell and winter once again came knocking on the doors of Amherst. Walks to Meeting were now met with wind and snow and horses pulling their carriages struggled to walk on the frozen cobblestones. Boughs of evergreen, pine cones, dried leaves, sprigs of holly and mistletoe filled the hearths and doorways as the Christmas season quickly approached.

Feeling a cold wind slap firmly against his left cheek, Benjamin Newton knocked firmly on the door to the Dickinson's Mansion. He heard a familiar laugh on the other side and smiled as Vinnie opened the door and invited him inside. He nodded and removed his hat and tucked the small package he was carrying under one arm.

"Can I take that for you, Mr. Newton?" Vinnie asked eyeing the parcel.

Benjamin had been working for Vinnie's father for the last three years and yet their conversations had been nothing more than cordial passings and polite conversation. On several occasions, she tried to ask him questions regarding his hobbies and interests, but Emily was always been there to cut in and steal his attention.

Vinnie was wise enough to know by now that he had no romantic interest in her, but she could not help but try when the opportunity presented itself.

"No thank you, I think I'll hold onto this one," he said smiling at Vinnie before gripping the small bundle tighter with one hand.

Vinnie shrugged and hung his hat and coat. Several guests were already gathered in the parlor for the grand occasion. After all, it was not every day that the favorite child of Edward Dickinson turned 20. As Benjamin entered the parlor, he immediately recognized Susan Gilbert and her sister Harriet. Susan stood next to Emily near the piano while Harriet sat talking to a middle-aged woman, whom he knew to be Mrs. Dickinson's sister, Lavinia, on the sofa. There were several other young women who were introduced to him as Emily's cousins, Fanny and Louisa, along with a young woman named Jane Humphrey and another named Abiah Root. A man he previously met in passing named George Gould stood next to Austin quietly sipping brandy.

Once he finished making his pleasantries, he began to make his way toward the general direction of the piano. Emily's face lit up as she saw him approaching.

"Newton!" She smiled, nearly throwing herself into his arms.

"Emily," her mother reproached firmly under her breath. "Compose yourself," she said through gritted teeth.

Emily ignored the chastisement and proceeded to loop her arm into Benjamin's and drag him off into one of the few empty corners of the room, leaving Susan standing alone next to Mrs. Dickinson.

"Happy birthday, Emily," Benjamin exclaimed, handing her the small package he had been carrying.

"You shouldn't have bought me anything, Newton. You know that," Emily said, gently taking the package and admiring its careful wrapping.

"Well, then you're in luck," he said smirking. "Because I didn't buy it."

Emily sat down in an empty chair and began slowly unwrapping the paper, taking care not to tear any of its edges. It was clear it was wrapped with great delicacy. The brown paper was folded neatly at the edges and a simple, brown string held it all together with a single bow.

A huge smile crept across her face as she saw the green, worn edges of the familiar book emerge. It was Benjamin's copy of the works of Ralph Waldo Emerson. It had been the fountainhead of their budding friendship years ago and its contents were the inspiration for many of her own poems.

"Oh, Newton," was all Emily could say as her mouth hung open.

She traced her fingers along the edges of the spine and held it firmly against her chest, before leaning over and hugging him.

***

From across the room, Susan Gilbert looked on, half in jealousy and half in curiosity about what Benjamin and Emily could be talking about with their heads tucked down so close, their voices no more than a whisper. She was so lost in her thoughts that she did not notice Austin Dickinson approach her until he was already at her side.

"How have you been, Susan?"

Susan immediately took note of the stark difference in the effect her name had when it came from Austin as opposed to when it came from Emily. To hear Emily utter the word, "Susan", was enough to send her into complete ecstasy. But hearing it come from Austin's lips felt as if she was hearing it from a friendly neighbor whom she hardly knew.

"I'm quite fine, thank you. And you?" Susan replied cordially.

"Oh, I'm very fine. I'm sure you've heard I have been teaching at the college? Business and Economics," Austin replied, tilting his head back, an air of confidence bursting from his chest as he spoke.

"Emily did mention that yes, congratulations, Austin," Susan continued, directing her gaze back to Emily and Benjamin.

She could hear Austin's voice vaguely echoing in her ears as he chimed on about his work, his students, and his plans, but all she could focus on was Emily and Benjamin still sitting in the far corner of the room. She watched as Emily giggled and threw her head back. She watched as she placed her hand on his arm and squeezed gently. She watched as his face lit up when she spoke and how he hung on her every word. She watched as Emily unwrapped something that he was giving her, though from where she stood, she could not make out what it was.

"What in the world are they talking about?" Susan asked abruptly.

Austin paused mid-sentence and glanced over to the corner of the room.

"Emily and Benjamin? Who knows with those two. Probably planning some mysterious elopement."

"Elopement!" Susan replied, her voice louder than she intended.

A few guests stopped to look at her and she simply smiled and nodded before turning back to Austin.

"What do you mean, an elopement?"

Austin shrugged. "Have you not heard? The other day he came into my father's office and said there was something *very important* he needed to discuss with him. I mean, what else could it be other than a marriage proposal? They're inseparable, those two."

Susan felt her heart drop inside her chest and her throat tighten. Still, she looked back over to the couple in the corner and continued to watch.

***

"Newton," Emily said quietly, glancing over at Susan who seemed genuinely miserable to hear whatever it was that Austin was saying. "I must tell you something."

Emily wanted to tell him all about her and Susan and this new happiness that she had found. She always felt as if she could tell Newton anything. He had been her constant ally and support when she was away at school and more than that, he was the one who had first encouraged her to begin writing poetry. He had been her kind and gentle preceptor for the past three years and most days she felt that there was nothing she could not share with him.

But there was another part of her that feared his disapproval and rejection more than anything. The idea of this friend, this tutor, this inspirational figure in any way condemning her or disapproving of her actions made Emily hesitate to be honest with him now.

Should I tell him about Sue? Should I let him read the poem I wrote for her? What will he think of me if he knows? Will he even care?

Before Emily could answer her inward dilemma, Benjamin spoke. "Ah. Well, that makes two of us with some news to share then."

Emily glanced around the room and saw that her mother was busy placing out more refreshments and that her father was entangled in what appeared to be a heated discussion with his law partner. This was their chance.

"Come with me," Emily said, grabbing Benjamin's hand and slipping out the side door to the parlor. Only Susan noticed them leave.

She followed Emily's movement with her eyes as they escaped unnoticed. She could not leave now and risk making a scene and Austin would surely follow her if she did. But she wanted to know where Emily had snuck off to with Benjamin and she desperately wanted to know what they were doing alone in private.

***

Once they were away from prying ears and down the hall, Emily spoke up.

"Alright then, Newton. Out with it."

Benjamin adjusted his cravat nervously and fidgeted with his hands. He had waited a few months to say this to Emily and now that the moment was here, he could not find the words. His palms began to sweat and he looked down at the floor, fumbling for words.

"Well, Emily. You know I have grown quite fond of our friendship these last three years."

Emily nodded but gave no hint of alleviating his angst in any way, so he continued.

"Anyways, I suppose that is what makes what I am about to say, so . . . well. . . so hard to say."

Emily tilted her head and raised an eyebrow.

"What are you getting at, Newton?" Emily asked.

"What I'm trying to say Emily is that. . ." his voice began to trail off at the end of his sentence and Emily leaned forward slightly to hear. "I'm leaving," he sputtered at last.

The words hung in the air and Emily felt as if someone struck her across the face.

"Leaving? Leaving where? Where are you going?" Her tone was desperate.

"Well, that's the other news," he continued, "I'm getting married! To a lovely woman named Sarah. I am moving to Worcester County where her family lives. I have a new job there as a prosecutor and I am hoping to start my own practice."

Emily could feel her head begin to spin. *Newton, married? Newton, a prosecutor? Newton in Worcester?* For the last three years, she confided in this man. She trusted him, shared secrets with him, and been vulnerable with him. And now, not only was he leaving but apparently, he was engaged? How could she have not known about all of this? How could he have kept something like this from her? Worcester was not very close to Amherst, even by train. Would she ever see him again?

Newton, seeing the pain his announcement caused her, spoke up.

"Emily, you're the first person I've told about any of this. Not even your father knows yet. I've asked to speak with him about it Monday, but I wanted to tell you first. Because the truth is, your opinion means more to me than even your father's. Please understand that."

Emily nodded. "I do understand Newton. It's just. . ." She paused for a moment.

"Just what?" Benjamin asked, bending down to attempt to read her facial expressions.

As Emily looked up at his cool, familiar blue eyes, she felt her eyes begin to well up with tears.

"It's just that I will miss you so much," she said, throwing her arms around his tall neck.

He bent over and scooped her up in his arms. He held her close for a moment, remembering the first time he met her – the bold, outspoken, teenage girl lying under the oak tree. She was a fine young woman now, and she had blossomed and changed in many ways. But he was so glad to see that she had not outgrown that precocious spirit she had on the day they met. And he hoped she never would.

"I'll miss you too, Emily Dickinson."

Emily could overhear her mother from the other room asking people if they had seen her and she knew it was only a matter of time before they were discovered. She wiped her eyes and looked up at her friend before turning back towards the parlor.

"Emily," Benjamin asked before she left. "What was it you wanted to tell me?"

Emily stopped and looked back at him. "Nothing, Newton. It was nothing."

Back in the other room, the entire crowd was gathered to present her with a large fruit cake that Mrs. Dickinson and Vinnie made together. She and Benjamin emerged from the other room and Emily smiled politely as they all wished her a happy birthday. She just hoped that no one could tell that she had been crying.

December 1850

"Why were you crying on your birthday?" Susan asked as she continued to thread what seemed like endless pieces of popcorn.

She wanted to ask her about it since that day, but they did not have any alone time at the party. Emily spent the rest of the evening clinging to Benjamin's side even more than usual and they walked around the house talking to guests as if they were husband and wife. Unfortunately, Austin did the same to her for the rest of the evening. The entire event felt unnatural to Susan. - she and Emily hanging on gentleman's arms.

Susan invited Emily over to help decorate their Christmas tree. William's gambling habits continued to get worse and worse and they recently had to fire even the stable boy which meant more work outside for William on the rare occasion when he was around. He also said they could not afford a Christmas tree this year, but for once, Harriett put her foot down. The tree was small and sparse but Susan was determined to fill it with lush decorations to make her sister happy.

Overall, Emily had surprisingly proven to be very helpful during the decorating. That is, when she was not pausing for long periods of time to stare out the window at the falling snow, or muttering lines of poems under her breath. Currently, she sat, fidgeting with a single piece of popcorn and looking out the window yet again.

"Emily?"

Emily jerked back to reality and faced Susan, "I'm sorry Sue, what did you say?"

Susan shook her head and peeked around the corner to ensure Harriet had not yet left the kitchen. She knew she was making potatoes and carrots for supper, but Susan was always extra cautious around her sister when Emily was visiting now.

"I asked why you were crying on your birthday?"

Emily frowned and looked down again. "I wasn't."

Susan huffed. "I don't believe you."

The words sent a shiver down Emily's spine and she was immediately taken back to their autumn day in the woods when she uttered the same thing to Susan. That day is what catapulted them into this new friendship, or relationship, or whatever it is they were now and it remained one of the happiest days of Emily's life.

"Alright fine. Yes, I did cry." Emily paused. "Because of Newton."

Susan dropped the string of popcorn and crossed her arms, her body raising slightly from her seated position on the floor.

"I knew it! He did something to you didn't he? Did he hurt you? What did he do? Shall I tell William? He knows just the sort who can straighten that man out. I never liked him, you know."

Emily looked over at Susan, whose face was now beet red and seething with anger. Emily laughed slightly and then reached out and placed her hand on Susan's arm. Susan immediately felt the tension release from it as she eased back down onto the floor into her prior seated position. Emily's touch always had an instant calming effect on her, but it was especially potent lately.

"Sue," Emily said softly, "he has not done anything to me. He simply had something important to tell me."

"Oh," Susan paused. "And this news is not something you want to share with me?"

She felt a slight pang of jealousy rising inside her again but she said nothing, already embarrassed at her first outburst.

"I suppose you think he has proposed to me? Is that it?" Emily asked, playfully raising one eyebrow.

Emily let her hand slide its way up Susan's arm and to the bottom of her neck and watched as Susan's skin shuddered beneath her fingers. She saw a slight hitch in Susan's breath as she inhaled and she saw her eyes turn from angry, to jealous, to aroused in a manner of seconds.

"Darling, he *is* getting married, but not to me."

Susan leaned in closer. "What do you mean?"

"He is marrying a young woman in Worcester named Sarah and he is moving there to be with her and work as a prosecutor in a few months."

Susan's jaw dropped. "Oh, Emily," she said, wrapping an arm around Emily's waist and pulling her close.

They embraced, the strands of popcorn lacing in their lap. Emily leaned into the hug even more and let her nose rest in the nape of Susan's neck. As she inhaled, she could smell the remnants of pine and earth from Susan's dress where she had previously been sweating and carrying the tree in it. She could smell the soft aroma of bergamot in her hair from her latest bath. She began to place slow kisses along the curve of Susan's neck.

Susan let out a small whimper in response before opening her eyes and remembering that they were currently in her sister's living room and that Harriet or even William, could walk in at any moment.

She placed her hands on Emily's arms and gently said, "stop."

Emily obeyed and sat back down on her spot on the floor. A few pieces of popcorn crunched beneath her as she moved and the two looked down at the damage and began to laugh.

"A casualty of love," Emily said, holding up the crumpled piece in her hand and popping them playfully into her mouth.

"So, you never had any feelings for Mr. Newton then?" Susan asked, changing the topic back to the original source of debate.

Emily bellowed. "Of course not, Sue! Is that what you've thought all this time?"

Susan felt silly having said the words aloud, but she nodded silently.

"I never had feelings for Newton, Sue.," Emily paused a long moment before continuing. "The truth is, I've never had feelings for any man."

Susan waited to be sure she was finished before continuing. "Neither have I."

They both exchanged a brief, knowing glance and continued threading their popcorn in silence. Emily had never thought there was anything necessarily *wrong* with her for not liking men, but it was still reassuring to hear that she was not the only one who had lacked the sentiments.

The two continued working in silence, gently inserting their needles through the hearts of the kernels sliding each piece delicately on the string watching as the line grew piece by piece. Only the faint sounds of Harriett singing as she worked in the kitchen below and the wind whipping outside broke the silence. Eventually, after what felt like ages, Susan's head shot up.

"Oh! Can I give you your birthday present now?" She looked down. "Well, I suppose it is also your Christmas present, so perhaps I should wait."

Emily smiled wide and jumped up, the sad remains of the popcorn strand she was working on spilling to the ground. "I want it now!"

Susan laughed and also stood, delicately placing her decoration on the ground.

"Alright then! It's up in my room. I'll go get it."

"Don't bother," Emily replied, "I'll come with you." She added a wink at the end of her sentence.

A shiver ran down Susan's spine and she quietly nodded, a slight smirk on her face as she grabbed Emily's hand and led her upstairs to her room.

On their way up, Susan paused at the stairs leading down to the kitchen. She could hear Harriett still singing to herself under her breath, her feet shuffling back and forth. Susan hoped she would not be leaving the kitchen anytime soon.

Once upstairs, Emily closed the door behind them and looked around. The last time she had been in this room was the day they *almost* kissed. She remembered thinking then that she would likely never see this room again. And now, barely a few months later, here she was, in the room with Susan again. And this time, she could kiss her any time she wanted, so long as they were alone.

Susan asked Emily to sit down on the bed, which Emily happily complied with. She giggled as the small bed made a loud screeching noise under her weight.

"So," Emily continued. "Hand it over, Miss Gilbert." Her dark eyebrow raised over her right eye and she held out her empty hands displaying a mischievous grin.

Susan smirked and swatted Emily's hand away telling her to be patient. She walked over to the small chest of drawers, and opened the top drawer pulling out a simply wrapped gift. Emily could tell by how it fell loosely in her hand that it was not contained in a box and she immediately began to analyze the shape to determine what it could be.

Noticing her efforts, Susan interjected and tucked the present behind her back.

"Hey! Close your eyes, Miss Dickinson, or you'll get nothing but coal this Christmas."

Emily rolled her eyes and flung herself backward dramatically onto the bed, resting the back of her hand on her forehead and sighing loudly.

"Don't make me ask again," Susan said, a tone of firmness in her voice.

Emily lifted her head and she could see that Susan was attempting to remain serious so she sat up and placed one hand over her eyes, desperately attempting to hide her smile.

Susan fidgeted with the brown paper behind her back for a moment. It was such a simple gift. What if Emily did not like it? Or what if she thought it silly, or even ugly?

Emily cleared her throat. "Everything alright out there?" She parted her fingers and looked out at Susan.

Susan grabbed Emily's hand and pushed it back over her eyes.

"Promise me if you hate it, you'll be honest with me, okay?"

Emily shook her head. "Sue, I'm going to love it. Now hand it here!"

Susan held it back for a few more seconds and then shoved quickly it into Emily's waiting hands. Emily opened her eyes and observed the wrapping. It was brown paper tied shut with a silk blue ribbon that ended in a neat bow around the front. Emily traced the soft lining of the fabric and looked up at Susan.

"Miss Mavis, the seamstress well . . . she had some leftover from a bonnet she was making so she let me have it."

"It's a very fine ribbon," Emily said gratefully.

"Well, that's not the present, silly. Go on, open it!" Susan proclaimed, biting down on one of her fingernails in angst.

Emily removed the ribbon first, setting it down gently on the bed beside her. After that the brown paper fell away on its own, slowly revealing a beautiful, finger-crocheted shawl. Emily held it up to the light and took in its details. It was a light, seafoam green, with loose tension between each connected opening. It had long, white tassels that hung at the end of each line. She let her fingers explore the pattern for a moment before throwing it over her shoulders and walking over the long mirror propped up in the corner of the room. Emily turned and saw that the back of it rested in a pointed triangle shape down the middle of her back. She turned to Susan and smiled.

"It's wonderful, Sue!" She said walking over to where Susan still stood, thumbnail nearly bitten down to the skin.

Emily lifted her hand and removed Susan's finger from her mouth and cupped both her hands in hers. "I love it," she said staring into Susan's deep, brown eyes.

Susan blushed and looked down but Emily dipped her head down and followed her line of sight, forcing Susan to look back up at her. Sometimes Susan found it hard to look at Emily Dickinson. She had tried for so long not to see her as anything more than her friend and now that there was no hiding the fact that they *were* more than friends, she still found it hard to look directly into her eyes most days. It felt like if she stared at her for too long, her heart may burst inside her body, or she might be swept away into the darkness of her deep brown eyes.

"I'm glad you like it," Susan replied, a soft smile creeping across her face.

Emily leaned in and kissed her, barely letting her lips linger for longer than a second, which sent Susan inwardly spiraling for more. Her eyes were still closed when Emily started to pull away and she had to blink quickly to realize that the kiss was already over.

"I said, I *love* it. And I'm going to keep it forever," Emily replied, leaning back in and resting her forehead on Susan's.

Emily breathed in, inhaling the smell of Susan. Being in such close proximity to her made Emily's constantly running brain be at peace, if only for a moment, and Emily closed her eyes and soaked in the serenity of the moment that she knew was fleeting.

Susan reached her hand behind Emily's neck and pulled her lips up to hers, slowly kissing her. Emily felt her body instantly react and she fought the urge to push Susan onto the bed and climb on top of her. Susan pulled Emily's body closer to hers and her heartbeat quickened with each kiss. Her body was yearning for more. Before her mind or her hands could go any farther, Emily stopped.

Emily stepped back and placed her hand on Susan's shoulder to steady herself as her head spun in thousands of large, dizzying circles.

"Are you okay?" Susan asked.

Emily nodded and put her hands on her hips, breathing heavily. "Yes, I just . . . needed to collect myself."

Susan frowned. "We don't have to . . . I mean if it makes you uncomfortable. . ."

Emily shook her head and immediately covered Susan's mouth with her hand, cutting off her words and sending a warm sensation down her spine and eventually resting in between her legs.

"It's not that. Trust me."

They both stood in silence for a few seconds and then Emily spoke again.

"I have a present for you too. Though it's nothing as fine as what you've given me."

Susan shook her head. "Really Emily, the shawl is so simple."

"Would you please stop qualifying your present? Now, close your eyes," Emily said, a familiar mischievous look now spreading across her face.

Susan smirked and shook her head. "That's not very nice of you, you know."

"Oh, you'll be alright," Emily remarked playfully.

Susan heaved a loud sigh. "Fine!" She bit down on her lip and closed her eyes tightly.

Emily leaned close and waved a hand in front of her face to ensure she could not be seen before reaching into her corset and pulling out a small, single, folded piece of stationary.

She told Susan to open her eyes as she held out the tiny square towards her in her open palms.

"Is this what I think it is?" Susan inquired, slowly removing the paper from Emily's hands.

"Open it and find out," Emily replied, lifting her finger to her mouth to begin gnawing out of anxiety and suspense.

Emily had allowed people to read her poems before. Austin was one of her first audiences and Newton, of course, had been a constant critic and editor of her work for several years now. But this was different. This poem was written *for* Susan. It was the first time she had ever attempted to put her feelings for another person down on paper and to have that person reading it was enough to make Emily explode.

What if she doesn't like it? What if she thinks it's stupid? What if –

Emily's internal turmoil was distracted when she noticed Susan beginning to unfold the paper.

Susan felt the crisp edges of the papers against the tips of her calloused fingers and she felt the urge to recoil as she noticed Emily looking at them. She didn't, and continued to unfold the page slowly.

Once the paper was finally open, she read the lines out loud.

> *Her breast is fit for pearls,*
> *But I was not a "Diver" -*
> *Her brow is fit for thrones*
> *But I have not a crest.*
> *Her heart is fit for home-*
> *I - a Sparrow - build there*
> *Sweet of twigs and twine*
> *My perennial nest.*
> *Emily-*

A single tear crept down Susan's cheek as she finished the last line. It was the most beautiful thing Susan could ever recall reading. Emily managed to capture every element of what she and Susan were, in just a few stanzas. Benjamin was right. Emily Dickinson was going to be a great poet.

She looked up from the page at Emily who had not stopped gnawing at her finger and pulled her close, kissing her.

"Do you like it?" Emily asked, their faces so close they could only manage a whisper.

"I love it," Susan replied.

Susan leaned down and kissed Emily again. She never wanted to stop kissing her.

May 1851

Emily rested her head in her hand and watched as a bee landed on the budding daisy in her garden while Carlo gnawed at his paw. The new spring air flushed against her skin and sent a chill down her spine. The sun was shining and the sky was a vibrant blue, but still, the faint remnants of winter clung to the wind. Emly pushed the thoughts of coldness from her mind and focused only on the hints of sunshine that now shot down through the tree branches as she admired the bright green leaves that lined the limbs of the old oak.

She and Benjamin sat beneath its bright branches, his beaver skin hat resting in his lap and his walking stick propped against the white picket fence in front of the Mansion.

They sat there for a few moments, chatting and laughing as if nothing was happening. As if it was just another cool, spring morning in Amherst. As if they would read lines of poetry or go for a walk together soon. But as time went on, the conversation began to lull and now they both sat in complete silence both wanting to absorb the last few moments they had together.

Benjamin was leaving for Worcester today and though they both knew they would remain friends, Emily knew once he was a married man, their friendship would naturally alter. She could no longer throw her arms around him whenever she wished. She could not loop her arm through his and pretend to be his wife. They could not banter and flirt as had become their second nature. No, once he left on that train today, he would be a District Attorney of Worcester County, a married man, and most likely a father soon thereafter.

A bright, yellow, lark flew down and landed on a lower branch of the tree, his vibrant chest puffing out as he whistled a morning song. Emily hated that her friend was leaving, but she especially hated that he was leaving when the weather was just turning nice. She would miss their frequent walks around town and poetry reading sessions in the meadows now more than ever.

Emily knew he would have to leave for the train station at any moment. She knew he had tarried there too long already. The carriage pulled up over five minutes ago and the driver was frequently checking his pocket watch and staring over in their direction. Carlo noticed the man looking in their direction at one point and let out a loud bark as if to tell him to mind his own business.

Finally, Newton let out a loud breath and then spoke. "It's time, Emily. I must be off or I will miss my train."

Emily nodded, rolling herself off of her stomach and onto her back before standing fully upright. She wiped off the loose pieces of grass that clung to her dress and looked up at Benjamin.

He smiled down at her and bent down, scooping her up as he had always done. Emily allowed herself to relax her body into his one final time. She would miss his warmth. He always made her feel so safe and she didn't know where her mental ship would wander without his constant anchor to keep her safe along the shoreline. As she let her nose rest on the high collar of his wool coat, the smell of tobacco and lavender filled her senses. She smiled, knowing the tobacco smell was the product of so many hours of working with her father. The dried lavender had been a parting gift from her and he tucked it into his breast pocket.

Soon her feet were back on the ground and she was wiping a tear from her eye. His sky-blue eyes looked over her one more time as he rested his large hand on the top of her head.

"Goodbye, Emily Dickinson," he said softly, "until we meet again."

He turned and walked over to the carriage, the driver hastily jumping onto the bench before Benjamin had even shut the door. The driver gave the reins a swift flick and the before Emily even had time to process what just happened, the carriage was pulling away.

She ran over to the gate and began waving frantically at him. He laughed loudly and leaned out as far as he could, waving back. Carlo began barking and chased after the carriage. She could see Benjamin's hand reaching out and trying to pat him as he jumped up and down until finally, the carriage was out of sight and Carlo came trotting back, panting. She sat down in the grass by the gate and patted his head while he sat down beside her and stared out towards the road.

Emily shut her eyes and listen for the horses' hooves to finally leave her ears and then, it was silent. A robin landed on the fence beside her and she smiled.

"At least I still have you, dear Robin," she said standing up and wiping a tear from her eye. "I have you, and I have the bees, and I have Carlo, and I have my poems and most of all, I have Sue," she said, reassuring herself.

"Who are you talking to?" She heard a voice say from the direction of the house.

In the doorway, Vinnie had emerged, her fat, fluffy grey cat curled up in her arms, purring loudly.

"I'm talking to Mr. Robin," Emily replied frankly.

Vinnie shook her head and sat down on the white rocking chair that now swayed freely in the spring air. She gently placed her cat on the stone walkway. The animal looked sleepily around at her new environment before sticking her flat nose high in the air and sniffing. Carlo trotted over to greet the cat who took a quick swat at his nose. Unphased, he shook his head, his long, brown ears flopping back and forth across his skull, and let out a loud huff before turning back towards Emily and laying down in the grass.

"I'm sad to see him go," Vinnie said, rocking back and forth staring in the direction of where Benjamin's carriage left.

"I'm sure you are," Emily chuckled, sharply inhaling the snot that was trying to escape her nose.

"I don't mean it like *that*," Vinnie continued. "I mean, I know how much he meant to you, and I'm sad that you've lost such a close friend."

Emily nodded. "Thank you, Vinnie. But I haven't lost him. He's only in Worcester after all."

Vinnie nodded silently and continued to rock. They both knew it was a lie, but it was a lie Emily needed to tell herself at that moment, and Vinnie seemed to sense that.

Vinnie rocked back and forth and watched as her cat cautiously made its way into the front yard, smelling various spots in the grass. Carlo perked an ear up as she began to approach him but otherwise, he remained unmoved.

"Care to go for a walk?" Vinnie said after a few moments of silence.

Emily was taken aback by the invitation. She and Vinnie never went on walks together and they had not spent much time together lately, admittedly most likely due to her recent, frequent rendezvous with Susan. Emily nodded.

Vinnie stood up from the rocking chair and picked up the cat who let out a loud hiss at being once again moved without her consent. Vinnie patted her large grey head, ignoring the crotchety animal, and walked inside the house. Within a few moments she returned, a fresh bonnet on her blonde head and a shawl draped around her shoulder.

The two women exited the ivory gate, while Carlo trailed behind them on his long, leather leash. They walked in silence for a few moments, with Vinnie politely smiling at the townspeople they passed, and Emily ignoring them altogether as usual. When they reached the Common, Emily let Carlo off the leash and he began to run freely through the large, flattened hay meadow.

His thick, tri-colored fur blew behind him in the breeze as he ran and his mouth pulled back in such a way as to give the appearance of a smile as he ran back and forth to recover the stick Emily had thrown.

Vinnie cleared her throat. For weeks she had dreaded the conversation she was about to have with her sister, and while the timing was not exactly ideal, she knew she could not put it off any longer.

"I notice you've been spending a lot of time with Susan Gilbert lately," she said vaguely.

Emily nodded. "She's my best friend. Of course, we've been spending a lot of time together."

Vinnie continued. "Yes, I know, it's just. . . well, don't you think you should also maybe spend time with some of your other friends? Like Jane? Or Abiah?"

Emily turned to her sister and raised an eyebrow. She had never taken any interest in any of Emily's friends before, not even when she and Benjamin had been inseparable and half of the town had whispered about their imminent marriage.

"What's this all about, Vinnie? Asking me for a walk. Asking me about Sue. What's going on?"

"Nothing," Vinnie replied, looking down.

She could tell her sister would not let her off the hook with such an uneasy answer so she straightened her back and turned to look Emily in the eyes.

"It's just gossip," she said casually.

Emily was still not satisfied and pressed further. "Gossip? What gossip could there be about Susan Gilbert?"

Her heart began to race at the idea of what the town could be talking about. Had someone seen them together? Had they been too careless? Had they sat too close together at Meeting? Had their hands grazed each other's at the wrong time on one of their frequent walks? Had someone followed them into the woods?

Vinnie looked around before she continued. "It's not exactly gossip about *Susan*. It's . . . it's her brother-in-law, William." She lowered her voice and then kept talking. "Everyone is saying people are looking for him over some gambling debts. They're saying he's in big trouble. It's quite the scandal."

Emily bit her lip and looked down, letting out a visible breath. She felt a slight wave of relief rush over her. The gossip had not been about her and Susan at all. Instead, it was only about her ridiculous, waste of space brother-in-law.

Then a new feeling of anger and defensiveness began to flood her mind. She couldn't believe people were talking about Susan just because of her relation to William. And he wasn't even technically her relative - not by blood anyways. It wasn't her fault her sister had married such a disappointment.

"Where did you hear this ridiculous gossip? At Church, no doubt?" Emily said, her voice elevated.

Vinnie looked behind her and then turned back to Emily. She had known the topic would upset her sister but it needed to be said nonetheless.

"Listen, Emily, I'm not saying this is Susan's fault. We all know it isn't. But if she knew about his . . . problem and that is why she's been working so many jobs. Well . . . it doesn't look good for a young lady."

Emily was seething now. "And what, now you're concerned about my reputation in all of this just because Sue and I are friends?"

Vinnie shrugged. "It just doesn't look good, Emily."

Emily turned back towards the Common and whistled for Carlo who came obediently trotting back to her side, a stick proudly jutting from his smiling mouth. She hooked him on his leash and turned back towards Main Street.

"Come on, Carlo, we're going home," she said, without looking in Vinnie's direction.

Emily proceeded to march in silence back towards West Street with Carlo by her side, stick still hanging from his mouth, and Vinnie trailing a few steps awkwardly behind her.

To say this day had not gone well would be a huge understatement. First, she had said goodbye to one of her dearest and most trusted friends and now she learned that the entire town was gossiping about her other closest friend. She needed to be rid of Vinnie. She needed to collect her thoughts. She needed to get her temper under control before she said something to her sister she would deeply regret. And most of all, she needed to talk to Susan.

***

The wind whipped down Merchant Row in a vortex of speed that blew the bottom of the skirts of ladies' dresses up above their knees. The clouds overhead had gone from a soft, wispy white to a menacing, dark grey all within the last hour. Horses began to whinny and neigh at the impending storm, as if urging their masters to return home faster and everyone in town seemed to have a new increased speed in their step. No one wanted to be caught in the late spring rain.

Susan looked behind her as she walked home from the seamstress' house. She could not help but feel like people were staring at her today for some reason. A woman wearing a bonnet that Susan had made for her months ago walked by with another woman Susan recognized from Sunday Meeting. They both smiled and politely nodded their head. Susan nodded back, but as she continued past the women, she could have sworn she overheard the name, "William", come from one of them. Susan looked over her shoulder to find them both whispering and looking back at her as they walked. When they noticed her looking, they quickly straightened up and walked away faster.

She stopped looking around then and simply lowered her head and quickened her pace. The wind was blowing harder now and she was ready to be home. She knew this would happen eventually. William's gambling habits had gotten out of control lately. Three nights in a row now, a large, burly man with a thick beard had banged fiercely on their door demanding to see him. Each time Harriett had bravely answered the door and lied, saying that her husband was away on business. Only she and Susan both knew he was downstairs in the kitchen, hiding like a rat.

As she turned onto Main Street, a gust of wind came up suddenly, ripping her bonnet from her head and sending it bouncing and flying down the street. Susan began to chase after it, but the hat didn't stop rolling until it landed at a familiar set of feet.

"Austin?" Susan said, looking up at the tall man now standing over her.

He bent down and picked up her bonnet and blew on it to rid it of dirt before wiping it down with his gloved hand and holding it out to her.

"Good day, Susan," he said, his usual cheesy smile plastered across his angled face. "How are you?"

Was this a trick? Why was he being so nice to her? Half the town had been staring at her all day, but here Austin stood as if nothing had changed since he had escorted her around his home on Emily's birthday months ago. He had written to her several times since then, but she had admittedly not written back.

"I . . . I'm fine, Austin, thank you." She reached out and took the bonnet back from him.

An elderly couple walked past them and Austin tipped his hat and nodded in their direction. They returned the sentiment but Susan noticed the way they glared at her. Austin seemed unphased by the interaction.

Austin raised an eyebrow as he extended an arm toward her. "Might I have the pleasure of escorting you home, Susan? It seems a storm is coming and you shouldn't be out alone in it."

Susan looked around. For once, the idea of Austin Dickinson's company was welcome to her and she gladly accepted his offer.

As they walked in silence, she wondered if he was going to ask her about William. Certainly, he had heard the rumors. His family was one of the most respected members of the entire town. There was not much that went on in Amherst that Edward Dickinson did not hear about first. And yet, as the moments went on, Susan began to relax at the realization that he had no intention of bringing up anything. He was content to simply walk beside her, her arm looped in his.

Susan had to admit, it gave her a brief moment of respite. She walked slightly closer to him, imagining him as a human shield, protecting her from the judging eyes of the townspeople. She knew no one would dare say a bad word about her in the presence of Austin.

By the time they reached the front door of Susan's house, Susan's shoulders had relaxed entirely and she was actually smiling.

"It was lovely seeing you again, Susan," Austin said, lingering at the front door.

She knew he wanted her to invite him inside. She also knew that's what Harriett would want if she caught sight of the two of them standing together at the front door. Perhaps she should extend the courtesy just this once? He had been kind enough to protect her from the rude townspeople and had not even asked her about William. What harm could a brief afternoon call do?

Susan opened her mouth and began to speak but before she could, the front door to her house swung open with an aggressive yank. Suddenly, another familiar set of eyes was staring back at her and she had not one Dickinson in her presence, but two.

"Sue!" Emily remarked, her face lighting up organically.

"Emily," Austin said.

"Austin?" Emily replied, "what are you doing here?"

"I might ask you the same thing," he said raising an eyebrow and glancing back at Susan with a brief smile.

Emily snapped back, "I'm here to see Sue."

"As am I," Austin stated.

Susan stood frozen between the two of them. She no longer wanted to invite Austin into her house at all. All she wanted was to be alone with Emily. But how could she politely maneuver this and not offend either Austin or Emily?

Harriett appeared from around the corner and, much to Susan's chagrin, resolved the issue quickly.

"Mr. Dickinson, what a lovely surprise! Please, come in, and let me make you a cup of tea. Here, let me take your hat, please."

Harriett nearly shoved Emily out of the way to open the door widely for Austin who nudged past her, entering the small, wooden house. Emily looked at Susan with a pleading look but Susan could only mouth the word, "sorry," before continuing inside herself.

Once inside, Susan removed her bonnet and hung it by the door, and took a seat on the sofa by the window. Austin sat in the tall, winged-back chair near the empty fireplace and Emily scooted over beside Susan, their legs nearly touching but for the dresses that prevented all contact. The three of them sat in silence while Harriet prepared the tea downstairs. She returned only a moment later and Susan breathed a sigh of relief when she began to hand out the cups.

Susan could see that the cup she was holding had a large chip in it, as did Emily's. She knew Harriet had given the good cup to Austin. Austin nodded and thanked Harriet and politely sipped the tea.

Harriet began. "So, Austin, how are things teaching at the College?"

"They're going well Harriett, thank you for asking. My father still wishes me to attend law school of course, and join him in his practice."

Harriett nodded, pretending to be interested while Emily scooted closer to Susan.

"And is that a path you think you will take?"

Austin paused for a moment, "I believe it might be."

Emily drowned him out. She was already well aware of her brother's pending admission to Harvard Law School. It was only a matter of time before he would be leaving her, just as Newton had. She did not want to think about Austin shipping off to Boston and not being down the hall from her room. Right now, all she wanted to think about was how to get Susan alone.

Susan looked down and noticed that Emily had inched closer to her. She could feel Emily's presence and the elevating tension between them was enough to make

Susan want to grab Emily right there in front of God and Austin and everyone and kiss her.

She resisted the temptation but allowed herself to get lost in the image of it all for just a moment. Suddenly the sound of her name snapped her back to reality.

"And you, Susan?"

Susan looked up and saw Austin and Harriet staring blankly at her. She had clearly missed the important part of the question.

"I'm sorry, Austin. What was that you said?"

Harriet shook her head and shot Susan a dirty look. "You'll have to forgive my sister. She can be a little absent-minded."

Austin waived Harriet off. "Not at all. Susan, I was asking how things were going for you with your tutoring?"

"Oh, yes of course. The Boltwoods are a kind family and they treat me very well. The children are fast learners. Soon they will have no need for our weekly sessions."

Susan sipped her tea, anxious to have the spotlight off of her.

"I heard Lucius Boltwood supports slavery," Emily chimed in, taking a loud slurp of her tea.

"Nonsense!" Harriet remarked, appalled at even the implication that someone from Amherst could support such an abomination.

The Boltwoods were as much of a pillar to the society of Amherst as the Dickinsons. The eldest son, Lucious, was five years older than Emily and graduated from Amherst College only a year ahead of Austin. It had been implied in recent years that perhaps Emily and Lucius might be married, but Emily put a swift end to that by threatening to run off and join the circus if even a breath of it was whispered.

Austin simply shook his head. He knew his sister well enough to know that she would say anything to shock a room.

"I am sure Emily's sources are far from reliable, Harriet," Austin said calmly and shot a warning look over his teacup towards Emily.

Emily shrugged and took another intentionally loud slurp. The room hung silent for a moment as Harriett continued to reel from Emily's scandalous implication. Emily smirked at the effect her announcement made and she could see a slight lift in Susan's lips indicating that she too found it humorous.

After a few more moments of pleasantries, mostly between Harriett and Austin, Austin stood and checked his pocket watch.

"I'm afraid I must be off ladies." He paused for a second before continuing. "Emily, perhaps you should come along as well and leave Susan and Harriet to their own devices?"

He extended an arm towards her and Emily looked over at Susan. Unexpectedly it was Susan who spoke first.

"She can't!" She struggled to collect herself. "She . . . she promised to help me with a quilt I'm making. Special order from Miss Mavis for the quilting competition. The family needs it completed by the end of the month and with all the tutoring I'm afraid I've fallen very behind."

Austin remained speechless and looked at Emily as if to confirm the story.

"Mmhmm, it's true, that's why I came over here in the first place," Emily said nodding her head violently.

"Surely you must be joking," Austin remarked. "You? Sewing?" Austin raised an eyebrow at Emily.

Emily nodded firmly. "I admit my sewing skills require work, brother. But who better to teach me than one of the finest seamstresses in Amherst?"

Emily shot Susan a quick wink and smirk causing an incontrollable blush to rise from Susan's breast and spread to her cheeks.

Harriet nodded, oblivious to their brief exchange. "What an excellent idea, Miss Emily! What an opportunity for Susan to teach you the proper ways to be a woman. My Susan is going to make a wonderful wife someday, Mr. Dickinson."

"Indeed." Austin nodded, skeptically raising another eyebrow toward his sister.

He collected his hat from Harriet and bowed before kissing Susan's hand. Watching her brother's lips touch Susan's skin was enough to make Emily's stomach convulse, but she held in her facial expressions as best she could and shoved him quickly out the door.

"See you at home, Oliver!" She yelled loudly once he was already in the street. A few people passing by stopped and stared and Emily laughed before shutting the door.

With the door firmly closed and Austin on his way back to West Street, Emily turned her attention back to Susan.

"Shall we get on with that quilt? I'm sure you have a lot to teach me," Emily said winking so Harriet could not see.

Harriet placed her hand on both of the girl's backs and ushered them towards the stairs.

"Yes, that's right Susan, you better be teaching Emily how to stitch in a straight line. That quilting competition is coming up soon and we won't have anyone saying that a Gilbert sewed something crooked."

Harriet shooed the girls upstairs and returned to the front room to clean up the tea cups.

Once upstairs, Emily followed Susan into her room and leaned against the door as it slowly closed behind her.

"So," Emily began, letting her body rest against the door. "Where is this magical quilt you need so much help with?"

Susan smiled, walking over to the chest of drawers. "It's right here," she said sliding open the bottom drawer. "I finished it last week."

Emily chuckled slightly and began to walk toward Susan. She could sense that Susan wanted to kiss her, but there was a fierceness behind Susan's eyes right now that she had never seen before. It looked as if Susan wanted to do more than kiss her. It looked like she wanted to devour her.

Emily stepped towards the middle of the room, completely forgetting why she came here to speak to Susan in the first place. Susan quickly filled the gap, grabbing Emily by the waist, and pulling Emily's body into hers. Emily gasped and pressed her lips firmly onto Susan's. Within seconds, Susan began to tear and pull at Emily's dress and Emily could not keep herself from reacting to Susan's touch.

Susan pushed Emily back against the door she had just been leaning against. Her hand slid down Emily's side and around her backside, grabbing a handful of flesh and muscle. Emily's leg instinctively wrapped around Susan's waist and Susan pressed her hips closer in between Emily's legs. Emily felt something come alive inside her as Susan began to push more and more in between her legs. She moved her lips down Susan's neck and Susan threw her head back, letting out a faint moan. Emily put her hand over Susan's mouth but even that couldn't contain the sounds of ecstasy escaping Susan's lips.

"I want more of you," Emily whispered into Susan's ear, biting down gently on her lobe.

Susan stopped for a second and took a slight step back, looking at Emily.

"What do you mean?" She asked, still panting.

Emily pulled her close again, "I . . . I don't know what I mean. All I know is I want more of you, all of you. I want you inside me, swimming in my veins, jumping up and down on my heart to make it beat, pushing up on my lungs to make them inflate with air. I want all of you, consuming me, engulfing me, saturating me."

Susan laughed slightly. Only Emily could describe something so intimate in such anatomically graphic terms.

"I want you too," Susan replied, continuing to kiss Emily's neck and down her chest.

She lifted Emily's leg and wrapped it around her again and slowly let her hand slide up, beneath her dress. She could feel Emily's firm thigh growing tense at her touch. She began to let her hand slide farther and farther up her dress until she could feel the round smoothness of her backside. She squeezed it firmly and began to kiss Emily again.

Emily threw her head back and allowed herself to be swept away into the dark sea that was Susan Gilbert. She wanted this for so long, probably even longer than she realized. Perhaps it had always been Susan that she wanted. Perhaps this was why she ;' never been attracted to any men. Her mind continued to wander as she felt Susan's hand move between her legs.

"Wait," she said softly. Susan stopped instantly and pulled back to look at Emily.

"Do you not want me to? We don't have to . . . "

"No, it's not that," Emily said, resting her hand gently around Susan's neck. "I want this more than I've ever wanted anything in my life."

Susan nodded. "What is it then?"

Emily bit down on her bottom lip. "I just don't want it . . . here. With your sister right downstairs."

Susan nodded understandingly. "Where then?"

Emily thought for a moment before lifting her dark eyebrows. "I think I know a place."

July 1851

Susan looked down at the letter before tucking it into her corset. She wanted to keep it close, as if any reader would be able to determine the subtext beneath the single sentence. But as soon as she had finished tucking it between her breasts, she reached down and yanked it out again, unfolding the tiny sheet.

Sue,

Meet me in the woods..

-E.D.

Susan folded it back up again and shoved it into its rightful place in her corset. She looked at herself in the long mirror in her bedroom, flattening and straightening out invisible wrinkles in her skirt. She was wearing her finest dress. It was a parting gift from Aunt Sophia, on her last day in New York three years ago and she had worn it only a handful of times since. Her aunt told her to save it for only the most special of occasions. She last wore it to Emily's birthday party in December, but she hoped Emily would not remember.

The dress was a deep, royal blue, with a neckline that swept across her chest and hung from her shoulders, making her small breasts look exceptionally plump. It had short sleeves that hung off of her shoulders with puffs of lace protruding from beneath them. The skirt of the dress shot out wide from the waist and covered the bottom of her ankles. There were pink roses in the pattern that crawled up from the floor, across her chest, spreading like vines across the entire design. It was made from a piece of very fine fabric and she knew it was foolish to wear such expensive materials into the woods, especially in the summertime, especially when it was going to be . . .

Susan let her mind wander for a moment. What exactly was she going to do in the woods with Emily? She was old enough to know what married men did with their wives, she learned that many years ago back in New York from her younger sister, Mattie, of all people. But she never heard of two women doing anything like *that* before.

She paid her insecurities no mind. When she was with Emily it was as if all of her questions and uncertainties were answered by the simple movement of her hands and the rhythm of their bodies. She wouldn't have stopped last week in her bedroom, had Emily not asked her to. But the logistics of what was about to transpire between them both confused and excited Susan.

She pressed her hands against her stomach, feeling butterflies dancing around inside of her at the thought of Emily's naked body pressed against hers at last.

Susan cleared her throat and stuck both of her hands on her hips.

"Just do it," she told herself.

She smiled in the mirror as she remembered the last time she had been this nervous to see Emily.

It was right after her return from New York, and she had gone all the way over to Emily's house only to learn that she was away at seminary in Holyoke. She gave herself the same words of encouragement back then. Only this time, she knew for certain that Emily Dickinson would be waiting for her.

Susan walked down the stairs quietly, making an effort not to disturb her sister, whom she assumed to be working below in the kitchen. As she reached the front door, she was alarmed by the soft sound of hushed voices in the parlor.

"Just in time," she heard a male voice say as she rounded the corner.

It was William. Harriett was seated at the table across from him, crying.

***

Across town, Emily Dickinson was racing off into the woods once again. She snuck around the Mansion all morning, being more quiet than usual. Her father even called her into his office to ask if she was ill.

"You did not say two words at breakfast today," he said. "Are you feeling quite well?"

Emily nodded aggressively and reassured him that she was only excited about a picnic she was having later.

"Who are you going with?" Austin asked, nosily.

"Abiah," Emily lied, "in the Common."

Austin let out a disappointed sigh and returned to his morning paper.

At noon on the dot, Emily quietly shut the door to the Mansion and crept across the backyard towards the woods, making certain that no one saw which way she left. She brought with her a large quilt, rolled up tight and cinched shut with a long piece of twine. Inside it, she tucked a small bottle of her father's whiskey. She had only tried spirits a few times before, but she hoped it would settle her racing nerves before Susan arrived.

As she walked quickly through the woods, she stopped to gather wildflowers that bloomed along the stream. The trees hanging overhead were now a deep, hunter green, and the fullness of summer had finally descended upon western Massachusetts. Their shade made a canopy from the sweltering heat and Emily regretted wearing such a heavy dress. She only wanted to look nice for Susan, but now she feared she would be covered in sweat by the time she arrived.

The dress was turquoise with a pattern of brown birds that flew all around her body. It hung just across the top of her shoulders and had long sleeves that belled out at her wrists, which allowed the warm air to flow to her arms freely. Her hair was pulled back into a long, loose braid that hung down around her shoulder and was tied at the bottom with the blue ribbon used for her birthday present from Susan. She looked more casual than she would have liked, but the last time she wore the dress, Susan remarked about how pretty she looked in it. And all she wanted right now was to look pretty for Susan.

After a few more moments of walking, and getting her boots and the bottom of her dress dirtier than preferred, she arrived at her destination. There, by the stream, was the same spot she and Susan had first kissed back when they were just 15. It was the same spot they ran into each other upon Susan's return to Amherst. And it was the spot they often snuck off to lately to be alone. It was their own little world back here. Emily had never once observed anyone else passing by in all her days this far back in the woods and she hoped the dense, thick trees would afford them the privacy they desperately wanted today.

She spread out the quilt on a green patch of long grass about 15 feet away from the stream. Once she finished spreading it out, she lay down and looked up, watching as the warm breeze made the trees sway and dance above her. She tried to be patient, knowing that Susan was likely on her way, but all she could do was listen to her heart beat faster and faster. She jumped up and began to pick more wildflowers to distract herself.

After gathering a fistful of black-eyed susans and daisies, Emily used the twine from the blanket to hold them all together. *A perfect gift*, Emily thought smiling to herself at the aptly named flower she gathered. She would give it to Susan when she finally arrived.

Emily looked up towards the sky. The sun was now far past the 12:30 marker that they agreed on. *She must be running late.* Emily bit down on her thumbnail and sat back down on the quilt.

What if she is not coming? Emily thought. *What if she got lost? What if something happened to her on the way? What if Austin went over to see her?*

She bent down and unscrewed the bottle of whiskey, taking a long, deep swig that caused her throat to burn all the way down to her lungs.

Emily's mind raced and raced and she stood up from the quilt and began to pace back and forth. She pulled out a small folded piece of paper from her corset. It was another poem for Susan. Over the last few months, Emily wrote many poems for Susan, but she was reluctant to show them all to her for fear that she would somehow scare her away. She saved this one to give her today. Emily knew today would be special for both of them, even though she was not sure in what way exactly.

All she knew was she wanted Susan Gilbert more than she ever wanted another human being. Emily kissed the tiny piece of paper clenched in her hand and tucked it back into her corset before sitting back down, to wait for Susan.

***

Susan raced across town, her heart beating wildly in her chest. She needed to get to Emily immediately. She hoped she was still there waiting for her, but deep down Susan knew that Emily would stay in the woods waiting for her through the night if she could. Still, she did not slow her pace.

Susan dodged a horse and rider as she darted across the street without looking.

"Hey! Watch it!" The man atop shouted as she ran on without looking back.

When she finally reached the edge of the woods she quickly looked over her shoulder before darting into the thick, dense trees. It would look peculiar, a woman dressed in her best gown racing off frantically into the woods, and the last thing Susan wanted right now was to be followed.

When she was only a few feet into the woods, she heard the church bells begin to ring indicating that it was 2:00. She was very late.

"Please be there, please be there," Susan spoke to herself running as fast as she could without ripping her dress.

She regretted wearing the heavy thing now. At the time, all she wanted was to look her best for Emily. Now all she wanted was to just see Emily. She *needed* to see Emily.

After a few more moments of running, Susan was dripping in sweat as her thick dress weighed down heavily on her and her damp chemise clung to her legs. By the time she finally reached the stream, she was dirty, tired, and panting. But as she walked closer, her heart again felt light when she saw Emily pacing back and forth, gripping a handful of wildflowers.

"Emily!" Susan shouted.

Emily whipped her head around. "Sue!"

Susan jumped across the stream and ran directly into Emily's outstretched arms. Emily pulled her close and listened as Susan's heartbeat began to even its pace and her breaths began to slow. Emily pulled back after a few seconds and grabbed Susan's face in hers before stepping back and admiring her dress and hair.

"You look so beautiful, Sue," Emily said.

Susan blushed and looked down at how dirty her dress had gotten. She could feel the sweat sliding down the spine of her corset now and she knew she must look a fright. And yet, to Emily, she really did look beautiful.

"Oh Emily," Susan began, before pulling Emily's face to hers and kissing her softly.

Emily felt her heart begin to race instantly. She could taste the salt on Susan's lips from where she ran to be here. She could smell the trace of rose petals from her hair mixing with the scent of the fresh dirt all around them. Emily dropped the bouquet of flowers and wrapped both of her arms around Susan's waist, pulling her closer to her body. Susan gasped slightly as Emily placed her hands on her hips and pulled them into hers.

Susan felt her head begin to swim as Emily's hands began to explore her body more freely. She did not want to do what she was about to do, but she knew she had to before it was too late.

"Emily, wait." Susan said, laying a hand on Emily's neck.

"Did I do something wrong?" Emily asked innocently, her brown eyes large and frightened at the idea of upsetting Susan.

Susan shook her head. "No, never."

A slight look of relaxation spread across Emily's face as she patiently waited for Susan to continue.

"Emily, something terrible has happened."

"What is it? What's wrong?"

Susan tried to speak the words, but when she opened her mouth, the only thing that came out was a flood of tears and sobs. She rested her head on Emily's shoulder and Emily held her close, patting her head and whispering, "shh."

It reminded Susan of the first time she cried to Emily in these very woods. Back when she first told Emily about William's gambling habits, years ago. It was nothing short of ironic that he also caused the tears she cried now in the same spot years later.

"It's William," Susan said.

She could not get out more before bursting into tears again. She could not recall a time when she had cried this hard, at least not since her father died when she was only eleven.

"His gambling debts have gotten out of control. He's sending me off to teach Math full-time . . . in Baltimore. He says it's the only way he can get out of this hole and Harriett is not educated enough to do the job."

Emily froze in disbelief.

"Baltimore?" That was all Emily could say as her eyes welled up and her voice began to shake. "There must be some other way. There must . . ."

Susan leaned forward and pulled Emily close.

"I'm afraid it's all arranged," she said.

"When?" Emily managed.

"In an hour. The carriage is being prepared now to take me to the evening train in North Hampton."

"I don't understand."

"I know, my love," Susan said softly, wiping a tear from Emily's cheek.

Emily's eyes shot up to Susan at the word and Susan smiled and nodded. "I love you, Emily Dickinson."

Emily began to cry more. "I love you, Sue."

Susan pulled Emily's face to hers and kissed her softly.

"I have to go," Susan said, tears flooding her eyes. "Write to me. Please, write to me?"

Emily nodded silently, still reeling in shock by the realization that she was losing Susan to a city she had never been to. A city down in the Chesapeake Bay. A city that took two days by train to even reach.

Susan pulled Emily close and kissed her once more before letting go. She felt as if someone had dug a knife through her heart. Susan was losing the person she loved because of someone else's vice. The entire situation was enough to make her both crumble from the pain and seethe with anger.

As Susan turned to leave, Emily grabbed her hand. "Wait!" Emily reached into her corset and pulled out the small, folded paper, and handed it to Susan. "It's for you."

Susan took it and pressed it to her lips before tucking it between her breasts.

Emily remained in the woods feeling numb, still and frozen, the bouquet of flowers already slowly beginning to die on the forest floor beneath her feet.

***

As the carriage pulled out of Amherst that afternoon, Susan found herself thinking about how Mattie had been when she found out she would be moving to Michigan and would be separated from her blacksmith beau. She remembered how she wailed and screamed and cried. How she swore she would not leave. How she was frantic to get in contact with him, to see him just one last time. She did not pity her then, but now, years later, she finally understood what it felt like to be ripped away from the person you love. To be shipped off like a convict to a far-off city for something that was in no way your fault.

Susan continued to look outside the carriage window as it plotted along, half expecting to see Emily galloping up on one of Austin's horses to rescue her. She chuckled at the idea. Emily was a fine equestrian but she knew even she was not foolish enough to attempt a stunt like that. Eventually, she sat back and stopped looking outward. When the carriage was about twenty miles out of Amherst and the sun was setting, Susan removed the small, folded paper from her corset and opened it.

Wild Nights – Wild Nights!
Were I with thee

Wild Nights should be
Our luxury!
Futile – the winds –
To a heart in port –
Done with the compass –
Done with the chart!
Rowing in Eden –
Ah, the sea!
Might I moor – Tonight –
In thee!

October 1851

Emily did not leave her room for most of that summer. Vinnie came to her door many times asking for a walk in the garden or down to the Common but she always politely declined. Her father paid a visit, reminding her that the birds needed company and her flowers in the garden looked overgrown, but she did not care. The only permitted visitor was her most loyal companion, her dog, Carlo, though even he was noticeably missing their frequent walks through town together.

This summer had been the loneliest Emily had been in her entire life. Her two closest consorts, Newton and Susan, had been scattered to the wind and Austin was off in Boston having just started law school.

To make matters worse, Susan had not responded to a single letter Emily had sent her since she left. The letters had not been returned, so she knew she had gotten them, but she could not understand why she had abandoned her so suddenly. They had exchanged vows of love just before she left, Susan had begged Emily to write to her, she had taken her poem and tucked it between her breasts. And now, almost instantly, she was gone. The depression had begun to consume Emily these last few months and even the sun shining through her window, or the birds chirping in her garden brought her no joy.

Nights turned to days, days turned to weeks and weeks turned to long, empty months for Emily as she watched the world pass by her closed window overlooking the cemetery.

Then, one day, a letter came from someone she had not expected.

Dearest Emily,

I write to you from behind the veil of marriage! How old I suddenly feel being called, "husband", and how much stranger it feels that I have now established myself here in the town of Worcester. The people here look to me in the way I once looked to your father – for answers to things I do not yet understand. I now understand his pain as I peppered him with questions as his law clerk.

How are you, dear friend? Has your summer been kind? I hope you are still finding time to write and that you are enjoying the beautiful weather we are having this season. Would you send me one of your latest poems? I have told my wife, Sarah, all about your poetic genius and I would love to share some of your prose with her. The next Emerson, I always call you.

Your faithful friend,

Newton

Emily smiled and folded the letter and kissed it gently. She did not realize how much she missed Benjamin's presence in her life. It was nice to know she had one friend who remained faithful through this dark, sunny summer.

Emily set the letter down on her small desk and stood up, peering out the window and into the cemetery. It was a clear, sunny day and the sky was a bright, light blue. Not a cloud could be seen and Emily closed her eyes and listened while the familiar song of a lark filled her ears. She smiled and tossed open her window fully, allowing the cool breeze of late summer to enter her room. She could not believe she had remained in this little room for most of the warm months that she usually cherished.

Emily stuck the entire upper half of her body out of the window and sucked in a deep breath.

"What are you doing?" She heard from down below.

Vinnie was in the yard, playing with Carlo as he tried to wrestle a stick from her.

"Breathing!" Emily replied.

Vinnie shook her head and stood, brushing off her dress as Carlo dropped the stick and obediently waited for it to be thrown. His tail seemed to wag harder at the sight of Emily.

"Why don't you join us?" Vinnie inquired.

Emily stepped back and slammed the window shut without saying a word. Vinnie shrugged and tossed the stick for Carlo. A few moments later, the front door burst open and Emily came racing outside.

Carlo immediately ran towards her and began jumping with excitement. Emily ruffled his long fur and began speaking to him.

"How are you on this fine day, my good sir?"

Carlo barked.

"Oh! What exciting adventures you've had! Do tell me more then?"

Carlo jumped and wagged his tail, circling Emily.

"You don't say . . ." Emily continued.

Vinnie crossed her arms and shook her head, smiling. "You know dogs can't understand English right?"

Emily shook her head. "Don't be absurd, Vinnie. Next, you're going to tell me that flowers can't hear me singing either and the birds have no idea when I send messages to the bees."

Vinnie's expression remained blank.

Carlo's ears perked up as Emily looked down at him and smiled. "Your Aunt Vinnie can be so crazy sometimes."

Vinnie rolled her eyes and followed as Emily walked past her towards the large oak tree in the front yard. She plopped down and began rubbing Carlo on the top of the head. Vinnie sat down beside her sister and joined in the petting.

"So," Vinnie began. "Tired of being the recluse of Amherst up your ivory tower?"

Emily laughed. "Is that what people are saying?"

Vinnie shrugged. "Maybe not in those exact words, but your absence has certainly been noticed at Sunday Meeting. The people around town always remark about how they got used to seeing you and Susan walking arm and arm every Sunday morning."

The mention of her name sent a jolt of pain through Emily's heart and she quickly jumped up and wiped off her hands on her dress.

"Well, I'm here now, so let's go for a walk and put that town gossip to rest, shall we?"

Emily held out her hand to help her sister up. Vinnie accepted the assistance and they giggled as Emily made an exaggerated heaving noise.

They walked in silence for the most part, though not arm in arm as she and Susan once did. Vinnie nodded politely to the passerby's and Emily ignored them and talked to Carlo which, of course, embarrassed Vinnie. Emily did not care.

They approached the Common and Emily found a stick in the smashed-down hay and tossed it for Carlo. The last time she and Vinnie had been here was when Vinnie warned Emily to stay away from Susan. Maybe Vinnie had been right all along. Maybe she would have been better off just staying away from Susan.

"Emily," Vinnie said, breaking their silence. "Why have you been locked away all summer? It's not like you to be indoors, especially during summer. Mother and father have been worried about you."

Emily knew it was a half-truth, for her mother only worried about the increase in chores Emily's absence caused. She believed the part about her father and felt guilty for causing him any concern.

"I don't know Vinnie, it's just that . . ." Emily stopped for a moment searching for the right words. "It's just, first Newton left and got married and then . . ."

"And then Susan left," Vinnie said finishing the sentence.

Vinnie paused for a moment as if considering whether she truly wanted the answer to what she was about to ask. Then she spoke. "Are you in love with Susan?"

It was out. The question it seemed like all of Amherst was wondering. Emily saw the judgmental looks from the people leaving Church as she reached out to grab Susan's hand and tuck her arm into hers. She heard the whispers as they walked down the streets together. She felt the eyes pressing inward on them as they snuck off into the woods. Sometimes it even felt like the birds themselves had become spies, their deep, black pupils burning down on them from up high in the trees. Emily told herself it was all in her imagination. That what she and Susan had was no one's business but their own. And yet now, to hear her sister confirm her fears was paralyzing.

"What a silly question, sister," Emily replied casually. "Of course, I love Susan, she's my best friend."

Emily hoped the feign of ignorance was enough to thwart her sister's inquisition, but she knew Vinnie well enough to know she could not be so easily thrown off the scent. Emily whistled for Carlo.

"That's not what I asked," Vinnie said, more firmly than before.

Emily looked down and bit her lip. She did not like to lie, especially to her sister, but part of her did not know if Vinnie could be trusted with such information. Or if Emily was even ready to share it with her. She missed the opportunity to share it with Newton, a choice she regretted to this day. Now it was too late, for she dared not risk putting such sentiments in writing.

"Yes," Emily said finally, looking into her sister's blue eyes.

Then Vinnie did something Emily did not expect. She reached out and grabbed Emily by the hand and held it. Emily felt the warmth of her sister's skin melding into her own and it was as if the heat opened an iron gate that had been holding back all of Emily's emotions all summer. Emily began to cry and Vinnie wrapped her arms around her sister and pulled her close.

"I know," Vinnie said, as she patted her sister on the back.

They stayed there like that for a few moments before turning back towards the house together. This time, walking arm and arm.

November 1851

Susan pulled the shawl closer around her chest and quickened her pace. The summer heat in Baltimore was much more intense than back in Amherst and she assumed that meant the autumn would be less frigid. What she had not taken into account, however, was the proximity to the ocean and the impact the wet, sea breeze would have on the overall feeling of the air. Back in Amherst, they experienced some incredibly cold winters, but here even when the mild, autumn breeze blew, it cut straight through your skin and down to the bone.

She was ready to be home – or at least the version of a home she had made here in Baltimore.

Susan was a boarder with an Irish family, the Mahers, who had connections with William and Harriet. Although, the longer Susan lived with them the more she realized that Mr. Maher was nothing more than a gambler, just like William. It was Mrs. Maher who kept the roof over the boarder's heads and paid the bills on time. Susan paid very little for the room and in turn was responsible for her share of washing the dishes, helping prepare the supper meal, and laundering the clothing. The arrangement was very similar to her situation back in Amherst, except now she made more money, which she put in the mail, instead of handing directly over to William in person.

Aside from Susan, there were four other boarders. There was a scrawny, white boy not older than 14 named Peter, whose family had sent him here from West Virginia where he had been working down in the mines. He had developed a bad case of black lung from so many years below the earth, and his parents had apparently hoped the fresh sea air of Baltimore would do him well. Of course, they must have not realized that the entire city of Baltimore was run on nothing but coal. As such, the boy walked around coughing most of the time and Susan, though she tried to be polite, avoided him whenever she could.

Jeremiah and Ezekiel were black twins from South Carolina. They were probably 18 years old, although she never heard them give their real age. They swore they had their papers and were free men, but no one ever saw any such proof. They were both quiet and kept to themselves, and they always looked outside the window and pulled their coats up high around their faces before they left the house. Susan hoped they truly were free men, and if they weren't, she hoped they would never be caught and returned down South.

Then there was Ingrid, who was 16 and from Michigan. She made Susan think of her sister, Mattie, but only because she was from Michigan where her sister still lived. They had no other personality traits in common. Where Mattie was wild and loud, Ingrid was demurred and timid. At first, Susan tried to bond with the girl to dispel the constant loneliness she felt in this place, but Ingrid was shy and seemed mostly too afraid of Susan to carry on a normal conversation.

Susan continued to walk and looked down when a man passing by stared at her. There were no friendly faces here in Baltimore and she did not look forward to the long cold winter that now faced her, both socially and physically. She missed Amherst. She missed her sister, nagging as she could be. She missed their local Church and familiar faces, judgmental as they may be. She missed her old bedroom and her bed, simple as it may be. And most of all, she missed Emily Dickinson, wild and crazy as she may be.

Initially, Susan did not know why she had not returned any of Emily's letters. She intended to write to her every day, but she soon realized that she would never have time for that and the postage would eventually exceed her weekly income. She told herself instead that she would write every week, but her weekends too seemed filled with menial tasks such as tutoring students for extra income and laundering.

But Susan knew that none of these were the real reason she was ignoring Emily. These were simply the excuses she made for herself. Susan knew deep down there was another reason for ignoring her – fear.

When they parted, Susan told Emily she loved her, and she meant it with all her heart. She read her poem so much that it was now withered and faded with small repeated folds. Perhaps that is what frightened Susan most of all - that she *did* love Emily more than she ever loved anyone, more than she *could* ever love anyone. After all, where could a love like theirs possibly end up?

The day Susan left Amherst they met intending to fulfill their love for one another. Back then the idea of making love to Emily did not frighten Susan at all; instead, it only excited her. Yet now it seemed that the farther away she got from Emily, the more clearly she could see things. It was as if she left her body and was looking down on them now, alone in the woods all those days. Kissing, laughing, touching. Mental images that once caused Susan's heart to beat with excitement now only brought her anxiety and dread.

Even if she and Emily had made love that day in the woods, what then? Were they expected to simply carry on like that for the rest of their lives? Sneaking off into the woods? Stealing moments alone in back hallways? Exchanging knowing glances from their pews at Meeting?

Susan knew that Emily deserved more than that. She deserved a husband and a family. And Susan knew all she was doing by continuing to love Emily the way she did was robbing her of even the chance of that. This time away in Baltimore helped her see that clearly now. She decided that it was best to use this time to separate herself from Emily. But every night when she fell asleep, it was Emily's face she saw in her dreams. Every morning when she rose, it was the smell of Emily's hair and skin that filled her thoughts.

After a few more moments of walking, Susan arrived at the Maher boarding house. It was a large brownstone with turrets that jutted out beside the front steps that rose to meet the two narrow front doors. She swung open the right door and the wind nearly knocked it loose from her hand. As she pulled it closed tightly behind her, she heard the familiar voice of Mrs. Maher.

"Why I never seen so much mail for a single gal in all me life!" Mrs. Maher proclaimed before Susan could even fully remove her bonnet, her heavy Irish accent lining every syllable.

Mrs. Maher had a thick head of red, wily hair that never seemed to move all in one direction, no matter how much she tried to tame it. It hit just below her shoulders and occasionally she would manage to tuck it all beneath her understated bonnet. Her bright, rosy cheeks matched her tresses and she had a permanently cheery disposition, as if she created her own private world inside her mind that helped her escape from the harsh realities of the present one.

Mr. Maher, on the other hand, was a quiet man who was rarely seen, except at the supper table when all the boarders would gather and discuss their work for the day. He only asked questions about their earnings and their work around the house. While not a cruel man, he was not rumored to be kind either, a trait that Susan contributed to his excessive drinking and gambling, much like William.

The only benefit to the living arrangement was that the Mahers were Catholic and did not force any of the boarders to attend weekly Mass, for which Susan was grateful. She did not necessarily mind attending church, but she had never been given the choice of not attending every week. And so, Susan enjoyed the freedom over her own religious practices for the first time in her life.

Susan finished removing her bonnet and smiled. "Thank you, ma'am," she said taking the thick stack of letters.

"How many times do I have to be telling ya? It's Bonnie." The woman smiled at her, with a slight twinkle that was always present in her emerald green eyes.

Susan nodded and smiled. "Yes, thank you, Bonnie."

Bonnie winked and left the room, singing an Irish jig under her breath as she walked, her plump hips swaying to the words.

Susan made her way up the large front staircase toward her room. The hallway in the house was long and dark but for a single window at the end that overlooked the busy street below. Shutting the bedroom door behind her, Susan walked over to her small window and pressed down firmly to ensure it was closed. The single pane of glass would not be enough to keep the cold winter air from breaking through and she would have to line it with newspapers soon.

Susan sat down on her bed, a loud creak releasing from its frail base at the weight of her slim body. She looked at the letters one by one. She read the one from Mattie first which was brief but kind, informing Susan that she was pregnant with her first child. Stephen was praying for a boy, of course. The idea of Mattie bringing another life into this world was enough to make Susan shudder, but she was happy at the thought of her sister finally being settled after such a wild childhood.

She moved to the next letter. Scribbled, sloppily across the front of the ivory envelope were the initials A.E.D. Amherst Massachusetts. *Austin?* Susan thought. How did he know where she was? Surely Emily would not have told him.

Susan ripped open the envelope carelessly and roughly unfolded the papers.

Susan,

I was most troubled to hear of your sudden departure from our fair town. It seems the metropolis of Baltimore has gained a new Math teacher and I am certain its pupils will grow all the wiser from your lessons. How long do you intend to remain in Baltimore? I hope not too long. Emily is beside herself with grief, and the entire family misses your presence. I hope it is not too forward to say, but it would please me if you would allow me to be your correspondent during your absence.

Yours,

A.E. Dickinson

Susan set the letters both down and breathed in deeply. She had been shirking Austin Dickinson's advances for years now. What started as a harmless flirtation had grown into something more for him. But she simply did not feel that way for him. Over the last few years, she learned that it was not just Austin she did not want, but any man - any human, for that matter - who was not Emily.

She looked down at the bed and opened the letter from Harriet next.

Susan,

You will never believe who paid us a visit a few weeks ago. Austin Dickinson! Oh, how that boy dotes on you. You would be wise to snatch him up now before a young socialite in Boston draws away his attention for good. One could do much worse than to marry a Dickinson you know. His sister too has visited us but only once or twice to see if you had returned or if we were holding any mail from you to her. It seems the girl was convinced this was all a trick of some kind. She could not accept you had actually moved to Baltimore. A strange one, that girl is. We do hope you are doing well in Baltimore and staying productive. William sends his regards and requests his monthly payment early.

Your sister,

Harriet

    She rolled her eyes. *Of course, she told Austin.* Susan paused and then let her hand slowly wander to the sole, unopened envelope remaining on the bed, tracing the ink gently with the tips of her fingers. The familiar "Ms. Emily E. Dickinson," was neatly inscribed on the back of the envelope. She could imagine Emily bent over her small, squared, wooden writing desk, her long auburn hair falling into her eyes as she wrote its contents with passion and vigor. She could not help but smile at the image and she closed her eyes briefly, allowing just a moment for the mental image of Emily to fill her mind.
    She imagined herself walking into Emily's bedroom, interrupting her writing the letter. She imagined coming up behind her, wrapping her arms around Emily, kissing her neck, her ears, and her hair. She imagined feeling Emily's body respond, watching her chest rise

quickly with each kiss. She imagined moving her hands lower, down the front of Emily's dress.

Suddenly there was a knock at the door.

"Yes?" Susan responded, trying to hide the quiver in her voice.

It was Ingrid. "Are you alright Susan? It's time to help Bonnie prepare supper."

Jerking back to reality, Susan nodded and stood up from the bed.

"One moment," she said, listening as Ingrid's meek, shuffled footsteps left the door.

Susan looked back at the letters sprawled out on her bed. There was Austin's, open and obvious, containing no mystery or meaning beyond the letters scribbled quickly onto the page. So, he wanted her to write to him while she was gone? She saw no real harm in that. Beside it, sat Emily's, unopened, delicately folded letter, sealed shut with red wax. Its contents were entirely unknown, full of suspense and wonder. Emily wanted far more from Susan. She wanted things that Susan wanted herself deep down, but that she now felt more afraid than ever to give to Emily. And what did Austin want from her? Correspondence? Courtship? Companionship? These are the things expected of a young lady in society. The things a young lady like Susan ought to want from a man. And yet, there was a large part of her that recoiled at the idea of all of it.

Susan sighed and pulled out a single sheet of paper from her dresser and began writing.

Dear Austin – she wrote.

March 1852

Austin Dickinson sauntered into the parlor with his head held higher than usual. Edward did not look up from his morning paper. He knew the look his son gave when he wanted to be the center of attention and refused to be baited. Mrs. Dickinson was not so steadfast in her convictions and immediately gave in to the boy's unspoken demand.

"Why Austin, you're looking chipper today," she remarked, offering to take his coat and hat as he lingered at the front door.

"Thank you, mother." Austin grinned his cheesy smile and nodded.

Edward sighed and turned the page. He already knew what the next question would be.

"What has you in such good spirits?" She asked.

There it is. Edward thought, smirking behind his paper. Emily and Vinnie were coming down the front steps now and Austin paused to let them reach the bottom before continuing his story, to ensure he had the largest possible audience.

As Austin began to open his mouth to reveal the cause of his excitement, his father spoke up.

"Has anyone else seen this?" He lifted the paper.

The women all shook their heads. Only Emily read the morning papers and only after her father finished with them completely.

Austin cleared his throat, hiding his annoyance at the interruption poorly. "What are you referring to, father?"

"A woman has been publishing a piece of literature in the newspapers in Washington and Boston. It seems it's a series all about slavery. Apparently it must be quite good because even the Springfield Republican has now commented on it."

"I've heard of that," Austin replied, honestly and eagerly. "It's by a woman . . . Beacher something."

Edward nodded. "Yes, quite right, Harriett Beacher Stowe. She calls it 'Uncle Tom's Cabin.'"

Austin visibly perked up at the slight sign of validation for his partially correct answer.

"I think all slavery should be abolished," Emily said suddenly from her spot at the bottom of the stairs.

"Me too," Vinnie replied firmly crossing her arms.

They stood side by side, both staring at their father as if challenging him to disagree with their stated position. Edward looked up and noticed the silent protest taking place in his living room and laughed.

"Well don't look at me! The Whigs have never approved of slavery, you know that."

"They could sure do more to fight it though," Emily replied, slightly under her breath.

Edward shot a stern glare at his favorite daughter but did not say anything. He knew she was only trying to get a rise out of him, as she always. Emily knew full well Edward did not support slavery, but there was talk of random acts of rebellion and uprisings in the South recently and Edward was never one for revolution. Mrs. Dickinson hushed Emily and cleared her throat.

The room hung in silence for a brief moment before Mrs. Dickinson once again cleared the tension with her unwavering manners.

"Austin, did you say you had some news for us?"

"Ah, yes, thank you for reminding me, mother."

Austin adjusted his silk cravat, a nervous habit he developed when he was a teenager. Emily noticed the familiar tick and chuckled.

"Out with it, Oliver," she said kindly.

Austin nodded. "Yes, well, you see it seems that I have been invited to study under a prominent attorney in Boston next term, Mr. William Carmicle. It's quite the honor as Mr. Carmicle has a reputation for being one of the finest litigators in the county."

Mrs. Dickinson began clapping in praise instantly, though they were all certain that Austin could have announced he was running away to join the railroad crew and she would have shown the same response. Emily ran towards her brother and hugged him, reaching up to tussle his hair playfully.

"Well done, brother!" She remarked, smiling.

"Very astute, Austin." Vinnie chimed in proudly.

The room turned quiet as Edward set his paper down and slowly stood from his chair. Steadily, he walked toward his son before arriving a few feet away. Austin swallowed hard and Emily thought she saw a small bead of sweat drip down his temple. Finally, Edward reached out and extended his hand to his son.

"Well done, Austin," he said smiling. "Mr. Carmicle is well-reputed. Congratulations on receiving such an honor. I have no doubt you will make the Dickinsons proud."

Austin smiled and took his father's hand, shaking it firmly. Edward patted him on the back saying well done once more and the room breathed a collective sigh of relief.

"I think this news calls for a celebration!" Mrs. Dickinson remarked. "Vinnie, Emily, run down to the kitchen and bring up the pie that we made for supper."

Austin and Edward began to make their way into the breakfast room with Mrs. Dickinson. As Austin turned to enter the room. Emily noticed him remove a single letter from his coat pocket and set it on the table by the door where all outgoing mail was typically placed. She waited for a moment as the room cleared.

"Emily, are you coming?" Vinnie chimed in from the door leading down to the kitchen.

Emily nodded but held up a finger to her mouth signaling Vinnie to not say anything as she snuck over to the front door and peeked down at the letter.

Susan H. Gilbert c/o the Maher Family, Baltimore, Maryland

The words felt like a huge lead blanket on Emily's shoulders as they seeped in through her eyes. Seeing her name, knowing that the letter was going to her, knowing that she would touch its pages and read it and even . . . respond to it? Was she corresponding with Austin all this time and not her?

Emily's mind began to spiral and she felt dizzy. Vinnie came up from behind her.

"Emily, what is it?"

Emily remained silent and pointed to the letter on the table.

"Oh, my." Was all Vinnie could say.

After what felt like an eternity of staring blankly down at the letter, Emily felt her sister's hand on her shoulder.

"Why don't we go down to the kitchen?" She said, gently pulling her sister's eyes away from the ivory envelope.

Emily complied and let her gaze be ripped away slowly. When they had made it downstairs, Emily began pacing quickly.

"Emily, just take a breath, okay?"

"Take a breath? Vinnie, she's been writing to him for the last seven months and hasn't sent me a scrap. What am I supposed to think?"

Vinnie nodded. "You don't know that they've been corresponding this entire time. Perhaps this is his first letter to her?"

Emily nodded quietly and kept pacing.

"And . . ." Vinnie continued.

"And what?" Emily snapped.

"Nothing it's just, I mean . . . you love Susan, right?"

Emily nodded again.

"And you love Austin. . . right?"

Again, Emily nodded.

"All I'm saying is that, well . . . perhaps it isn't the worst thing in the world, Austin and Susan. I mean, we all know he's been pining over her since we were children and we know what a kind and doting husband he would make."

"Husband?" Emily erupted. "You can't be serious. Vinnie, you think I want my brother to marry the love of my life?"

Vinnie approached her sister and grabbed her arms gently to stop her from walking. Her bright blue eyes seemed to pierce a hole into Emily.

"Emily, I know how much you love Susan. I've seen it for years. When we were little girls, I envied her so much for getting all of your love and leaving none of it for me. I was happy when she moved away to New York. Then when she moved back, I knew you two would fall back into old habits. Perhaps a part of me always knew that those habits would grow into something more. Something deeper. Or perhaps I knew those feelings had been there all along. The truth is, I have nothing against Susan Gilbert, but I won't let my only sister be hurt like this. Susan is a grown woman, as we all are, and she has to choose the life she wants to live and who she wants to live it with. And if that person, isn't you, then . . ."

Vinnie paused, looking around as if to ensure no one was listening even though the room was completely closed off to outsiders. Emily looked back in anticipation.

"Then she's even more of a fool than I assumed she was when we were children."

At that Emily let out both a laugh and a tear and she pulled her sister in close to her.

"You're my favorite sister, you know that?" Emily said in Vinnie's ear.

Vinnie laughed and pushed Emily away. "I'm your only sister, nitwit."

Emily wiped the tears from her eyes and nodded. "Well, I suppose the competition wasn't that stiff then."

She winked at Vinnie as they gathered the pie, plates, and silverware and brought them upstairs. She could hear Austin's booming voice talking to their parents and as much as she hated the idea of him corresponding with Susan, she knew no part of her could ever hate her brother.

She just hoped Austin was not the only Dickinson who would be getting a letter from Susan Gilbert soon.

May 1852

Emily set the pencil down and breathed in a deep breath of fresh, spring air. She threw open the window by her writing desk earlier that morning and now the sound of the larks and finches filled her ears. It was a beautiful day in Amherst and the sky was a pale blue with whisps of far-off clouds being dragged across the atmosphere like brush strokes lazily drawn across a blue canvas.

She folded the poem she just wrote and tucked it into an envelope before sealing it closed with red wax.

"Mr. Benjamin F. Newton, Esq. Worcester, Massachusetts", she carefully wrote across the front of the envelope. She no longer sent Susan her poems, as she had a nagging feeling that they all went unread, and the idea of her poems ending up ignored or disregarded was almost as painful as the idea of Susan and Austin corresponding for the last year.

Benjamin quickly returned to his original role as preceptor and she was grateful for his consistent friendship over the long, dark winter they just escaped.

Last winter, Vinnie caught a cold so bad they had to call the doctor to ensure it was not consumption. After that, both Vinnie and Emily were forbidden from leaving the house. Vinnie filled her days playing with her judgmental cat, cleaning, practicing piano and doing needlepoint. Emily, on the other hand, spent the winter feeling like a lion trapped in a cage at the circus and she found herself having new pity for the beasts who had never chosen such a career for themselves.

She did however use the time to develop a new hobby of baking and was quite proud to serve her newly developed Jamaican black cake at Christmas that year. It was so dense and difficult to mix she had to enlist the help of both her sister and mother for the task. The recipe alone contained two pounds of flour, 19 large eggs, five pounds of raisins, two pounds of butter, two pounds of sugar, one and a half pounds of currents and one and a half pounds of citron, among other things. It was by far the most physically demanding task of her life, but the reward was well worth it as she watched her friends and family smiling and enjoying her massive creation.

But even with her new found interest in baking delicious and excessive treats, by the time spring arrived Emily was eager to leave the confines of the Mansion and even more eager to feel warm and free again. She watched outside as Carlo ran back and forth inside the fence of their yard. He knew better than to leave the boundary alone so she never worried about him when he was out there unattended.

Emily heard a knock on her door and informed the person to enter without turning around.

"How about a walk?" She heard her sister's voice echo over her head.

Emily looked over her shoulder and smiled. "A walk sounds lovely."

She grabbed the mint green shawl that Susan had given her and tossed it over her shoulders. She still refused to wear any other.

Vinnie set down her fluffy grey cat at the top of the steps and it immediately dropped to the ground and began to bathe right in the walkway, attempting to rid its long fur of the scent of Vinnie's skin.

"Carlo would never be so gross," Emily chimed in as she shook her head and eyed the cat, meticulously cleaning the same spot over and over again.

"Carlo eats his own vomit," Vinnie jabbed back, tossing a golden curl over her thin, pale shoulder.

"He does not!!"

Vinnie nodded insistently. "Oh yes, he does. It's in the Bible. 'As a dog returns to his vomit, so a fool repeats his folly," Vinnie pronounced proudly. "It's in Psalms."

Emily stuck out her tongue, feigning to gag. "Great, now you sound like my teacher back at the seminary."

"Well, maybe if you still attended Sunday Meeting with the family, you'd know that your dog is gross."

"I keep my own church," Emily remarked as they made their way to the front door and each grabbed their bonnets.

Emily stopped attending church with her family after Susan moved away. Much to her pleasure and surprise, her father never gave her any grief for it. Even her mother remained silent on the issue.

"Oh really," Vinnie began, cinching the silk ribbon under her neck tightly. "And where might this church be?"

Emily swung open the front door so wide that it nearly struck the wall of the house. A crisp wind wafted into the main hall and Emily stepped outside, throwing her hands freely above her head.

"It's right here!" She yelled, spinning around in the front yard as the breeze made her dress fly up well above her knees.

"Emily Dickinson!" Emily froze as the familiar, shrill voice of her mother echoed out of the upstairs window. "You shut that door right now! I can feel the draft up here!"

"Maybe you feel the draft from your open window, mother!" Emily shouted back, smiling.

Mrs. Dickinson ignored her baiting and simply yelled, "right now!" Before disappearing.

Not wanting to test her mother's patience and risk spoiling such a fine day, she complied and shut the door.

Vinnie shook her head and took her sister's arm in her own. Carlo trotted happily beside them as they left the front gate and turn to head towards Main Street. He no longer needed a leash to stay by their side and it seemed to most that he would follow Emily right off a bridge, his loyalty was so clearly tied to her.

They had not gotten more than a few steps down the road when a long-forgotten, but familiar face greeted them.

"Emily Dickinson?"

Emily looked at the man's face for a moment in silence before realizing his identity.

"George Gould?" She replied, still uncertain if she had reached the correct conclusion.

George Gould was a classmate of Austin's back at Amherst Academy but he had graduated with Austin two years ago and she had not seen him since. He was constantly lurking around their house the last few years of their schooling together, and Emily thought he must have taken a fancy to Vinnie, given how often he had hung around. But when graduation came, George left along with so many other young men, to pursue bigger dreams out west. The last time she had seen him was at her 20th birthday party, though she admittedly did not speak to him much then. Not with both Susan and Newton also being present at the event.

"It's been quite a while, Emily," George said removing his hat.

Vinnie cleared her throat.

Emily spoke, "George, you remember my sister?"

George bowed politely, his long, curly mouse-brown hair falling slightly into his face as he did. As he stood, he tucked the rogue strand behind his ear, displaying his dark, hazel eyes that seemed to pop out from beneath his olive skin in the sunlight.

"Of course, it's so lovely to see you again, Lavinia."

"You can call me Vinnie," she replied, a wide, flirtatious grin spreading across her face.

George was taller than Emily remembered, though she knew that to be an illogical conclusion. He had been a man of 22 when she had last seen him at her party and had surely finished all of his growing by then. Yet somehow now he seemed very tall. Perhaps she had been comparing him to Benjamin the last time she saw him, whose broad shoulders and wide frame made most men look small and frail. Or perhaps she had never taken any notice of his height at all before now.

Unlike Benjamin, George was thin and slender, his frame seeming to stretch unnaturally into the sky. Where Newton's eyes blazed with bright blue intellect and mystery, George's were soft, kind eyes that had flecks of gold and green mixed in warm hues of brown and amber. Also, unlike Newton who was fair-skinned like Emily, George's olive skin seemed only to absorb the sun instead of burn and he was much darker than she remembered when she saw him a few years ago. He had long, thin fingers that shifted nervously around the brim of the beaver-skinned hat he was holding and thin sideburns that ran down to the bottom of a sharp, angled jaw. She could not say he was an unfortunate-looking man; in fact, most would say George Gould was objectively handsome.

"What are you doing here, George? Austin is away at law school in Boston, haven't you heard?"

"Ah yes, of course, I did hear that. I'm back in town for my own business actually," George said. "But, since I have missed your brother, perhaps I can accompany you two ladies on a walk this morning? It is a fine day after all."

Vinnie jumped in and answered with an immediate "Yes! That would be lovely!" Before Emily could even open her mouth.

Emily interjected, "but we're going to the cemetery. Creepy place, probably wouldn't interest you much, I'm afraid."

"Or," Vinnie chimed in, "we could walk to the pond. It's a longer walk and surely more appropriate for such a fine, sunny day as this."

Emily bit her lip. She did not want to walk to the pond with George Gould, handsome and nice as he may be. She wanted to walk to the cemetery, maybe get some inspiration for another poem, throw a stick for Carlo, greet some robins, and go home. Not make small talk with a man she hadn't seen in years with whom she had little in common, even in their youth.

Clearly, Vinnie had different ideas swirling around in her mind, based on her eagerness for the man to join them. And so, with a single look from her sister, that seemed to say "don't you dare say another word," Emily nodded and the three of them continued their quest in the direction of Main Street.

After a few moments of what felt like ages of long, painful silence, Emily spoke.

"Where have you been all this time, George?"

"I've been traveling actually. Out west mostly. Made it as far as Oklahoma believe it or not, but had to about-face. The Comanche in that area are becoming pretty aggressive with all the white settlers invading their land and I knew better than to try to hold my own. I'd like to go back through and hopefully settle on a farm. When I get a wife that is."

The idea of being so far away from Amherst both excited and terrified Emily. The farthest she had been was her time at Holyoke – only 11 miles away - and that had certainly not turned out well.

Vinnie, however, was more than intrigued.

"You mean you saw *real* Indians out there? What were they like? What did they wear? What kind of houses did they live in? Father says Indians live in teepees. Did you see any of those out there?"

George laughed at her genuine enthusiasm. He told Vinnie all about the natives he encountered, their lifestyles, religious customs, clothing, and foods. He talked so much that his voice began to grow hoarse and by the time they made it down to the pond, he was completely parched.

"I beg your pardon, ladies," George began, clearing his throat. "It seems my throat has run dry from so much chatter. I should let you do more of the talking from now on."

"No!" Vinnie remarked, looking into his tall eyes dreamily. "Do go on."

George laughed and Emily remained silent. She stopped listening to him over a mile back. She was simply enjoying listening to the birds and the breeze as they danced in unison through the budding trees. George's story was benign to her but she liked that Vinnie seemed so enthralled with his tales of adventure.

"Would you like me to go on, Emily?" He asked suddenly, breaking her from her inward reverie.

"What? Oh, Uhm . . ." She looked over towards Vinnie who nodded rapidly in her direction. "Yes, yes, of course, do go on George."

They turned to walk back to the Mansion and George carried on with his many tales of the wild west, the settlements taking place, the restless Indians, the jobs for young, able-bodied men, and the wide-open plains, ripe for settling and raising a family. Emily returned to her internal conversations with the birds and Vinnie continued to hang on George's every word.

When they finally reached the front door to the Mansion after what seemed like an endless walk, Carlo trotted over to the large oak tree and laid down. Emily wanted nothing more than to follow him and lay in the grass, brushing the blades through her fingers, but George lingered beside them.

"It was lovely to see you again, George," Emily began politely. "Do look us up next time you are in town."

Vinnie shot her a dirty look, annoyed at her obvious attempt to be rid of the man.

"Or," Vinnie interjected, "you are welcome to join us for some tea inside. I know mother would love to see you again."

Emily looked at Vinnie in annoyance but Vinnie ignored her and continued to stare doe-eyed at George. George looked at Emily who quickly re-composed her face and smiled in a friendly, yet uninterested manner. George cleared his throat, sensing the awkwardness of the invitation.

"Uhm . . . perhaps another time, ladies. Although I would love to see your mother and father again."

"Are you certain you can't stay?" Vinnie asked again, making her intentions too obvious for Emily's liking.

George again looked at Emily who remained silent and smiled blankly, her arms tucked behind her back.

"Yes, but thank you for the invitation."

George reached out for Emily's hand and she reluctantly removed it from behind her back and allowed him to kiss it. Vinnie generously extended her hand without the need of asking and he kissed hers briefly as well.

"Until next time," George remarked, winking at Emily.

When he had turned the corner out of the front gate, Emily wiped her hand off her dress and gagged.

"Why do men think we want their saliva clinging to our hands all day? We cook with our hands! Do they expect us to simply cover their bread in spit too? Because that's exactly where these hands are going next." Emily continued to wipe until her hand was red.

Vinnie seemed to not hear a word of it, and simply stared up at the sky dreamily.

"He's very tall, isn't he?" Vinnie remarked.

Emily stopped wiping. "Who? Old George there? He's always been a gangly one. Remember when he and Austin were in school and they would try to join us in hide and seek? Poor George's only safe place was behind the apple tree and we caught him every time."

She chuckled to herself slightly remembering the ridiculous memory.

Vinnie sighed again. "But he was just a boy then and we were just little girls. Now we are women and he is certainly a fine man. Can you believe how far he's traveled all alone? That takes so much bravery."

Emily shook her head. "Whatever you say, Vinnie."

She walked over and splayed on the grass next to Carlo. As she lay there, she was reminded of the time she first met Newton. She had been lying under the same tree, plucking a blade of grass when she first heard his voice. She remembered thinking how handsome he was at first sight; how the look of him unnerved her. And yet, how even with that seemingly instant attraction, they had grown to be nothing more than the closest of friends.

And then, entirely without her consent, her mind wandered to Susan. She did not want it to, and she tried most days to not let it. But sometimes, when she was least expecting it, Susan simply came into her mind without any permission. This time, she laid down beside Emily on the grass, propped up on her shoulder. She lifted her hand to trace the soft outline of Emily's jaw and let her hand slide slowly down her clavicle. She traced the straight sternum of Emily's corset.

Emily felt her breath hitch as she closed her eyes and let herself fall deeper into the daydream.

Susan's hand found its way between her legs and Emily's mouth parted slightly. Susan was so close to her now she could smell her skin and the sweet smell of orange on her breath. Emily's mouth opened more and then –

"Emily!" Her sister's sharp voice broke her from the vision and she sat up abruptly.

"What?" She said looking around frantically and confused.

Only Carlo laid lazily at her feet. Susan was not there, she quickly reminded herself. She was in Baltimore. *Sue is gone.*

"Did you fall asleep?" Vinnie asked.

"What? No, I . . . maybe. Why?"

Vinnie just shook her head as she turned to walk in the door. "You are the strangest sister I've ever had."

When Vinnie had gone through the front door, Emily shouted, "I'm your only sister, nit wit!"

Emily lay under the tree for another hour, counting the leaves and writing lines of poetry in her head. She refused to let herself close her eyes again, even though her lids felt heavier with each stanza she recited in her mind.

She did want to rest, but the idea of seeing Susan in her brain again was too full of both pleasure and pain. She was starting to hope Susan would stay in Baltimore forever so she could just fade out of her mind completely. Certainly, that would be better than the pain she felt every single day she was not with her in Amherst.

"I don't know why it matters so much anyways," she said to Carlo who did not move from his slumber. "I hope she never comes back."

July 1852

You are to return to Amherst.

Susan read the letter several times, opening and closing her eyes firmly as if to ensure it was not some optical illusion. But no matter how many times she rubbed her eyes or read the sentence back and forth, the words never changed.

Dear sister,

I have some wonderful news for you! William's debts have been paid off in full and you are to return to Amherst. He has taken up a job at the local blacksmith's shop and while the work will be hard, he has promised the work will be honest. We will still need your help around the house when you return, of course, but it seems the spring has brought us a fresh new start at long last! William will pick you up at the Northampton train station when you arrive in September.

All my love,

Harriet

Susan contemplated the subtexts of the letter inwardly and bit down on her lip. How did William manage to pay off all of his debts? And how did he get a job at the blacksmith's shop? He had no experience in such a trade and was surely too old to learn.

She would be returning to Amherst, after being away for a year. She would be returning to her sister, to her old room, to her old job at the seamstress's house. She would see Austin and Vinnie and . . .

She stopped at the next thought.

And Emily.

Susan's breath caught short as the image of the auburn-haired woman flashed in her mind uncontrollably.

She spent the last year shoring up her convictions that she was no good for Emily Dickinson. Her love was no good for her. Her devotion was no good for her. All she would do is hurt her or hold her back from true happiness. That it was for the best, that she slowly fade into the background of Emily's mind, or that if she did return to Amherst one day, they would simply behave as young ladies of society ought to behave. That their days of sneaking off to the woods together were at an end.

And so, as she vowed early on in her exile, she did not respond to Emily. Rather, she did not send any letters. The truth was that Susan had almost an entire drawer full of letters to Emily, none of which had been sent.

But now, as she read the words over and over again, Susan felt flooded with a sea of emotions that she repressed ever since her departure from Amherst.

She would be returning to Amherst. She would see Emily. She would see her smile, hear her voice, smell her hair. She imaged Emily's hands as they gently plucked a flower from her garden and it was enough to send Susan spiraling all over again.

Susan was safe from her emotions here, locked far away in the dark boarding house. She managed to find herself almost constant distractions. Cleaning, cooking, making nice with Ingrid, telling stories to Bonnie. Even Mr. Maher was kind to her as of late, remarking on how delicious her chocolate cakes were. She wrote a few letters to Austin, all of which were nothing more than cordialities and pleasantries, even though she knew his affections ran deeper.

Somehow, in her mind, Susan was able to separate him from his sister. To identify him now as a new, independent being, not simply the elder Dickinson boy as he had once been. She would be lying if she said she had not enjoyed his correspondence, mostly for the role it played in her need for constant distraction from Emily. He had proven to be a great friend to her over the past year and she found that his presence in her life no longer annoyed her as it once did. She had come to see what Emily admired about him for so many years. He was dedicated, loyal, honest, and kind. Any woman would be lucky to have him as a husband. Any woman who was not already in love with his sister, that is.

Because alone, late at night, when Susan could no longer keep her hands and her mind occupied with chores and lectures and lessons and cooking, Emily always returned to her. She would see her pale skin bouncing off the sunshine in the orchard behind the Dickinson's Mansion. She would hear her high-pitched giggle as Susan poked at her ribs and she bent over from laughter. She would feel her lips kissing her cheek, her neck, and sometimes even farther.

The idea of seeing Austin did not phase Susan whatsoever. The idea of seeing Emily paralyzed her. It had been barely one year since they last spoke, but it felt like a lifetime. In many ways, it felt even longer than when she moved away to New York for so many years. This time it felt as if there was an ocean between them, where before there was only a river.

Susan closed her eyes and remembered back to the last time she saw Emily. They were alone in the woods – at their spot in the woods. Emily gave her a poem that Susan had now memorized by heart. Susan kissed her and told her she loved her. And then . . . she abandoned her. There was no doubt in her mind now that Emily Dickinson no longer cared for her. Not after all of that. She would be lucky if Emily even wanted to see her when she returned, let alone still felt any affection for her.

No – thought Susan – *that part of her is dead now all thanks to my deafening silence. She is free to go off and marry a statesman and have children.*

Susan looked at herself in the mirror and held her chin up high. She did what she set out to do. She had driven Emily away. Emily hadn't written to Susan in months, so clearly her efforts worked.

Susan continued to stare at her face in the mirror attempting to evoke some demeanor of pride or self-assurance. But the empty, brown eyes that stared back at her began to swell with tears and suddenly she dropped her face into her hands.

What have I done?

There was a soft knock at the door and the recognizable voice of Bonnie Maher rang from the other side.

"Supper be waiting for ya, Miss Sue," she said cheerfully.

Emily was the only one who ever called her Sue, until Bonnie. At first, she corrected the woman, to yet again try to keep Emily out of her thoughts. But as time went on, she found that she liked how the single syllable soothed her ears when combined with the woman's thick Irish accent.

"Coming," Susan said, unable to hide the shaking in her voice.

Bonnie cracked open the door slowly. Susan looked up at the woman's round face as she popped her head inside the doorway and began to weep even more.

"Why, what's got you so down, Miss Sue?" Bonnie asked, entering the small room and closing the door behind her.

"It's nothing," Susan said, the letter from Harriet still resting on the bed behind her.

Susan held up the letter to Bonnie and Bonnie sat down beside her and read.

"Why, don't be sad. Though I am happy as a lark to see you'll be missing me as much as I'll be missing you."

Susan smiled. "It's not that, although yes, of course, I will miss you dearly."

Bonnie nodded. "Then I reckon you better tell old Bonnie what it is that's got ya crying."

Susan paused a moment, unable to find the right words. Bonnie took the opportunity to fill the silence with her voice, as usual.

"I can't help but notice that you're quite popular with a certain family back in Amherst," she began.

Susan nodded silently.

"And I can't help but notice that only one of them gets return letters."

Susan nodded again.

"And I can't help but also notice that your linen drawer be bursting with letters to the Dickinson lass, although they have not been mailed."

Susan looked up at Bonnie. "You've gone through my things?" She asked skeptically and slightly defensively.

"Oh, no it's nothing like that. I seen the letters when I was putting away your clean dresses the other day for ya. You gave me the permission, don't ya remember?"

Susan nodded, feeling slightly foolish at her accusation. "Yes, of course, Bonnie, forgive me."

Bonnie looked around the room blankly. "Do you mind if I ask ya why you never sent the letters?"

Susan thought for a moment, wiping a tear from her cheek before answering. "Because I thought it was best that she didn't hear from me anymore," she said frankly.

"I see . . ." began Bonnie.

"What?" Susan asked.

"Well, it just seems a shame that you think that is all," Bonnie replied.

Susan raised her eyebrows, confused. "But why?"

Bonnie bit her lip and paused a long moment before responding. "Because it seems to me that you've got a whole lot you want to say to her."

Bonnie's voice hung low at the end of the sentence and she reached out and pulled Susan close, her round, warm arm wrapped entirely around Susan's small body. Susan began to cry once more and it made her miss her Aunt Sophia's maid, Abigail. She remembered always feeling safe when Abigail was there to hold her and rock her, just as Bonnie was doing now. She found herself crying and wondering what ever happened to Abigail back in New York, and hoping she would see her again one day.

Bonnie stopped rocking Susan after a few moments. She wiped the tears from Susan's face and stared directly into her eyes.

"I may not be an educated woman, Miss Sue," she said, "but I think I know love when I see it. And it sure seems a shame to me that something as grand as love should stay locked away in a drawer."

August 1852

If there was a breeze that summer, it blew exceptionally slowly through the town of Amherst. Cows swished their tails in the fields in a never-ending effort to keep the flies from landing on them. Horses lazily grazed and the sheep's short wool hung thick with sweat. People in town moved slower than usual as if the very street itself was made of quicksand. Men's collars wilted on their way to Sunday Meeting and they untied their cravats as soon as they returned home. Women wore lighter bonnets and carried fans to wave in their faces constantly to avoid fainting from the restriction and pressure of their corsets.

Emily and Vinnie made a new habit of walking to the pond every day. Emily told her sister that the faster they walked, the cooler the breeze would feel against their skin. Vinnie had not been so convinced and only joined because of the other person they happened to see almost every day on the same walk.

George Gould made himself a permanent fixture in the Dickinson household ever since his return from out west. While Emily could not say she disliked his company, she could affirmatively say she preferred to be alone than with him. Her sister, however, was completely smitten with the man, which seemed obvious to everyone except poor George Gould.

At first, they met through sheer happenstance, much as they had on their first encounter. They were walking past the mercantile on Merchant Row as George was exiting and Vinnie hailed him over, much to Emily's chagrin.

That day they once again walked and talked and Emily managed to retreat inwardly and exchange knowing looks with Carlo. But then George asked them if they would be doing the walk again the next day and Vinnie ratted out their secret, growing the group from two to three.

That was over a month ago now and Emily was growing tired of walking with George Gould.

"I think I'll stay at home today," she said one day when he came to their door. "I seem to be catching a cold," she said forcing out a low cough.

"Oh heavens," George announced, true shock and concern on his face. "Perhaps I should call for the doctor? Or tell your father? Would you like me to bring you some water? A cool rag maybe?"

On and on George fawned until finally, Vinnie chimed in.

"I'm sure she's just fine," she said curtly. "Besides, it would be strange indeed to have a cold." Her eyes lingered on Emily's in a knowing and skeptical way as she finished her sentence. "In August."

Emily nodded, covering her mouth again and forcing out another loud cough.

"Yes, I'm sure it's just a bug of some sort. Nothing a day indoors won't fix. But please, you two enjoy your walk."

But George would have none of it. He insisted on seeing that she was taken care of and the anticipated day off turned out to be nothing more than a day of confinement while George sat in the parlor talking to Mr. Dickinson and Mrs. Dickinson forced Mrs. Winslow's Soothing Syrup down Emily's throat, sending her into wild hallucinations.

Though she produced several profound poems in her delirium, she decided that it was the last time she would feign illness to try and avoid a man.

Vinnie was cross with her for a few days after that, but soon enough the three of them returned to their walks, as usual.

But today was probably the hottest the temperature had been since they began their tradition, and Emily could feel the line of sweat dripping down the front of her whalebone corset. She breathed in as deep as the binding around her ribs would allow, still finding herself short of breath.

Carlo panted heavily beside her as they walked and she never identified more with a dog than in that moment of true exhaustion. It seemed as if the street would never end and the cool pond would never present itself to them. Emily looked up into the sun as it beat down on her and she closed her eyes imagining she was back at her favorite spot in the woods by the stream.

She imaged taking off her hot, leather shoes and stockings and dipping her feet into the cold, icy water. She had not returned to that spot since . . . suddenly Emily's mind wandered to the place she knew it should not. *Since I was there with Sue.* Her mind flashed uncontrollably back to their final day in the woods together. The thoughts made Emily's heart race faster with both passion and anger. With the sun beating down on her unprotected eyes, her mind began to race unexpectedly at a rapid pace.

How could she do that to me? How could she tell me she loves me, promise to write to me, and then not say a word? And worst of all how could she write to Austin, of all people, instead?

Emily's mind was truly unraveling now and black spots began to creep into her vision like spilled ink slithering slowly across a blank page. Emily began to breathe heavier, her inhalations growing shorter with each step. Then suddenly, without warning, she was falling. She could see the ground rising to meet her face, but her arms hung limp, paralyzed by her side. Slowly she fell, helpless to stop the pull of gravity that had overcome her body.

The next thing she remembered was a horrible smell filling her senses and the sounds of mumbled voices gathered over her head.

Was she dead? No. Surely Heaven would not smell so bad. Unless she was in . . . her mind was cut short by the familiar sound of her name echoing across the black void and into her ears.

"Emily? Emily?" She heard it say.

"Sue?" She felt her mouth utter as she opened her eyes and began to see moving shadows and figures overhead.

She blinked and the figures turned slowly into faces. A lot of faces. It looked as if half of the town was looming over top of her and she sat up slowly.

"Easy," George said, cradling her head delicately.

Emily felt dizzy and began to fall back slightly, but caught herself.

"Sue?" She said again, looking through the faces for the one she wanted to see.

"It's me," Vinnie said, repeating her name. "Sue isn't here, remember?"

Emily rubbed her cheek. It was covered in dirt and a bruise was starting to form where she hit the ground face first.

"What happened?" She asked, looking around, blinking wildly.

"You fainted," a man wearing all black said as he put a cap on the tiny vile of smelling salts and placed it back into his medicine bag.

"You called a doctor?" Emily said looking at Vinnie.

"Actually," the man replied, "I was just passing by when it happened. And you're quite lucky I was. A few more moments out in this heat and I am afraid you would have been much worse off."

Emily looked around and felt embarrassed. People were still staring at her and she gave Vinnie a pleading look. Vinnie, sensing her sister's embarrassment took charge.

"Yes, well thank you, Dr. Miller, for your aid, and thank you everyone for your concern. As you can see my sister is quite well. Please, everyone be on your way."

She began making a quick ushering motion with her hands and reluctantly the people dispersed. Emily took George's hand and he helped her stand.

"I . . . I'm sorry," Emily said when she regained her footing.

"Whatever for?" George asked, gently brushing the dirt from her cheeks.

She looked up at him and smiled, his warm hazel eyes seeming to wrap around her, even farther than his long arms could ever reach. She did not know how or why, but at that moment, she didn't mind being so close to George Gould.

"We should get you home," Vinnie said.

"Indeed, we should," George agreed. "Wait here."

Vinnie and Emily moved to the side of the road to stand beneath the shade of a tree. They talked for a few moments about the weather being the cause of Emily's fainting, but only Emily knew what internal torment had truly prompted the event. Not long after, a small carriage arrived in front of them and George stepped out.

"Here, please, let me bring you both home."

He extended a hand for both of them and Vinnie let her hand linger on his just a second longer. By the time they made it home, all Emily wanted to do was be in her room, alone.

She didn't want to think about what a fool she had made of herself in front of the entire town. She didn't want to think about George. She didn't even want to think about her sister or Carlo. And she certainly didn't want to think about Susan Gilbert. All she wanted to do was be alone and write.

As they reached the Mansion, George exited the carriage and followed them both inside. He removed his hat as if he meant to stay but he could sense that Emily wanted him to leave.

"Well, I'll leave you now, please let me know if there is . . ."

Suddenly and without warning, Austin burst through the front door. Carlo began barking loudly and jumping all around at the noise.

"You will never guess the news!" He shouted.

Mrs. Dickinson came racing up from the kitchen and Edward raced around the corner from the refuge of his office.

"What is the meaning of all this?" Edward said.

Emily quieted Carlo who still looked uneasy. Upon seeing George, Mrs. Dickinson quickly removed her apron and tossed it down the kitchen stairs. The entire house hung quietly as Austin cleared his throat and held a letter up high above his head.

"Susan is returning to Amherst!"

Emily's heart began to race uncontrollably again and she looked over to Vinnie whose mouth hung open. She came over to Emily and placed an assuring hand on her arm.

"How do you know?" Mrs. Dickinson asked.

"She wrote to me of course," Austin proclaimed, lifting his chin in pride and adjusting his sweat-stained jacket.

Emily felt the black spots seeping into the corners of her vision again and she clutched the banister of the staircase to stay upright.

Susan. Coming back. Here. Her mind began to race and she focused intently on breathing. A loud, ringing noise filled her ears making the voices in the room turn to mumbles. Vinnie's nails dug deep into her arm now, the only thing keeping her from slipping back into that empty darkness.

"That's wonderful dear," Mrs. Dickinson said, polite as ever.

Edward simply shrugged and returned to his office, seeming annoyed at all the fuss. What difference did it make to him if Susan Gilbert was in Amherst or anywhere else in the world for that matter?

The room hung silent for a moment and slowly the ringing in Emily's ears began to fade. She turned and walked up the stairs without saying a word to anyone.

"Emily?" She heard George's voice echo faintly behind her but she did not stop or turn.

"Forgive my sister," she heard Austin say when she reached the top of the stairs. "She's always been an odd one."

Once she reached the safety of her room, she shut the door and walked over to her the small, square desk that sat by her window. She did not stop writing until the sun came up the next morning.

September 1842

As the carriage pulled into Amherst, Susan thought back to when she first returned from New York. Ironically, Emily Dickinson consumed her mind back then too. And now, it was no different.

The heat which raged violently for months on end suddenly stopped seemingly overnight and the cool scent of a late New England summer filled her nose as she stepped out of the carriage. She missed the smell of home and even the pines that hung low around the town seemed to welcome her in. Hariett and William were both waiting outside the house to greet her.

"Welcome home, Susan," William said, uncharacteristically friendly.

He did not look as pale and sunken in as when she left and Harriet also seemed to overall healthier; her cheeks full, her waist plump.

A man arrived to take their bags and Susan shot Harriet a look as if to say, "we have a groomsman again?"

Harriet simply smiled wide and hugged her sister.

"It has been far too long, sister," Harriet remarked, stepping back and taking in Susan's appearance. "Although you do look a bit peaked," she continued, pinching at Susan's cheeks.

"Did the Mahers not feed you well?" William asked as they entered the house.

"They were perfectly pleasant," Susan responded. "Especially Mrs. Maher."

Susan would live to be a thousand years old before she would say an unkind word about Bonnie Maher. The truth was, Susan hadn't eaten a bite since receiving word of her impending return to Amherst last week.

As they entered the front room, Susan immediately noticed a new carpet and fresh upholstery on the high, wing-backed chair that rested near the fireplace. As they proceeded upstairs, Susan noticed a painting hung on the wall that she had never seen before. And when they finally reached Susan's room, there was a new, larger framed bed and a new chest of drawers waiting for her.

"What's all this?" Susan asked.

The last she heard William was in such debt, that she had to leave town. Now it seemed as if they were doing more than well financially.

William gave Harriet a knowing look and nodded politely at Susan before leaving them alone in the room.

"Sit down, dear," Harriet began.

Susan reluctantly obeyed and the new bed remained mostly silent under her weight. Harriet took Susan by the hands.

"The truth is . . ." She began ringing her hands nervously. "The truth is, it was Austin Dickinson who paid off William's debts and asked that you come back to Amherst."

"What?" Susan said, her voice elevated.

"I knew you might be upset. Austin knew it too, that's why he asked us not to tell you. But you know I've never been one for keeping secrets and I just thought you really should know. I hope you're not angry with the man for wanting to provide for you."

She could not believe her ears. *How dare he? How could he?* She did not know what to feel. The insolence of this man to try and buy her affection. Was she expected to feel gratitude? Was she indebted to him now? Did his family know? Did Emily have something to do with this?

Was she just the charity case over at the Dickinson house now?

"Angry?" Susan started, her voice now shaking. "Angry does not even begin to cover it."

Harriet stood. "I know it's a lot, but please try to understand I do not think he intended it to be as you perceive. Austin simply cares for you. Truth be told, he doesn't seem to have a bad bone in his body."

The blacksmith's job. Of course, she thought. Austin had been good friends with the local blacksmith since he was a teenager. *That's how William got the job.*

"And if I can just say one thing more," Harriet added. "William has been clean as a whistle since he got that new job and he seems truly happy. Please don't do anything that might spoil that for us? We've been given a fresh start, don't you see? A second chance. That's more than most get in a lifetime."

Susan stood up and walked over to the window, her arms crossed over her chest. She was irate at Austin, but Harriet did have a point. This was the best she had seen either of them looking in years and she didn't want to do anything foolish that might ruin that for them.

"I understand," Susan managed to say through gritted teeth.

Harriet turned and left the room. Everywhere she looked, Austin's presence lingered now. That was Austin's chest of drawers, Austin's bed, Austin's painting hanging in the hallway. What else had he inseminated into her life against her will?

And yet, as the anger subsided, she found herself feeling somewhat grateful. What Harriet said was true. He had given her family a second chance when they truly needed it the most. Was it so bad that he did it out of affection for her? That he did it because he cared for her? Would having Austin Dickinson take care of her be such a curse?

Susan shut her eyes firmly and pushed the thought from her mind. Suddenly the walls began to cave in around her and the air seemed to grow thinner with each breath. She needed to get out of this room immediately.

She flew down the stairs and out the front door in a fury. Of course, the buildings all looked the same. Nothing ever changed here in western Massachusetts. She marched down Main Street and past the seamstress's house where she used to work. She passed the Church where she went and worshipped every Sunday. She passed the mercantile where she sent and received her postage. She passed the Common where she . . .

Susan froze.

Just across the street and down the road, she saw her. Emily. She was bending over to pick up a stick, her auburn hair standing out brightly against the sun. Susan ducked behind a tree and continued to watch unnoticed, feeling her heart racing quickly inside her chest. She tried to forget her face for almost a year, but now there she was, so close she could walk over and grab her if she wanted to. Or if she had the nerve.

She could hear Emily's laugh from where she stood and it was enough to send a flood of warmth into her belly. Vinnie was with her and Carlo and . . . a man?

Standing close to Emily was a tall, gangly man she thought she faintly recognized from Emily's 20th birthday party, although she had admittedly been focusing her entire attention on Emily and Newton at that event. She had barely seen the man for more than a moment back then, yet now here he was standing bold as brass right next to Emily.

He had dulled, brown hair and a wide, optimistic smile. He wore a grey coat with a linen, white shirt and a lavender cravat. His long, lean legs jutted out from the bottom of the jacket like the trunks of a mighty tree and he lingered by her side, looking down at her softly, even when she looked away from him. Vinnie's eyes seemed focused on nothing but the man, but his eyes barely noticed the beautiful blonde standing in front of him. All he seemed to notice, was Emily. Her Emily. Susan clenched her fist and released it to alleviate the twinge of pain and envy that spread through her veins like vines.

She watched as Emily tossed the stick into the Common for Carlo, who chased it excitedly. She watched as Emily's hand casually grazed the man's arm. Susan felt a lump of familiar pain rise in her chest as she watched the man's face light up at the mere touch of her hand through the fabric of his coat. She knew that feeling. The feeling of electricity that shoots through the point of contact and straight to your heart. She knew what it was like to be in love with Emily Dickinson. The powerful, enrapturing feeling.

This is what you wanted; Susan told herself as she lurked behind the tree. *This is the reason you stopped responding to her. You wanted her to find a man. To marry a man. You have no right to feel this way.*

"Susan!" She heard a shrill voice from down the road.

Susan's attention shot over towards the voice. It was Miss Mavis, the seamstress.

"Good afternoon," Susan said politely but quietly.

She glanced quickly over her shoulder to ensure Emily had not heard her name being shouted.

"I heard the news you were coming back to us and here you are!" The old woman pronounced excitedly. "Will you come back to the shop with me? I could certainly use your help; we have just been flooded with work this season."

Susan ushered the woman in the opposite direction of the Common.

"Uhm . . . I'll come by tomorrow and see if I can be of assistance," she said, glancing over her shoulder yet again to ensure they remained unseen.

"Oh wonderful, just wonderful! And will you be at Meeting this Sunday?"

Susan nodded, quickening their pace so fast that the old woman nearly tripped on the dirt road.

"Yes, yes of course. If you will excuse me, Miss Mavis, I must be going now. It was lovely to see you again," she said dropping the woman off at the door to the shop.

Miss Mavis waved at her and paused to catch her breath before walking up the stairs and inside. Susan walked quickly down the street towards the woods, not stopping again to look back in Emily's direction.

***

By the Common, Carlo began barking wildly in the direction of Merchant Row.

"What in the world has gotten into him?" Vinnie asked.

"I'm not sure," Emily responded, patting the dog on the back and looking over at the large tree where his nose was so adamantly pointed. "Maybe he saw someone he knows."

October 1852

Austin Dickinson held his hat firmly onto his head as he walked down the street. The crisp, autumn wind blew sharply against his wool coat, causing his cravat to blow freely. Aggravated, he shoved the bottom of the silk tie beneath his coat as he pressed on against the wind. He had grown accustomed to strong wind after spending so much time in Boston over the last few years, but for some reason the wind today was of the utmost annoyance to him.

Of course, if he was being honest with himself, he was annoyed at more than the wind. His father continued to chide him about joining his law firm when he graduated from Harvard the next year and Austin continued to be afraid to tell him about his new dreams of moving west and starting his own practice. To make matters worse, Susan Gilbert had not spoken two words to him since she returned to Amherst last month. He called on her several times, but every time her sister said she was out for a walk.

Where does one woman go in such a small town? He thought on the third unsuccessful attempt.

***

Susan dipped her fingers into the icy water. She returned to this spot every day since she came back to Amherst. Their spot. She didn't know why or how she even ended up here at first. She came here the day she saw Emily with that man, whose name she learned from her sister was George Gould. She came here that day to both remember and forget the pain she felt in her heart at seeing them together. But she returned every day since for a different reason. She returned secretly hoping to see Emily here.

It was a cowardly thing to do, she knew. She could just as easily have gone over to her house and knocked on the door like a normal person. She could have walked up to her in the street that day six weeks ago when she saw her with Vinnie and Mr. Gould. She could have even used Austin she wanted to, to be invited to the Dickinson Mansion. For some reason, the idea of using Austin so shamelessly did not sit right with Susan and so she elected to hide here instead, hoping the Fates would intervene.

But, for the last month, only Susan had been present at their sacred spot in the woods by the creek. She watched as the leaves turned from the deep green of summer to the bright red and orange of autumn. She smelled the wet, damp air turn fresh and crisp. She felt the sweat that dripped down her back turn into a chill that ran down her spine. But she had yet to see Emily Dickinson.

She decided that today would be her last day coming to this place. That it was time to truly let Emily go and leave everything that they once were behind her. And so, after sitting for hours on a fallen tree, Susan stood up, wrapped her cloak around her shoulders, and turned to leave at last. She took a small, folded piece of paper out from her corset and knelt down by the water.

It was Emily's poem that she took with her to Baltimore. It was barely able to be called a piece of paper now from so much use. Susan thought that this final act would be what she needed to truly say goodbye to any lingering romance between her and Emily. She intended on releasing the paper into the creek and watching it float away. Then she would reach out to Emily in a purely platonic way and they could begin some form of new friendship together, hopefully. If not, she would respect that, though she imaged it was only a matter of time before their paths did cross.

As she leaned over the water, her fingers gripped the page tighter. *Just do it*, she thought to herself. She leaned so close that the paper was almost touching the water, but try as she might, she could not open her hand to release the page. Annoyed, Susan stood up and shook her head.

"This is ridiculous!" She said to the empty woods, crumbling up the paper tight in her fist. She marched around in circles and continued muttering to herself. "It's just a piece of paper Susan. Throw it away. Forget about it. Forget about her."

"Forget about who?"

The voice caused Susan to jump.

There, standing across the water, not ten feet away from her, was Emily. She wore a dark green, wool dress and matching bonnet. Her face looked the same as when she left but was somehow changed. Where there was once softness and vulnerability in her dark eyes, she now saw bitterness and resentment.

"Emily?" Susan said, still reeling in shock at the proximity of her presence.

"Susan," Emily said, her voice as sharp and cold as the air between them.

Susan. The name stung as it shot out of Emily's mouth. She was no longer, Sue. She was simply Susan. Just as she was to Austin and Harriet and everyone else in the world. But this is what Susan wanted, or so she had told herself. She could not protest it now.

"What are you doing here?" Susan asked.

"I'm collecting leaves for my herbarium. What are *you* doing here?"Emily's arms remained crossed and her voice distant and formal.

"I wanted to . . . get away for a bit," Susan replied.

"Is that why you've been coming here every day since you got back?"

Susan froze and looked up at Emily. She'd been caught. "How did you -"

Emily cut her off. "Austin told me he'd called on you but that you were 'out for a walk' every time. I put two and two together pretty easily. He didn't, of course. Might take up too much of his manly brain power."

Susan stuttered nervously. "I suppose I should be home next time he calls."

"Perhaps you should be," Emily snipped back. "Wouldn't want the great Austin Dickinson slipping through your fingers."

Susan raised an eyebrow. "What exactly does that mean?"

Emily rolled her eyes. "I think you know exactly what it means, Susan. We all know he's the only reason you're back here. Your sister goes on and on about your 'courtship' to the entire town."

Susan's cheeks flushed red with embarrassment. This is exactly what she had feared upon learning of Austin's generosity to her family. She was the charity case of the entire Dickinson family and once again she was the center of the town's gossip. Why had Harriet been lying and telling everyone Austin had been courting her? They had not spoken of any formal courtship in any of their correspondences.

"What has told you?"

"He's my brother," Emily replied, "he's told me what I need to know."

The last words seemed pointed, as if to tell Susan that she knew that the two of them had been writing for the last year. That she knew about how William got the job at the blacksmith, and that she knew every detail of the upgrades made to Harriett's house, down to the last tea set in the cupboard.

"I should be going," Susan said, gathering up the bottom of her dress. She was embarrassed and felt like a fool for ever coming here.

"As you wish, Susan," Emily said, bending down to pick up a large maple leaf that had recently fallen.

Her face was steely and nonchalant as she turned the large leaf over in her hand and held it up to the sunlight to observe its veins.

Susan did not know what else to say. She came here in hopes of seeing Emily. But now she saw that she had been right to dread it. Standing before her was the result of her hard work in Baltimore. She had officially succeeded in pushing Emily away. She injured her in the worst way imaginable - she abandoned her. Susan knew already that there would be no rekindling of the romance they once had, but now she saw that it was also unlikely that they would even be friends again. Being this close to Emily and seeing the hatred she felt for her now was too much for Susan to bear.

She hopped across the creek to where Emily stood to leave the forest. Emily stepped to the side and let Susan pass on the narrow walking path between the trees but as she did, her shoulder slightly brushed against Emily's sending an uncontrollable shiver down her entire body. She hoped Emily did not see her reaction to it and after a slight pause, she continued to walk. As she was almost out of reach, Emily stuck out her hand and grabbed Susan firmly by the arm.

"Who are you trying to forget?" Emily said, her face so close she could feel Emily's breath on her lips.

Susan swallowed hard and blinked, taking a step back as Emily released her grip.

"Nobody," Susan replied, crossing her arms and pursing her lips together.

Emily nodded her head and looked down.

"Nobody," she quietly repeated under her breath.

Susan paused for a moment, fighting the urge to grab Emily's face and pull it to hers. Then she turned quickly and continued to walk out of the woods, once again leaving Emily standing alone by the water. As she walked, she tucked the wrinkled-up poem back into her corset. Apparently, she wasn't ready to let go of it after all.

December 1852

George Gould straightened his cravat and cleared his throat as he stood outside the intimidating Mansion on West Street. He gulped slightly as he looked up to the top floor, the only room on that floor still illuminated by full candlelight being Emily's. George knew it meant that everyone was already down on the lower floor preparing for the meal that evening. Everyone of course, except Emily.

He thought of how silly he must look, staring up at a window from outside, but still, he lingered in hopes of catching a glimpse of the mysterious woman he had fallen in love with these past few months.

Emily Dickinson started out as his friend's strange, younger sister. Then, throughout the years, she became his friend's strange, somewhat attractive sister. But when he saw her at her 20th birthday party two years ago, she had become her own, still strange, beautiful, independent woman. He hoped to have gotten a chance to speak with her alone that day, to tell her how his feelings for her had suddenly changed, and to express his intention of courtship with her, but she and a man named Benjamin Newton were inseparable and the entire party labored under the impression that their betrothal was imminent.

George Gould took a job out west the following week, seeing no future or prospects for him in Amherst.

It wasn't until Austin wrote to him last year that he even knew Emily was very much *not* betrothed to Benjamin Newton - or any man for that matter. Austin had all but insisted that he return to Amherst as the town needed good, working gentlemen, and George was on the next train home the following week.

So much time had passed since his return to Amherst in the summer, and yet he could not help but feel that Emily Dickinson was just as far away from him now as she was two years ago on her 20th birthday. Even with the disappearance of Benjamin Newton, she seemed just as uninterested in him.

Austin assured him that there was no man in Emily's life and that he just needed to be straightforward with her and make his intentions known.

And so, tonight, before supper, George would ask Edward Dickinson to speak with him alone in his library. He would ask for his blessing to propose to his eldest daughter, Emily. The thought of the conversation made George feel sick with nerves and he shook his head, cleared his throat once more, straighten his back, and knocked on the front door.

***

The air outside the Dickinson Mansion was so cold Susan could see smoke pouring out of her nostrils with each breath. It already snowed several times and a thick coat of powder clung to the roof and ground of every house in Amherst.

This was a mistake, Susan thought as she stood outside the large white house, staring up at the upper window. The candles glowed heavily and Susan knew it meant Emily was still upstairs while the rest of the party was already downstairs. She could imagine how angry Mrs. Dickinson must be at her daughter's blatant impropriety.

Why did I even come here? Susan's mind raced again.

Because you were invited, her mind responded, answering her own question.

Austin invited Susan to the annual Dickinson Christmas Eve supper a few weeks ago and he quite literally would not take no for an answer. The first time he asked, Susan politely declined. The second time he asked she lied and said Harriett would be lonely without her. The third time he asked it was to inform her that Harriett and William were also invited and that they had accepted on her behalf. She was out of excuses.

Again, she had been cornered by Austin Dickinson's persistence, but the idea of seeing Emily again filled her once again with both dread and excitement. She had not been inside the Mansion in over a year and she wondered how, if at all, the place had changed. Did Emily move her desk? Did the shawl she made her still hang permanently on the back of Emily's chair? Did she even still have that shawl? Did her bed still rest against the back wall . . .?

Susan shook her head and told herself to stop thinking about Emily and her bed. She was here at the invitation of Austin. She would be on such good behavior that even her old Aunt Sophia would be proud of her.

"What are you doing?" A familiar voice broke Susan from her reverie.

"Hello, Harriet," Susan said looking down at her dress and clearing her throat. "Just waiting for you to arrive," she lied.

William walked up beside Harriet and rested his hand on her back, smiling at Susan.

"You both look lovely," he said kindly.

Susan could not ignore the obvious shift in William's behavior since Austin had entered their lives. He had not touched a drop of liquor or entered a billiard hall in months. He was helpful around the house and his body had grown strong from the honest work at the blacksmith shop. He was kind and polite to Harriet and Susan, which had in turn made Harriet happier than Susan had ever seen her. She could not deny that Austin Dickinson had truly given her family a blessing. Her kindness towards him in return was the least she could do.

"Well, let's get inside then," William continued. "It's freezing out here."

Austin met them at the door after a single knock, a familiar, wide grin plastered on his face.

"Welcome!" He said excitedly, moving out of the way and ushering them all inside.

He took Susan's cape and hat and hung them on the wall while William did the same for Harriet.

"I'm so glad you could join us this evening," Austin said, his voice sounding more chipper than usual. "Happy Christmas!"

"Thank you for inviting us, Mr. Dickinson," Harriet remarked slowly looking around the large house.

"Nonsense," Austin replied, reaching out and shaking William's hand firmly. "You are like family after all. And please, call me Austin."

As soon as the door was closed, the uncontrollable thought of the auburn-haired girl who lived here crept into Susan's mind and she instantly began to scour the rooms with her eyes for Emily. She saw Mrs. Dickinson in the parlor, talking with people Susan knew to be Mrs. Dickinson's sister, Lavinia Norcross, and her daughters, Fannie and Louisa. The last time she had seen them was two years ago at Emily's 20th birthday party, but like Emily and Susan they had very much grown into women since then.

In the library Mr. Dickinson sat smoking a pipe with several men she did not recognize, and one of whom she recognized as the young man who was doting on Emily at the Common several months ago – George Gould.

She felt like a millstone dropped around her neck at the sight of him. She could not help but feel the way she had once felt at the sight of Benjamin Newton standing in the same parlor at the same time of year, two years prior. Would there ever be an end to the men who pined for Emily's affection? And would she ever not envy them the way she did?

"Austin," Susan asked, "who is that young man in there with your father?"

"Who? Old George? He's a friend from school. But truth be told he isn't here for me at all. He's had his eyes set on Emily since we were kids. They've been spending all their time together this past summer."

The millstone grew heavier and Susan felt like her skin would rub raw with the weight of its invisible tether around her neck.

"I see," was all Susan could manage to say.

"Don't tell me you're jealous, now," Austin said playfully.

She looked up at his dark brown eyes defensively. "What do you mean?"

"I knew it!" He continued, still smiling. "Everyone thinks old George is more handsome than me. Always have. But I have the brains where he has the brawn, that's what I always say."

Austin winked at Susan who, for the first time, realized that Austin had been correct in detecting her envy but incorrect in the understanding exactly whom she envied.

"I'm sure that's true," Susan said reassuringly, touching Austin briefly on his arm.

She could see his eyes light up in response and she let her hand drop.

Suddenly, she saw George Gould stand up from the chair where he had been seated and usher the rest of the gentlemen from the room and close the door behind them. The gentlemen all snickered amongst themselves as they exited.

Susan's heart dropped lower in her chest.

***

George's palms were clammy with sweat and his heart beat so fast he began to feel nauseous from the smell of the cigars that filled the room. He set his cigar down in the ashtray on the small, mahogany end table next to the fireplace that roared furiously in the otherwise dark room.

"You see, the thing is, Mr. Dickinson . . ." George began.

Suddenly he stood up and began pacing in front of the fireplace, wiping his hands furiously on his pants.

Mr. Dickinson sat back and crossed his leg in front of him, puffing steadily on his pipe. He smiled a little bit at the boy's obvious nerves, remembering when he had been forced to have this exact conversation with Mrs. Dickinson's father.

After several more seconds of stuttering and pacing, Mr. Dickinson broke his misery.

"Out with it boy," he said firmly. "Ask me what it is you want to ask me and be done with it. You'll make both of us feel much more at ease, I assure you."

George flushed with embarrassment. "Mr. Dickinson, I would like to ask permission to marry your daughter."

"Which one?" Edward replied, sadistically.

Edward knew it was Emily that George fancied. Edward knew George fancied Emily even before he left for his adventures out west. It was no surprise to Edward that their house was his first stop on his return to town.

What was also becoming common knowledge, however, were Vinnie's feelings for George. She followed the poor man wherever he went, constantly peppering him with questions about his experiences out west and how long he intended to remain in Amherst. She would wear her finest dresses to Sunday Meeting and ask that he sit next to her every Sunday, which he, of course, obliged.

The only thing that remained clouded in mystery to all, was Emily's feelings for George. Mr. Dickinson knew his eldest daughter to be a particular type of woman and as good of a man as George Gould was, he did not know if he could see her truly being happy with him.

"Emily, sir," George replied, breaking Edward from his thoughts.

"Ah, I see," Edward said, removing the pipe from his mouth and resting it on the tip of his forehead.

He remained silent for a few seconds, which to George Gould felt like an eternity, before finally slapping both of his hands on his knees and standing up.

"I'll tell you what George. You go on and ask Emily. Whatever her answer is, will be my answer as well."

George was taken aback by the frankness of the man's reply. Mr. Dickinson had a reputation in Amherst as an intellectual and influential man, yet his answer had left George completely perplexed as to what his opinion truly was on the matter. It was custom for a man to seek the blessing of his future father-in-law before proposing to a lady. It was also custom for that father-in-law to give his blessing verbally or on the other hand, to vocalize his disapproval, thereby ending the man's efforts. But Mr. Dickinson had done neither.

"Does this mean you give me your blessing sir?" George asked as a point of clarification.

"I do not think it is my blessing you need, my good boy," Edward replied, slapping the tall man on the back and smiling. "Why don't we join the party now? Supper should be ready any moment."

***

The door to the library opened and both men stepped out of a cloud of smoke. George looked ashen white and like he may faint at any moment. A quizzical look rested across his brow and Susan could not tell if he was simply confused or gravely ill.

Mr. Dickinson followed soon behind him smiling ear to ear and chuckling slightly beneath his breath, his pipe casually dangling from his mouth.

"Father," Austin chimed in, placing his hand on the lower part of Susan's back. "You remember Susan and of course her family, Harriet and William Cutler."

Susan felt the heat of Austin's hand burning through her thick gown like a fire poker and she wanted to slither away from his touch, but did not for fear of being rude and fear of the thought of what Harriett would do if she saw such a reaction.

"Ah yes, of course, Miss Gilbert needs no introduction around here," Edward said taking Susan's hand and bending politely.

Edward exchanged pleasantries with Harriet, William, and Austin while Susan continued to look around the room.

As if reading her mind, Vinnie entered the room and asked if anyone had seen Emily.

Blank glances passed around the now quieted room and the universal shrugs of shoulders filled the party.

"Perhaps I should go check her room," Susan said, though she was not sure why.

"No," Vinnie said defensively. "I'll go."

Vinnie shot Susan a hateful look before turning towards the staircase.

"No need," a small voice from the bottom of the stairs said, "I'm here."

Emily entered the room and smiled, as Vinnie walked quickly to her side, grabbing her hands. Vinnie leaned over and whispered something in Emily's ear and Emily looked over Vinnie's shoulder towards Susan as she did. The look was not unpleasant, but certainly not warm or kind.

They've certainly grown closer, Susan thought.

George was soon at Emily's other side and the two flanked her like a small army, protecting her against only one intruder – Susan Gilbert.

Susan cleared her throat and returned her attention to Austin, Harriet, and William.

A few moments later Mrs. Dickinson entered the room and announced that supper was ready. Susan and Emily were seated at complete opposite ends of the table and she was not surprised upon learning that Vinnie had been in charge of the seating arrangements.

The supper was extravagant, as most Dickinson holiday suppers were. Roasted Goose with cranberry sauce, roasted potatoes, mince pie, and oyster stuffing filled the table for the main meal, and apple sauce, plum pudding, and Emily's massive Jamaican black cake were passed around for dessert. Susan felt so full by the end of the event, that her corset would barely allow her room to breathe. Emily, she noticed, barely ate a bite at the other end of the long table.

After supper, the women retired to the parlor and the men to the library for more smoking and port. Emily announced that she was going up to her room, which gave Susan a slight breath of both relief and disappointment. She could not bear to be so close to her any longer, but neither could she stand the idea of her leaving and sleeping in a room just upstairs from her. Either way, Susan would be tortured but at least with her out of sight it would be easier to avoid staring at her.

"Might I ask you to join me outside for a moment?" George announced as Emily was heading up the stairs.

"Good Heavens, George. Right now? It's late and it's freezing outside. Even Carlo isn't out there in this weather."

George looked around embarrassed, feeling the eyes of the room on both of them. "May I offer you, my coat?" He asked reassuringly.

Emily looked into the parlor and saw Susan staring back at her. Her dark eyes seemed to follow her throughout the evening and she felt if she did not get away from her right now, she might scream or run over and kiss her in front of everyone.

"Actually, the cool air sounds refreshing now that you mention it," Emily said, allowing George to slide his coat around her.

Susan watched as they exited the front door.

"What do you think is so important?" Vinnie asked the general audience as Mrs. Dickinson poured tea for the ladies.

"Don't be daft Vinnie," Lavinia Norcross spoke up. "Is it not clear?"

"What do you mean?" Susan chimed in, producing another dirty look from Vinnie.

"Now, it's just rumors, ladies, let's not put any pressure on the boy," Fannie Norcross interjected, smirking.

"Will someone tell me what on Earth is going on?" Vinnie snipped.

Mrs. Dickinson cleared her throat and rested her hand on her youngest daughter's shoulder.

She knew her daughter's affections for the gangly man had grown deep these past months and she wanted to try her best not to cause her any pain by the potential of George marrying Emily.

"We believe George may be proposing to Emily, sweetheart," she said as kindly as she could.

"What?" Susan and Vinnie exclaimed in unison.

Before anyone could say another word, the front door was opened again and Emily and George were both back inside.

The entire room of women waited anxiously for some shred of news, some announcement, some smile or frown, or indication that a proposal had been made, and better yet accepted.

Instead, George tipped his hat, took his coat back from Emily, bid everyone a Merry Christmas, and left while Emily went up to her room in silence. He did not even take the time to put his coat on before leaving through the front door.

Vinnie and Susan exchanged a worried glance and Susan looked down and sipped her tea.

"I'm going to bed too," Vinnie said before following her sister upstairs.

How Susan wished more than anything that she could follow them too. She needed to know if George proposed. She needed to know if Emily accepted. She needed to be alone with Emily. But she knew that now, more than ever, that was impossible. All she could do now was wait in the misery of her own making.

February 1853

Frozen rain and sleet pelted the window of the Mansion and Emily watched as the naked branches began to sink lower and lower with the weight of the precipitation. She could not help but feel as if each droplet was weighing down her spirits just as equally.

George Gould proposed to her on Christmas Eve. She hadn't said no, but she hadn't said yes either. The truth is she hadn't said anything. She simply said she was too tired to discuss such serious matters and returned inside the house. Poor George didn't know what to do with himself and after that he just went home.

That was two months ago, and George came by almost every day since then. Most days she would say she wasn't feeling well. Other days she would come down and exchange pleasantries with him, but he did not mention the proposal again.

Vinnie's heart broke on Christmas Eve and she hadn't spoken to George since Christmas. When he paid a visit, she left the house or hid in the kitchen or in her room with her cat.

She assured Vinnie that she had no idea that George had feelings for her, and while Vinnie told Emily she understood, she could not help but notice her absence as well. Emily felt alone this winter more than ever. Susan was still gone, although she lived only a few streets away again. Austin returned to Boston for law school. Vinnie hated her and George loved her.

Patting Carlo on the head, Emily turned to the one friend she felt she had left in the world.

Dear Newton,

I suppose you have heard about the drama that befell our simple Christmas Eve supper this year. George Gould has proposed to me. I have not yet given him an answer. The truth is, I do not know what to say. I once thought I would marry for love or not marry at all. But now I wonder if that was simply a young girl's fairy tale playing out in my mind.

Perhaps I am simply destined to be alone with my poetry. Perhaps that should be my great love in this life. I do wish you were here now, so we could sneak off into a dark corridor and write stories, or perform Shakespeare together. But more than that, I wish you were here to give me counsel on this great quagmire of my life. How I miss your company now more than ever my dear friend. Promise to write to me soon?

Always,

E.E.D.

Emily set down the pencil and folded up the letter to be mailed with tomorrow's post. She pulled the teal shawl of Susan's around her tighter. There was a deep chill in the air that day that seemed to cut through the thin windows of the Mansion and straight to the bone.

She hated this never-ending winter. She hated that Newton lived so far away. She hated that there were no green trees or sunshine. She hated that the only flowers she saw were between the dried pages of her herbarium. She hated that George proposed to her. And most of all, she hated that she could not stop missing Susan Gilbert.

Seeing her at her family's table at Christmastide felt like the most natural thing in the world. But having her at the other end of the table, seated beside her brother felt equally unnatural. Why had Susan stopped writing to her when she went to Baltimore? What had she done wrong to drive her away? Was it something she did or said? It couldn't be. Susan said she loved her first. She kissed her back. Surely Emily could not have made it all up in her mind, right?

These are the thoughts that played endlessly through Emily's mind every day. Being around George for the summer helped distract her in some way. Listening to him chatter on about his life, his dreams, his ambitions. It was as if she found a little outlet of escape within his stories. And when she did not feel like listening, she could simply drown him out and enjoy the butterflies and the bees and Carlo. But now that winter had set in - now that this proposal was spoken out loud - it was as if all of those loud distractions were suddenly silenced and her mind once again was only filled with the sounds, the sights, and smells of Susan Gilbert.

Perhaps the worst part of all of this was that she had actually grown quite fond of George lately. She considered him a good friend and though no one could ever replace Newton, she had grown to enjoy their conversations and banter, much in the same way she did with Newton in the past. But could she love him? Could she marry him? Could she share a life with him? Was it really that complicated? Or was she just overthinking it? There was only one way to find out for sure.

As she looked out her window, she could see the familiar sight of George Gould entering the front gate. The poor man even walked to see her in the freezing rain. Surely, she could not turn him away today.

Emily looked down at herself. She looked a mess, not ready to be presented to such a fine young gentleman. She shrugged and tossed open the window as a blast of freezing air slammed into her face.

"George!" She shouted.

He leaned back, holding onto his hat, and looked up smiling.

"Hello, Emily!" He said waiving.

"Shh. Don't knock. Just come up," she said firmly slamming the window shut.

George froze in position, dumbfounded by what he had just been instructed to do. It was highly improper to enter a house unannounced and it was unheard of to see a woman in her private bedroom unaccompanied. But Emily asked him to do it.

He looked around as if to see if anyone overheard the scandalous request before walking up to the front door. He removed his hat and hesitated for a moment before gently opening it. As he stepped into the entryway he sheepishly looked around. The house was quiet except for Carlo who trotted up and greeted him briefly before returning to the library where he had no doubt been sleeping. The tick tock of the grandfather clock and the steady beating of the falling rain were the only audible sounds in the hallow house. George stood still for a moment, waiting to see if his presence remained unnoticed before walking up the stairs towards Emily's room.

Once there he waited outside and lifted his hand to knock. He felt his heart beating furiously in his chest. He had not been upstairs since he and Austin were in school and this certainly felt different than those days.

Before he could make contact with the door, it was opened from the other side. There before him, Emily stood, still in her nightgown. She opened the door and whispered for him to come inside.

He tried not to stare at her and nervously gripped his hat in his hand as he entered.

"Emily, I don't think your father - " Emily pressed her finger to his lips and he stopped speaking.

"My father is away on business and my mother is out shopping. She won't make the walk home until the rain lets up. Vinnie is in her room across the hall."

George gulped at the touch of Emily's finger on his lips. He began to fidget with his damp hat once again.

"Here, let me take this for you," Emily said, taking his hat from his hand and resting it on her bed.

As George stood there in her bedroom, she noticed for the first time how large of a man he really was. He was so tall he seemed too small for her intimate little space. His head nearly grazed the ceiling, even with his hat removed and she could only imagine how his feet would dangle off the end of her bed. His mass seemed to take up half of her entire room and Emily began to feel suffocated at his proximity. The strands of his brown hair were dripping wet from the rain and he had slight goosebumps all over his neck and hands from the cold, yet somehow, he did not shiver.

"You look lovely," George said sincerely and Emily laughed softly.

"George, I'm in my nightgown and my hair is a mess."

"And even still, you look lovely," he said.

His eyes were warm and she could almost feel his nerves begin to relax.

"I know you need an answer, George. And I'm sorry I've been so cruel and ignoring you for so long. I swear I would never intentionally torture you like this."

George nodded looking down wishing he had his hat to cling to.

"I just . . . I needed to do one thing first," Emily said, taking a step closer toward George.

She reached out and grabbed his hands and placed them in hers. She looked down at the large, long, hairy fingers as they engulfed her own. She could feel the callouses from days of hard work out west and the bristle of his hair as it tickled against her soft palms.

"You wanted to feel my hands?" George said, chuckling slightly as Emily continued to play with his hands, studying them like a botanist inspecting a new species of plant.

"No," Emily said.

Without warning she leaned up and pulled his face down to hers, kissing him firmly on the lips.

George kissed her briefly then stepped back, a look of confusion plastered on his long face. Then within seconds, he was back, towering over the top of her and kissing her. She could feel his tongue slide quickly between her lips, filling her mouth. It wasn't like kissing Susan. Unlike Susan, whose tongue would dance around for a few kisses and then ask permission before entering, George's burst its way into her mouth without a moment's hesitation. His lips too were so large they seemed to engulf both her top and bottom lip all at once and he moved them in such a quick, aggressive fashion that it made it hard for her own lips to keep up. She felt his large hands begin to quickly make their way down her back and up to her shoulders.

Mechanically, she forced her hands to move up to his chest and around his tall shoulders as well, all the while ignoring every instinct in her body that screamed how wrong it felt. She focused instead on ignoring the thoughts flashing in her mind of Susan's body, Susan's lips, Susan's hands. After a few moments, Emily began to feel the manifestation of his excitement pressing against her stomach. There it was, erect and unignorable between them. The unmistakable sign of a man who is aroused.

Upon feeling its impending presence press closer into her, she pulled back.

"I'm sorry," she said, covering her mouth. "George, I'm so sorry."

"What's wrong? Have I hurt you? Should we stop? I did not mean to upset you I . . ." George stepped back, placing his hands over his crotch looking ashamed. "I did not mean to . . ."

"No," Emily said grabbing his hands from their protective place and holding them in hers. "It's not you at all, I swear you did nothing wrong."

"Of course, I did. I've upset you," he said, his hazel eyes filling with tears as he gently touched her cheek.

"It's not you," Emily said, fighting back tears of her own. "It's me. I'm so sorry but I can't marry you, George."

"I see," George said, a small tear now trickling down his cheek. "Is there . . . is there someone else?"

Emily paused for a moment considering her reply carefully. "It's nothing like that," she said finally. "I just can't."

George cleared his throat and pushed back his wet hair. "I understand," he said gently.

His eyes looked as if they were filling with more tears and he inhaled deeply through his nose. After a few seconds of silence, he wiped his left eye, then he reached out and kissed her hand lingering for a moment as if he was searching for the words to somehow erase what just happened. Unable to find them, he silently left the room.

Emily went to the window and watched as he walked out of the front gate, his head hung low as the rain fell on him. She contemplated sitting down and writing something. A poem maybe. Or a letter to George apologizing again for her actions. But when she tried, no words would come.

Instead, she found herself across the hall knocking on the door to her sister's room. Seeing Emily standing at her doorway in tears, Vinnie let her in with open arms.

"I don't know what's wrong with me," Emily said to Vinnie as she cried on her shoulder telling her everything that just happened.

"You don't love him," Vinnie said patting her sister's head.

"I know, and I know you do," Emily replied.

Vinnie sighed. "But he doesn't love me. And at the end of the day, I would rather be alone than be with someone who does not want to be with me. Wouldn't you?"

Emily nodded. "I think I'd rather be alone than be with any man at all."

"I think maybe there is someone you'd rather be with," Vinnie said.

Emily began to cry again. "But she doesn't want me anymore."

Vinnie sighed again, stroking her sister's hair. "Then she is a fool after all."

***

Susan,

Since becoming acquainted with you, I have been every day more pleased with your company, and I hope you will allow me to enjoy more of it. If you are not otherwise engaged, will you kindly do me the honor of meeting me in Boston next month? I know it is very inconvenient for you, and I will arrange for your travel and board, of course. There is an important question I must ask you.

Regards,

Austin Dickinson

Susan let the letter drop to the floor. She knew what it meant. She also knew Harriet had already read it and *not* visiting Austin in Boston was out of the question. There was only one reason Austin would be so forward with her, and Harriet knew it as well as Susan did – Austin Dickinson intended to propose to her.

March 1853

Benjamin Newton read the letter and smiled. It was no surprise to him that Emily had a gentleman knocking on her door asking for marriage. As far as he was concerned there was no better catch in all of western Massachusetts than Emily Dickinson.

His wife, Sarah, entered the room and placed her hands on his shoulders.

"You should be in bed, dear," she said softly.

"Yes, darling, in just a moment. I just want to write a response to Emily, here."

Sarah patted his shoulder and left, picking up the basin of water that rested beside the nightstand. She could not bear to look down at the color of it as she removed it from the room. A few weeks ago, Benjamin came down with a nasty cold after a long walk home from the office late one night. Then the cold turned into the flu. Cold sweats in the night, fever, and nausea followed. Then the long fits of coughing came. By the time they called the doctor, the consumption had already gripped both of his lungs and all they could do now was wait and pray.

Newton pulled out a pen and paper and began to cough. This spell was worse than most and when he was finally able to stop coughing, he looked down at his handkerchief. It was soaked through with blood. Sarah returned to the room, insisting he get back into bed immediately. She brought him clean water and wet rags for his forehead.

"Emily will just have to wait until you are better," she said reassuringly. "Your letter will still be there when you are well."

Sarah rested a clean rag on her husband's sweating forehead and tried to ignore the pale, green hue of his skin.

"She's going to be a great poet you know," Benjamin said, fighting off another cough.

"Yes, so I've heard," Sarah said smiling and patting his hand. "Just rest for now. You'll be better soon."

Benjamin nodded and closed his eyes. He would write to Emily first thing in the morning.

***

"Has she seen it yet?" Edward asked, folding the morning newspaper onto the table and rubbing his forehead.

"I don't think so. You're always first to read the paper," Mrs. Dickinson replied.

Vinnie came down the stairs, her blonde curls bouncing playfully behind her. Immediately she sensed the dreary mood of the room.

"Who died?" Vinnie asked in jest.

Edward shot her a glaring look and peaked up the stairs before handing Vinnie the paper.

"Oh God," she said covering her mouth. "Does Emily know?"

"Does Emily know what?" Emily said rounding the corner into the breakfast room.

Vinnie tucked the paper behind her back quickly and shook her head. Emily looked to her mother and father who both had solemn looks on their faces.

"What's going on?" She asked.

"I think you should sit down dear," Edward said, standing and pulling out a chair for his favorite child.

"No," Emily said resolutely. "I want to know what's happened."

Edward hung his head and sat back down. "It's Mr. Newton, Emily," he stated gently.

"What about him? I just wrote to him a few weeks ago," Emily said, her shoulders beginning to relax.

There was nothing wrong with Newton. If there was, she would know about it. He was her closest confidante. There was nothing they kept from each other at this point, except for the fact that she was in love with her best friend of course.

Edward looked to his wife for help but she simply hung her head and covered her mouth.

"Emily dear, I'm afraid Mr. Newton has . . . been called back."

"Called back," Emily repeated.

"It must have been the consumption," Mrs. Dickinson chimed in, her voice cracking slightly. "It's spreading like wildfire this season."

Vinnie stepped forward, the newspaper now showing in her hand, "I'm so sorry Emily, I know how much he meant to you," she said placing a hand on her sister's shoulder.

Emily snatched the paper from Vinnie's hand.

"No," she said, "you're wrong. It's wrong. It's the wrong Benjamin F. Newton. Newton is fine, he's been writing to me like normal. This is wrong. This is a mistake."

But there it was. Staring back at her in undeniable black and white print.

> Worcester, Massachusetts. Benjamin Franklin Newton. Died March 1853, aged 32. Mr. Newton possessed excellent abilities and was one of our most promising young lawyers. He was universally esteemed for his suavity of disposition and high moral integrity.

Emily felt the entire world begin to spin as a familiar high-pitched sound began to fill her ears. She saw dark ink begin to fill the corners of her vision and her breath began to hitch in her chest. She refused to let herself faint again. She was stronger than that. She shook her head and sat down next to her father, still gripping the newspaper.

This is not happening. Newton is fine. He's sending you a letter any day now. This is a dream. This isn't real.

She stayed like that, rocking slowly in silence for what felt like an eternity assuring herself that Newton was fine. Eventually, her father rested his arm on her shoulder. With that simple contact, it was as if the entire world became clear and the truth became undeniable. She stopped rocking.

Newton was dead. Her friend was gone forever. Emily shut her eyes and imagined his beautiful, strong body, now rotting in a wooden box six feet beneath the ground. She imagined herself in the grave beside him, her hand curled around his thick, warm neck, the sound of his heart still beating in his chest. She thought of the dirt being thrown in and burying them together, the air slowly leaving her lungs as they slipped into eternity together.

But when she opened her eyes, she saw only the flowered wallpaper of the Mansion and the sea blue of her sister's eyes.

After a few moments of sitting in continued silence, her father's arm around her shoulder, her sister's hand resting in her lap, Emily stood up and walked towards the door.

"Emily?" Vinnie said, watching as her sister placed a bonnet on her head and her dirty boots on her bare feet. "What are you doing?"

"I need to be outside," Emily said before walking out the front door in her long, white nightgown.

The cool spring air blew through the front door and Vinnie chased after her.

"Emily!" She shouted.

But her sister was already gone, sprinting in the direction of the woods.

***

Susan set the morning paper down and covered her mouth in shock. Mr. Newton was only 32 years old. Such a strong, healthy man to be taken at such a young age. But more importantly, she wondered if Emily had heard the news and if so, how she was handling it. She was one of the few people who truly understood what Benjamin was to Emily. Emily had not suffered deaths as Susan had in her family. She would take this loss particularly hard; Susan knew. She immediately set the paper down and walked to the front door.

"Where on Earth are you going at this hour?" Harriet asked from the breakfast table.

"Out," Susan snipped back.

"But your train for Boston leaves in just a few hours!" Harriet said frantically.

Susan ignored her and grabbed her thick, wool jacket and bonnet, and left. She thought of going over to the Mansion on West Street but soon altered her course. If Emily did hear the news she knew exactly where she'd be.

***

Emily chipped at a piece of ice that hung to the edge of the creek with her bare finger. In a few months, the birds would be chirping over her head and this thin stream would be a rushing river. But for now, the winter was still thawing and the water was barely a trickle. She knew it was too cold outside for her to be wearing as little as she was. She knew dressing like this made her run the risk of the same disease that had taken the life of her dear Newton. But she did not care if she lived or died today. She would stay out here until she felt something again or until she felt nothing at all. She would stay until the pain went away.

She did not know how long she had been there when she heard the sounds of sticks and dried leaves cracking and crunching from behind her. She turned to see Susan Gilbert standing only a few feet away from her.

They stayed like that for a moment. Just looking at each other, both with a renewed look of vulnerability in their eyes. Emily did not have the energy to keep up her icy façade towards Susan today and Susan did not have it in her to push Emily away. Today, if only for today, they both let their guards down.

Susan approach Emily without speaking and held out her arms. Emily walked towards her and pressed her entire body into Susan's. She inhaled the sweet smell of her hair and felt her warm heart beating against her chest. And for the first time since hearing the news of Newton's death hours earlier – she wept.

June 1853

That spring was one of the cloudiest and wettest springs in western Massachusetts that Emily could remember. The clouds hung low nearly every day and a permanent drizzle fell over every town in the entire area. Birds chirped as they always did, but with weaker, fainter cries. Trees budded slower and by the time the sun finally did begin to make its presence known, summer was well upon them.

Emily didn't care about missing her favorite season this year. She didn't care about most things she used to since the loss of Newton. She stopped writing her poetry altogether that spring. Her words didn't help anyone. They didn't even matter at all. Poetry had not saved her friend. Poetry had not stopped Susan from choosing Austin over her. And poetry couldn't abate this emptiness growing inside her.

George stopped by a few times that spring to check on Emily. She only saw him twice. She had no reason to avoid poor George. After all, she was the one who hurt him, yet still, much like her dog, Carlo, he remained loyal to her. But for some reason spending time with Newton's quasi-replacement only made her feel lonelier. In the time they spent together since his death she was been reminded of how very much *unlike* Newton he was. And how she would never be able to replace his loss in her heart.

Susan wrote her a few letters and brought her food as any friendly neighbor or church member would. The letters were empty, the ones she did read. There was no sentiment, no passion or feeling behind them, and

Emily eventually began throwing them away without even reading them.

    Vinnie was the only person she permitted into her room and she would often bring in Carlo and her cat to play together. The cat had gotten fatter over the last year or so and her thick, grey fur was now even more exaggerated in places where her belly protruded from too much food. Their "playtime" together mostly consisted of the cat lying lazily on Emily's bed, hissing at Carlo, as Carlo raced around the bed wagging his tail and barking.

    One morning in the late spring, they performed the usual ritual and this time the cat was brave enough to take a swat at Carlo. Unfortunately for the poor feline, Carlo was too quick and she went tumbling to the ground only to land on her feet and race out the bedroom door with Carlo chasing playfully after her. Emily burst uncontrollably into laughter after watching the scene unfold. It was the first time since Newton's death that she laughed.

    Their mother was particularly kind to Emily that spring and she did not scold her for burning the bread and forgetting the pies as she normally would. This, Emily decided, was the best way she knew how to show sympathy.

    And so, the days of spring passed for Emily like an endless wave crashing on the shore. She didn't bother to keep track of the days or weeks as they passed her by. In fact, she only recently realized it was even summer at all.

    Emily sat in her room, her head rested on her desk, looking out her window. Vinnie stopped by this morning to bring her breakfast and she patted Carlo on the head to say her usual good mornings to him. Then they left her alone. She currently watched as the puffy, white clouds passed by overhead and she lifted her head from her desk and tapped aimlessly on the glass. A few seconds later she returned her head to the desk and sighed.

Then there was a soft knock on her door.

"What is it, Vinnie?" Emily asked lazily, not lifting her head.

"It's Sue."

Emily's head shot up and she inhaled frantically. *Sue? What is she doing here?* She began to panic. She jumped up from her seat reaching for her robe and throwing it around her. She looked in the mirror and smoothed her hair as best she could. Her eyes remained swollen and red from nightly crying but that could not be helped.

Why do you care what you look like? Emily's mind raced. *She is being courted by Austin. Not you.*

Ignoring her inner saboteur, Emily pinched her cheeks briefly to bring some color to them before sitting back down calmly at her desk and turning to face the door.

"You may enter," she said attempting to sound aloof.

The door creaked open slowly and Susan Gilbert stepped delicately inside. She wore a purple and white pin-striped dress with buttons that ran from her breast down the front to the floor. It had long sleeves with gold embossing between the pinstripes and was a shiny sort of fabric that seemed to sparkle in the sunlight. Her dark hair was pulled back into a low bun that covered the tips of her ears.

She could not help but observe how Susan looked in her bedroom compared to how George looked several months ago. Where George's size and demeanor seemed to fill the space so much that it lacked oxygen, Susan seemed to bring fresh air into the stale room. She fit perfectly like a fixture on the wall or a book on the shelf. She seemed to almost belong here.

"What do you want, Susan?" She said curtly.

Susan shook her head. "For you to stop calling me that first of all."

"That's your name," Emily replied frankly.

"Yes," Susan began hesitantly. "But not with you. At least it didn't use to be what you called me."

"A lot of things used to be different between us, Susan," Emily replied, her voice sounding sadder than she had intended it to.

Susan nodded looking down. "I know," she said sadly.

Emily looked at her hands. She couldn't stand to look at Susan like this. She couldn't stand to even be around her. She had spent months trying to rid herself of all emotions; trying desperately not to feel the pain and agony and loss of both Newton and Susan. And now, seeing Susan here, standing in her bedroom, it seemed as if all of that effort was wasted. Just once glance at Susan Gilbert had rendered her guards useless.

Right now, all she wanted to do was shove her against the back of her bedroom door and kiss her. She stood from her desk and crossed her arms, slowly stepping closer to the area where Susan stood.

She felt her inhibitions dropping slightly, though whether it was from a lack of sleep or some other factor, she did not know.

"How did you get in here?" Emily asked stopping in the middle of the room about two feet away from Susan.

Emily felt her head begin to swirl slightly. She felt like she was drunk. Drunk on not caring what Susan thought. Drunk on the pain of losing both her and Newton. Drunk on numbness and regret. Drunk on love and hate and everything in between.

"I uhm . . . Susan hesitated looking down again.

Susan could barely look at Emly the closer she got. She could see the red swelling of her eyes and the hollowness of her cheeks now. She could almost smell the sweet lavender oil that Emily placed behind her ears and it was enough to make Susan go wild with lust. She had to look down or up or anywhere but into Emily's eyes.

"I snuck in through the kitchen door," Susan admitted finally.

Emily let out a slight chuckle and Susan could not tell if she was mocking her or not.

"Why on Earth would you do that?" Emily asked, her voice now returning to the familiar, playful tone Susan had grown to love years ago.

Susan smiled cautiously. "Because I wanted to see you. Just you. And I was petrified that if I announced myself, you would turn me away or sick Vinnie on me."

At that Emily laughed fully. "Sick Vinnie on you? Are she and Carlo a duo now?"

"Oh, don't play coy with me, Emily Dickinson, I've seen the looks your sister has been giving me since my return to Amherst. I know she knows . . . things about us."

Emily paused and crossed her arms. "And you're concerned about that?"

"Yes . . . well . . . no," Susan stuttered.

It wasn't the idea of Vinnie knowing about them that bothered Susan. It was the things Emily had told her. Had she spoken only poorly of her? Had she told her intimate things they had done? Had she made . . . complaints about those intimate things?

"You can relax, Susan," Emily remarked her voice now back to its new, steely tone. "I haven't divulged any details. She only knows that I love you and that you hurt me."

Susan's eyes shot up to Emily's.

"*Loved* you," Emily said, correcting herself. "She knows nothing that would harm your prospects with my brother, don't fret."

Emily turned and sat back down at her desk.

"I didn't come here to discuss your brother," Susan said, hoping to change the direction of the conversation.

"And why did you come here? To 'check on me' to 'see how I'm doing'"? Emily snipped. "Newton is dead. George hates me. Vinnie hates me. And Austin is courting the only person I ever loved. How do you think I am right now, Susan?"

Emily turned to look out the window, unable to bear the sight of Susan in her room any longer.

"When my parents died, I thought my world would stop turning," Susan said from the safety of her spot across the room. "I used to lie in bed and pray I would just stay asleep forever. Because I was convinced that it was the only way I would ever not feel the empty, swelling pain inside my chest. I would imagine walking into a freezing river just to feel the cold shoot through my legs and into my heart, numbing me with each step."

Susan took a small step further into the room. "But through all of that time, I held on to one thing that gave me hope that someday that pain would pass."

Emily remained facing the window. "What was that?"

"You. Your . . . your friendship."

Emily looked over her shoulder at Susan briefly. Is that what she was what they were now? Friends? Jane Humphrey was her friend. Abiah Root was her friend. Benjamin Newton had been her friend. Susan Gilbert had always been more and she knew it.

"Back then I was only Suzie to you," Susan continued, "we were just children. Then I grew into being Sue. Your Sue. And we were something else entirely."

At least she admits it.

"Now it seems Susan is the name you have deemed best for me and I suppose that is not my choice to make. Call me whatever you will. Suzie or Sue or Susan or any other name you can imagine. I know we are not as we once were, but just know that I will always be here for you, Emily. The way you were always there for me."

After a few seconds of silence, Susan sighed and turned to leave. Emily fought every instinct that told her to stop her from leaving. To tell her that she was still in love with her. To slam the door shut and throw her onto her bed.

Instead, Emily stayed frozen, staring out the window in silence. She couldn't look at Susan. She couldn't expose herself to that kind of pain anymore. Not now. Finally, Emily heard the door close slowly behind her.

A few moments later she watched as Susan made her way across the front yard. When she reached the front gate, she turned and looked up at Emily's window. Emily did not wave and neither did Susan. They simply remained like that for a brief moment, looking at one another, before Susan turned and left. She did not know if she would ever trust what Susan just told her, but she was at least glad she said it.

Emily remembered when Susan returned to Amherst after Baltimore. She remembered seeing her in their spot in the woods.

Why did she go there of all places? Why did she say she was trying to forget somebody then? No, not somebody – Nobody. The word clung to the back of Emily's mind ever since Susan uttered it. *Nobody. Nobody.*

When Susan was completely out of sight, Emily picked up her pen and began to write. It was the first time she wrote since Newton's death.

I'm Nobody! Who are you?
Are you - Nobody - too?
Then there's a pair of us!
Don't tell! they'd advertise - you know!
How dreary - to be - Somebody!
How public - like a Frog -
To tell one's name - the livelong June -
To an admiring Bog!

July 1853

After Susan's visit last month, Emily began to make her way out of doors slowly, though she still preferred to spend most of her days either alone or with Carlo. She wrote furiously now and she constantly carried pieces of paper and a pencil with her wherever she went. She would stick a scrap of paper into the side of her bonnet and keep a worn-down pencil tucked behind her ear, or hidden in the top of her corset. She would use anything she could find as paper. Kitchen recipes, candy wrappers, used envelopes, or even the letters of business her father threw in the waste basket.

Her father eventually caught onto her schemes when he saw her sneaking out of his office one day and upon learning that she was carrying the privileged remnants of notes all over town, insisted she tear off the blank parts of the paper to use, or leave the documents in the garbage.

Susan resumed her job at the seamstress' shop with Miss Mavis, even though thanks to Austin, her family was more than well off. Susan liked the work and more importantly enjoyed feeling like she was in some way contributing to her own destiny.

William continued to work long, hard hours at the blacksmith shop and also seemed to benefit from the labor. It gave him no free time to distract himself with his vices and he enjoyed coming home at the end of a long day feeling utterly exhausted.

Austin came to Amherst more and more frequently to visit Susan. Each time he stopped by he had some lavish gift to bestow upon her and when he could not be there in person, he would send a courier with flowers, nuts, sweets, colorful fabric, anything a woman could ever want. She distracted herself trying to not think about Emily and especially not think about Austin. To not think about what happened when she visited him in Boston last March. She was so busy worrying about Emily, that she had little time to think about the trip, or what it potentially meant for Susan's future.

"Perhaps we should consider moving soon," Harriet said one day as Susan was peeling carrots in the kitchen with her.

"Whatever for?" Susan replied.

"Well, we are certainly moving up the ranks of society these days. I'm just not sure this humble house fits our social class any longer."

"And how would you propose paying for this new extravagant house, sister?" Susan asked pointedly.

"Austin would pay for it, of course," Harriet replied.

Susan slammed the knife and carrot down on the wooden table. She could feel the heat boiling inside her and rising to her head. She endured the gifts from Austin. She endured the new furniture and the silverware and the paintings. She endured the new job he gave William. She had even been grateful to him for all of it. But now Harriet had gone too far.

"Austin Dickinson will *not* be buying you or me or anyone a new house," she said through gritted teeth.

"And why ever not? The man is in love with you. It's only a matter of time before you're wed."

"Oh, it is?" Susan retorted turning to face her sister.

Harriet took a step forward and grabbed her sister by the arm, roughly. Susan was taken aback by the aggressive act. Harriet was always kind and gentle and she never dared lay a finger on Susan. Even William, in all of his drunken stupors, never raised a hand to either of them before.

"Yes," Harriet said leaning over Susan. "For the good of not only your own future but this entire family's future, you *will* marry Austin Dickinson."

Susan jerked her arm away from Harriet's grip and Harriet returned to the fire to stir the stew that brewed in the large pot over top of it.

In an instant, Susan wiped her hands, took off her apron, and left out the kitchen door before Harriet could turn back around.

Susan walked down Main Street, unsure of where she was even going. She could pop in at Miss Mavis' shop and do some extra work, but her fingertips were still tired from her earlier shift this morning. She could walk to the post office and pen a letter to his sister, Mattie, but she did not know what she would say to her.

Eventually, she made her way over to the mercantile on Merchant Row and simply sat on the bench out front. She would sit here long enough to clear her head and then return to the house – or prison, as it currently felt.

Susan watched for a moment as horses pulling carriages trotted by and men carrying large sacks of grain loaded a nearby wagon off the side of the store. It looked like hard work and Susan felt guilty for pitying her simple fingertips after watching the men perform their duties.

She tried to imagine Austin doing their work. Loading and hauling sacks of grain. Wheeling massive barrels of whiskey and rye. She tried to imagine him bent down in a field, sowing crops, tossing wheat up in the air to separate the grain from the chaff. The mental image of Austin Dickinson on a farm made her laugh. She could see it now, his silk cravat becoming wrinkled with sweat, his combed hair getting messy in the wind, his fair skin burning under the rays of the sun. Austin Dickinson was many great things, but a laborer was not one of them.

And then, as it usually did, her mind wandered to Emily performing the same tasks. Emily pulling a plow, Emily sowing crops, Emily picking apples. She imagined her in a field wearing men's clothes, sweat dripping down her slightly opened flowing white shirt, her legs firm and tight in her breeches, the tall, leather riding boots hitting just below her knee.

"Hello, Susan," she heard a voice breaking her from her daydream.

She did not have to look up to know that the voice belonged to none other than Emily Dickinson. Standing by the bench with her arms folded in front of her stood the auburn-headed girl that Susan was daydreaming of. Instead of the imagined menswear, she wore a baby blue and white linen dress that hung just off of her waist. The buttons cut low down the front of her chest and Susan had to stop her eyes from tracing the line of the hem and look down.

"Hello, Emily," she said.

Much to Susan's surprise, Emily smiled and sat down on the bench next to her. Susan remained silent, almost afraid to speak for fear that any word from her would send Emily into another angry rant or verbal lashing. Emily had not spoken kindly to her since her return to Amherst and she did not think she could handle another confrontation today.

"How are you?" Emily said.

Susan paused for a moment reflecting on the tone of Emily's voice. It was polite, yes. And while not as warm as it once was, Susan could not deny that she sounded almost . . . kind.

"I . . ." Susan began. "I'm fine, thank you."

"Why are you lying?" Emily replied as they sat side by side staring out at the main road. "I've known you since we were small children. I've held you as you wept, I've bandaged your scraped knees and elbows, I've stolen cakes and pies with you from my mother's kitchen." She said.

"I've felt your lips parted against mine," she said more quietly. The sentence sent a shiver down Susan's spine.

"So, why do you lie and tell me you're fine when I know you better?"

Susan let out a small sigh and felt her shoulders relax. She did not know what Emily's intentions were with the conversation, but at least it didn't feel like she was in for a verbal lashing today.

"It's nothing you want to hear about," Susan stated plainly.

"Because it's about Austin," Emily remarked.

Her voice hardened slightly at the mention of her brother, but she continued to keep her face gentle and her voice soft. Susan paused and then nodded.

"He intends to marry you, you know," Emily continued, leaning down and picking at the lace in her brown boot nonchalantly.

Susan nodded again.

"But you do not love him?" Emily asked.

Susan looked at Emily. "No," she said, "I don't."

It was as if they both knew how the sentence really finished. They both knew what Susan meant to say was, "because I love *you*."

Emily stood up and looked down at Susan. "Come with me," she said holding out her hand.

Susan hesitated for a second and then placed her hand in Emily's. They had not held hands in two years. It had been two years since Susan left Emily standing alone in the woods. Two years since she left for Baltimore. Two years since she decided to give her and Emily a fresh start. But now, two years later the familiar sensation of Emily's skin touching hers sent sparks and flames down Susan's fingertips and into her spine. It was as if no time had passed at all, and yet there was a large canyon still lingering between them. Susan had to work to contain the shiver that now ran down her back.

Emily dropped Susan's hand as soon as she stood and Susan could not help but want more. They made their way down Merchant Row towards Main Street and within minutes Susan knew exactly where they were going.

The trees in the woods hung like a thick, dense canopy. Their leaves were a dark green and only a few specks of sunlight beamed down through small holes where their branches were left exposed. It was a hot, summer day just as it had been on the day Susan left for Baltimore.

The creek trickled steadily and the sounds of birds chirping and singing overhead was the only thing to parallel the sound of slowly running water. They did not speak until they finally reached their sacred spot by the water.

Then, without warning, Emily turned and said, "George Gould proposed to me."

Susan's mouth dropped. "When?" She managed to say.

"When you were at my home for Christmas."

Susan nodded slowly. "I see."

Is this why she dragged her to their sacred spot in the woods? To tell her she was engaged to another man? To get revenge for her relationship with Austin? To hurt her the way she hurt Emily?

"Do you not want to know what my reply was?"

Susan nodded again, not looking at Emily. She felt a knot growing in the pit of her stomach now. Marrying someone like George was exactly why Susan elected to not respond to Emily's letters in the first place back when she was in Baltimore. She wanted Emily to marry a kind, successful man like George Gould. She wanted her to grow old with a husband and bear his children. It's what she wanted for Emily all along. So why, now that it was a realistic possibility, did it seem so painful to her?

Emily paused for a moment and leaned back against the tree. "I told him no."

Susan let out an audible sigh of relief.

Emily stood up straight and walked a few steps closer to Susan. "Why does that make you happy?" She asked, one eyebrow raised.

Susan shook her head. "It . . . it doesn't. I'm sorry to hear that, he seemed like an upstanding gentleman."

"Stop it," Emily said, "stop lying to me. Tell me why you're happy to hear it."

Her voice was slightly elevated and she continued to approach Susan slowly and steadily. She was only a few feet away now and Susan could feel the air being sucked out of the quickly disappearing space between them.

"I'm not lying," Susan protested.

Emily stopped a foot away from Susan. "Tell me why you don't want to marry my brother," she said furrowing both brows.

"I . . ." Susan tried but she couldn't find the words to speak.

Emily being this close to her was making her head swirl. She could smell the lavender from her hair and the oil she dabbed behind her ears. She looked down but before she could, Emily's hand was on her chin to lift her head back up. She was so close now she could smell the orange on her breath.

"Say it," Emily said, forcing Susan to look directly into her eyes.

Susan mustered all of the energy she had left in one final effort and then when she opened her mouth, the one thing she did not want to say, came out.

"Because, I love you."

Susan felt like a massive weight was lifted off of her shoulders as the words came out and Emily dropped her chin from her hand. Susan began to look down again but before she could, Emily's lips were on hers, pressing against her strongly and desperately.

It felt like lightning struck her heart and was now coursing through her entire body. She felt herself levitating from the ground where they stood and she instantly kissed Emily back. Without her mind's consent, her hands began groping, pawing at Emily like a wild animal grasping for flesh to consume. Backward and backward, they stumbled until Emily was pushed against the tree she had been leaning against earlier.

Instinctively Emily's hands began grabbing at Susan's backside and pulling her closer in between her legs. Susan followed Emily's cue and began to move rhythmically against Emily feeling her entire body respond with each motion. Emily let out a slight moan as Susan moved and she continued to kiss her neck and ear. Susan could taste the sweat dripping down Emily's neck from the summer heat and the exertion. She licked up each salty drop as if it were a sweet treat from the mercantile.

Emily grabbed Susan's face and began kissing her again, slower and steadier this time. Then, Emily spun around so that it was Susan who was now pressed against the tree.

Emily kissed Susan's neck slowly, intentionally, before pulling up at the bottom of her dress and letting her hand slide beneath it. She could feel Susan's thin chemise against her fingers as she made her way up and between her legs. Susan's only response was to wrap her leg around Emily's body, granting her access to whatever part of her she wanted. The wetness between Susan's legs told Emily that Susan wanted this as badly as she did. Slowly she began to move her hand against Susan. She watched as Susan threw her head back and whimpered with pleasure. She continued in the same, rhythmic motion until finally, it was as if something erupted inside of Susan. Wildly, she clung to Emily's back, pulling her closer and closer against her until there was a loud moan and then, finally, release.

Afterward, Emily kissed Susan's neck and forehead and Susan pulled Emily close against her, panting and sweating, trying to catch her breath.

"I love you," was all Susan could manage to say in between breaths.

After a few seconds, she stood up and flipped their bodies around so it was now Emily who was pressed against the tree.

"I've wanted to do this for so long," Susan said, kissing Emily's neck.

"How long?" Emily asked while nibbling at Susan's ear.

"Since the first time we kissed in the woods when we were 15." Susan continued, her hands making their way in between Emily's legs. Emily let out a loud gasp at the contact.

"What took you so long?" Were the last words she was able to speak, before slipping off into repeated, rapturous bliss.

August 1853

"What are you doing over there?" Susan asked poking her toe at Emily.

They were both sitting beneath the large oak tree in front of the Mansion. Carlo sat beside them sprawled out in the shade, breathing heavily. The sun was beaming down on them and Susan sat propped against the tree while Emily sat a few inches away, hunched over a piece of paper furiously writing. Vinnie's cat had even been allowed outside to enjoy the weather as well and she now laid near Carlo, incessantly bathing her round, furry belly. Vinnie had been invited to sit outside with them as well but had refused and shot Susan a subtle, but dirty look.

"She's still angry with you for hurting me," Emily said when Vinnie dropped off her cat and turned back around to go inside.

"I'm quite angry with myself for that as well," Susan replied.

Emily ignored her and continued to look down at what she was writing. "Done!" Emily proclaimed as she looked up for the first time in what felt like hours.

"Done with what?"

"This," Emily said, handing Susan the sheet of paper.

Quickly, Susan's eyes began to scan the page.

I have never seen "Volcanoes" --
But, when Travellers tell
How those old -- phlegmatic mountains
Usually so still --
Bear within -- appalling Ordnance,
Fire, and smoke, and gun,

Taking Villages for breakfast,
And appalling Men --
If the stillness is Volcanic
In the human face
When upon a pain Titanic
Features keep their place --
If at length the smouldering anguish
Will not overcome --
And the palpitating Vineyard
In the dust, be thrown?
If some loving Antiquary,
On Resumption Morn,
Will not cry with joy "Pompeii"!
To the Hills return!

"Oh, Emily. It's beautiful," Susan said wiping a tear from the corner of her eye. "It's even better than your last one."

"My last one?" Emily raised an eyebrow and laid-back resting on her elbow.

"Well, the last one you wrote for me, I should say. I'm sure there have been hundreds since then," Susan went back and began reading the verses over again.

"You mean the one I gave you in the woods the day you left for Baltimore?"

"Wild nights, wild nights, we're I with thee . . ." Susan began reciting.

"I do love it when you quote me." She giggled. "But in all seriousness, I'm glad to hear you liked it. You never said as much."

"I know . . ." Susan continued, picking at a blade of grass nervously. "But I kept it with me always and I read it every single day when I was in Baltimore."

Emily sat up and scooted closer to Susan. Ever since that day in the woods, they were even closer than before Susan left. They walked everywhere together, arm in arm, wrote letters to one another, and spent all of their free time together. But they both knew something had changed between them. They were not young and free as they were before Susan left. There were other people to consider now. There was Austin first and foremost, who continued to fall more in love with Susan each day. There was George who still clung to some faint hope that Emily might change her mind and come running back to him. There was Harriet whose entire life seemed to rest on Susan marrying Austin. There were Emily's parents who had also taken quite a fancy to the young woman as their potential future daughter-in-law. There was Vinnie who now hated Susan thanks to what she had done to Emily.

They were no longer free beings who could sneak off into the woods whenever they pleased. There were always eyes on them now. Not only that, but they both changed and grown so much since then. Emily lost her dearest friend, Newton. She rejected a marriage proposal from George. Susan had grown fond of Austin as a companion and friend, and she cared for his feelings and did not want to hurt him. And then there was William and Harriet who were truly happier people now.

"Can I ask you something?" Emily started, not waiting for a reply. "When I saw you that day in the woods after you returned from Baltimore. Why did you go there of all places?"

Susan sighed deeply and sat up straight. "The truth is, I went there because I saw you the day I got back. You were standing by the Common with Vinnie and Mr. Gould and . . . it impacted me. I wanted to be close to you but I knew I shouldn't be, so I went there often. That day I had gone there because I told myself I had to let you go. To forget you. I even planned on letting your poem float down the river. But when the time came I just . . . I couldn't let go."

"Why did you think you shouldn't be close to me?" Emily asked.

"Because . . . I knew something like *this* would happen," Susan said blushing. "I wanted to give you a chance at a new life without me holding you back, weighing you down. I wanted you to be free of me. That's why I stopped writing to you in Baltimore. I thought you were better off without me."

Emily reached out and placed her hand on Susan's.

"It's my turn for a question," Susan said, changing the subject. "Why did you go from hating me when I first returned and at Christmas time, to . . . you know . . . that day in the woods last month?"

Now it was Emily's turn to blush. She reflected for a moment, looking up at the sunlight poking through the tree branches that now covered them like a canopy.

"When Newton died, it felt like there was this big hole inside me that would never be filled. Like I was destined to walk this earth and never feel heard or understood again. But then after a few months, I realized that there was someone else who had once made me feel heard and understood and loved besides Newton. And I realized that all I was doing by being angry at that person was losing precious time. Because losing Newton has shown me that life is too short to spend it not being with the person you want to be with."

"And that person is me?" Susan said softly.

"Yes, Susan," Emily replied.

"I do wish you would go back to calling me, Sue," she said crossing her arms and leaning back against the tree.

"Ah, but you are not just my Sue anymore, are you? You are more his Susan now than mine." Emily looked down and bit her cheek.

And there it was. The elephant in the room that sat between them daily. Susan was still getting her weekly correspondence from Austin and she was still responding. The entire town was awaiting the day that they would announce their engagement officially. The only people who did not seem enthused by the match were Emily and Susan.

"I don't belong to him," Susan remarked, raising an eyebrow.

Emily frowned. "If only that were true. Then you *would* be my Sue again." She reached over and traced the outline of Susan's cheek with her hand.

"Emily . . . there's something I need to tell you. About . . ." Before she could finish speaking, Vinnie emerged to inform Emily that her help was needed with preparing supper.

"Very well," Emily yelled across the yard. "But tell mother I am preparing a plate for Susan too. She is family, after all."

Emily winked at Susan who shook her head and looked down. Vinnie rolled her eyes and went back inside.

"Will she ever forgive me?" Susan asked.

"I don't know. Vinnie has been known to hold a grudge. She once didn't speak to me for a month when we were girls because I ate her share of dessert after supper."

"Will *you* ever forgive me?" Susan asked, her voice more serious than before.

Emily looked at Susan, contemplating her answer for a moment. "Only if you promise you won't leave me again," she replied.

Susan reached out and grabbed Emily by the hand, "I promise."

Emily smiled and stood, holding out her hand to help Susan up.

"Do you promise . . ." Emily continued searching the large yard with her eyes. Suddenly she ran over to the opening of the fence surrounding the yard and yelled. "To never be this far from me!"

Susan giggled and shook her head. "Yes!" She yelled back.

Emily continued moving farther and farther back and now stood across West Street entirely.

"Will you promise never to be this far from me?" She yelled even louder.

Susan was grateful it was nearing supper time and there were no visible passersby in the vicinity. The town of Amherst may have grown accustomed to Emily's antics by now, but that did not mean Susan stopped being embarrassed by them at times.

"Yes!" Susan shouted after looking up and down the street quickly.

Emily darted across the dirt street and back into the yard.

"Very well then, that's all settled," she said wiping her hands as if she just spent the day tilling a field or chopping down a large tree. "If you're coming for supper, you must help with the preparations. That will give you and Vinnie plenty of time to kiss and make up."

Susan swatted at Emily who dodged the contact barely and managed to circle Susan poking her playfully in the ribs.

"Pardon my interruption," a man's voice said from the front gate. It was none other than George Gould, who had returned for his weekly visit.

"Nonsense, George," Emily replied kindly. "You're not interrupting at all. We were just about to head inside, but would you like to join us for supper?"

George's face lit up at the invitation, "I would be delighted." He bowed low and stood awkwardly clutching his hat.

"Well, don't just stand there George, do head inside. My father is in the library and would enjoy the company."

Susan looked at Emily confused as she watched George bow again and walk into the house. His long legs seemed to swallow the few steps leading up into the house as he walked.

"You should not lead the poor man on," Susan whispered under her breath.

"I am doing no such thing. I have every intention of setting George up with my lovely sister, Vinnie. And what better way than to seat them right across from each other at supper tonight? She fancies him and has for years now. What harm could come of a little matchmaking?"

Emily playfully shrugged her shoulders and began to twirl her dress in the wind. Susan smiled. She hadn't seen Emily look this happy in years.

"If you say so," Susan shook her head and sighed.

As the four women worked in the kitchen Mrs. Dickinson took painstaking efforts to make conversation with Susan. Vinnie took the same amount of effort to be pleasant towards her in front of their mother and Susan made every effort not to stare at Emily too lovingly, even when she had a dash of flour on the tip of her nose that made her look adorable.

"I've always found that a good housewife should know her kitchen as well as she knows the back of her hand," Mrs. Dickinson said when the girls were doing their assigned tasks.

"I couldn't agree more, mother," Emily replied before suddenly looking down at the back of her hand and exclaiming in feigned shock. "Oh my! How long has that been there?"

Susan and Vinnie laughed in unison and Mrs. Dickinson tisked under her breath and shook her head.

George sipped tea with Mr. Dickinson in the parlor until the meal was brought up by all four women at once. Emily had snuck up earlier and placed name plaques at each setting to ensure that everyone was seated according to plan. George remarked about the formality and the penmanship of the inscriptions before his plate and Vinnie simply shrugged, smiling as she delicately sat down across from George and next to Emily.

Edward said the blessing over the meal and Mrs. Dickinson waited in silence for the men's rehearsed reactions to their hard work. Emily slid her foot beneath the table and rested it on Susan's. She watched as a look of excitement raced over Susan's face and she bit her lip to hide any further visible reaction.

"Quite the weather we are having," George began.

Everyone nodded in polite agreement.

"George," Emily began. "What would you say is your favorite season?"

George perked up at the question and contemplated it a moment.

"I believe I'd have to say, autumn."

"You don't say! Why that's the same as yours, isn't it Vinnie?"

Vinnie wrinkled her nose and cocked her head. Everyone knew Vinnie was partial to the warmth of the summer months and hated when the seasons started to change for the colder. She had even once said the sound of the leaves cracking beneath her shoes irritated her.

Emily firmly nodded her head. "Isn't it Vinnie?"

Catching on to the ruse, Vinnie nodded quickly, "Oh! Oh, yes, yes, of course, I have always loved the fall. The crisp, coolness of the air, the sound of the leaves crunching beneath your feet."

Vinnie cringed a bit as she said the last part, but only those who knew her well would have noticed it.

"I couldn't agree more!" George proclaimed. "There is something so exhilarating about knowing the thick, white winter is approaching."

"People die in winter," Mr. Dickinson chimed in, bleakly.

"People die in spring too, father," Emily remarked, thinking grimly of her dear Newton.

"What about the new President? Franklin Pierce?" Susan interjected, attempting to shift the conversation away from the dreary subject of death.

"Bah," balked Edward. "Another Democrat who thinks the abolition of slavery is a threat to the Union. That man will do nothing but drive us to the brink of war, mark my words. The Democrats have no interest in the unification of this nation," Edward continued.

Looking over at Emily, Susan quickly realized the error of her ways as Emily hid a smirk with her hand. She knew her father, a staunch Whig, to personally hate the new Democratic President. Emily did not have much of a mind for politics, but she abhorred slavery and she knew enough about this particular president to know if she did have the right to vote, she would not have cast it for him.

"Have you ever heard of this Kansas-Nebraska Act they're debating right now in Congress?" Edward continued, pointing a fork at poor George.

"Well, sir, yes, I have heard of it, although I have heard it intends to open up the land for a transcontinental railroad." George replied, firmly but respectfully.

"Propaganda," Edward groaned after popping a piece of carrot into his mouth. "I'm as against slavery as the next Massachusetts man, but this President of ours will do nothing but divide this nation and the Kansas-Nebraska Act is just the first step on the road to war."

The room hung silent for a moment before Vinnie broke the awkward tension.

"George, why don't you tell my father about that time you ran into an Indian out west and bartered with him for his fur coat?"

Emily slightly shook her head and smiled, shooting a sideward glance at Susan. She knew this topic would not settle her father's famous political passion, but she was looking forward to the fireworks that were sure to follow.

As George droned on about his days out west, Edward's face grew redder and redder as he nodded and listened, not wanting to be an inhospitable host. It came as no surprise to her when, before dessert, her father politely excused himself from the table and retired to his library.

After the meal, George lingered and helped clear the plates, although Mrs. Dickinson insisted that he rest his feet while brandy was poured for him.

"My mother would never allow me to sit by while women worked," George remarked.

"Vinnie," Emily said as she carried the plates down to the kitchen. "Perhaps Mr. Gould would like the opportunity to see your beautiful rose garden out back?"

"But it's dark," Vinnie remarked, blankly.

Emily shot Vinnie another reproachful look. "Then bring a lantern, sister," she said through a forced smile.

Vinnie nodded again, finally understanding the subtext of her sister's suggestion.

"Oh, yes, of course, the color of the flowers will be even more illuminated by the flames. Please, Mr. Gould, let me show you!"

Vinnie grabbed him by the arm, leading him out the front door. When the pair finally left Susan looked at Emily and shook her head.

"Subtly is not your strong suit, is it?" Susan remarked smirking.

"Have you met my sister? Subtly isn't exactly hers either."

Emily looked around the house. Vinnie and George were safely outside. Mr. Dickinson was off in his library probably snoring in his armchair by now and Mrs. Dickinson was down in the kitchen.

Emily took the opportunity and pulled Susan close to her, stealing a quick kiss in the dining room. Susan's body began to melt into Emily's arm and she felt her heartbeat quicken with each passing second. Then, suddenly, Emily pulled back and winked at Susan. Susan rested her hand on her chest and steadied herself on the fireplace mantle.

"That was cruel!" She said to Emily, hiding a smile and furrowing her brows.

"And what will you do about it, Miss Gilbert?" Emily replied playfully. "Punish me?"

"Maybe I will," Susan said winking as she followed Emily down to the kitchen with a hand full of plates.

She was surprised that no one had mentioned Austin throughout the entire evening. The thought of his name in her head gave her a deep, sinking feeling in the pit of her stomach. There was something she had not told Emily about her and Austin. Something she knew she must say soon, but something she knew would alter the course of their friendship forever.

September 1853

"Guess what guess what!" Vinnie exclaimed as she ran into the breakfast room that morning.

Emily only yawned in response.

"Please, Lavinia, compose yourself. Be a lady," Mrs. Dickinson chirped from her seat.

Vinnie cleared her throat and straightened her hair attempting to hide the excitement.

"George Gould has invited me to go on a picnic with him today!" Vinnie jumped up and down and waived a folded piece of paper.

Dear Lavinia,

It should be fine weather tomorrow; I wonder if you might join me for a picnic down by the pond? I shall bring a fishing pole for us. If you have any interest, perhaps I can teach you some tricks of the trade from out west?

Your friend,

George Gould

Well, well, well. Emily thought to herself. Looks like her not-so-subtle efforts at matchmaking were paying off after all.

***

Susan dried the clean, white plate a third time before placing it on the wooden rack in the kitchen. She still could not get used to this fine China they now used but Austin insisted they take it. Austin was insisting on a lot of things lately, but he was never unkind about it. It was clear to Susan that he had genuine feelings for her and she had grown very fond of him as well, just not in the way he wanted.

The truth was, Susan would never feel that way about Austin or any other man. She had only and would only feel that way for Emily, she knew. Whether that was a sustainable way of life was another story.

"Letter for you dear," Harriet said entering the kitchen in a more chipper mood than usual.

Susan wiped her hands and looked down at the inscription. It was from her sister, Mattie. Susan grabbed a knife and sliced open the red wax seal and began reading.

Dear sister,

I write to you with more happy news. I am with child again! Our eldest is barely old enough to toddle around the house and yet I can already feel my belly grow with his younger sibling. Stephen hopes it will be a boy so we can have extra help around the farm. I hear you and Austin Dickinson are still courting. I await your reply and am anxious to hear of your recent trip to Boston.

Your sister,

Mattie

Susan closed the letter annoyed and shot Harriet a dirty look. "Do you think you could keep your gossip to yourself just once?"

Harriet pressed her hand to her chest, shocked. "What on Earth do you mean?"

"I mean telling Mattie about Boston, about Austin, about me."

"Of course, I've told her about you and Austin, she's our sister, Sue."

"Don't call me that," Susan spat.

Harriet ignored her and continued. "And as far as telling her about Boston, how could I? You haven't said a word about it yourself. One minute you're packing a big carpet bag and taking the Northampton Express to Boston and two days later you're back, quiet as a church mouse. I *wish* I had some gossip to share about that trip but you won't say a word about it to any of us."

Susan sighed and bowed her head in exhaustion.

"Perhaps Miss Emily will tell me next time she comes around. She's bound to know."

"No!" Susan snapped, lifting her head and staring angrily at Harriet. "Don't you say a word about any of that to Emily, do you hear me?"

Harriet shook her head, feigning ignorance. "Seems strange you wouldn't tell your best friend about a romantic weekend away with her own brother."

Susan stood up straight and threw the rag down on the wooden table.

She walked over to her sister and looked her straight in the eye. "Harriet, do everyone a favor and for once, keep your mouth shut."

She left out the back door, letting it slam behind her in her sister's face.

October 1853

    Susan tucked her legs up in front of her chest and nestled her cold nose into Emily's neck. Emily pulled the large quilt around both of them tighter and wrapped her arms around Susan. They snuck away to their secret spot in the woods this morning "before the first lark sings," as Emily described it. They enjoyed an intimate morning together in a way that had now become more comfortable and accustomed to their meetings, though no less thrilling and satisfying physically.

    Susan no longer grew red when Emily's fingers slid beneath her dress and Emily didn't close her eyes when Susan undid her corset.

    Emily told Susan that they only had a few more precious days of sunshine left and they needed to take advantage of every moment.

    "The sun isn't going away you know," Susan said as they trekked out in the early hours of the crisp autumn morning.

    "I didn't say the *Sun* was leaving," Emily retorted, "I said the *sunshine* is."

    "And what exactly is the difference?"

    "The Sun is a ball of burning gas hanging precariously in the sky. It's there year-round, whether we see it or not. Sunshine comes only in the warmer months. When the birds are singing their morning songs and the buzz of bumbles and crickets' legs rubbing together make the forest an endless sea of white noise. When you can leave your house without a cape or shawl and not feel a chill run down your spine. When you lay beneath a tree and feel a single ray of light beaming down onto your skin and you don't move because you hope if you leave it there long enough, the energy will seep into your pores and make you immortal. *That* is sunshine."

Susan simply sighed and kissed Emily. She was constantly falling in love with the way Emily spoke and wrote, and lately her poems were only improving with intensity, passion, and eloquence.

"Did you ever think of being published?" Susan asked as they rested beneath the tree together.

"How do you mean?"

"Well, you know the Springfield Republican is always running poems from artists in Massachusetts. Why not publish one from a local Amherst girl? The daughter of the great Edward Dickinson – a published poet," Susan went on.

Emily leaned her head back against the bark and breathed. "Can I tell you something and you not be mad?"

Susan felt a pang of pain in her heart at the words. This was it. She needed to tell Emily now.

"Yes, if I can tell you something with the same conditions," she said, trying to hide the quiver in her voice.

"Deal," Emily said, reaching her arm around Susan's and shaking her hand.

"Well, my secret is, that spring when you were away working in Baltimore . . . I did submit something to the Springfield Republican. And well . . . they published it! Under a pseudonym of course."

Susan sat up straight, the cold air now slicing between them.

"Emily! That is amazing news! I can't believe you didn't tell me! What did your parents say? What poem was it? Do you have a copy?"

Emily giggled and smiled at Susan's enthusiasm over her small accomplishment.

"The truth is, nobody knows but you. Well, I did tell Newton of course, but he never told a soul, and now with him gone . . ."

Susan nodded as the sentence went unfinished. A thin silence hung in the air with the mention of Benjamin Newton's name.

"You must miss him terribly," Susan said, reaching out her hand and placing it gently on Emily's.

"Every day," Emily replied, sighing as she looked up at the thinning trees hanging overhead. "But I believe he is with me just as you are," she said, smiling slightly.

"I didn't think you believed in God," Susan said.

"This *is* God," Emily replied breathing in deeply, tilting her head back and staring up into the sky.

Susan followed Emily's line of sight and looked around, listening to the sound of the wind slicing through the trees and filling her nostrils with the crisp, autumn air.

"Susan grabbed Emily's hand and kissed the back of it, wrapping her long, pale arm around her neck so tight she could barely breathe. She didn't care about air right now. She wanted Emily's body as close to hers as possible beneath the heavy quilt.

"Emily Dickinson," Susan said sighing gently. "A famous poet."

Emily knocked Susan playfully with her knees before wrapping bothers of her legs around her like a frog.

These were the moments Susan loved the most. When it was just her and Emily deep in the forest. When they could be free with one another. When the whole world ceased to exist. In these moments, Susan was happy. But each time they emerged from the woods, or the sanctity of Emily's bedroom, or from whatever dark corner they had managed to tuck themselves away in, Susan felt a crushing weight come crashing down on her again, and ever since last March she had found it harder and harder to find any peace even when she was with Emily.

Now as they sat curled beneath the familiar maple tree, Susan could feel the weight beginning to grow on her chest.

She sat up suddenly and turned around, staring at Emily.

"Emily, there's something I need to tell you," Susan stared at the dark, warm eyes of the woman she loved and imagined the look of pain that would spread across the lines of her perfect, fair skin when she heard what Susan needed to say. *Just do it.*

"The truth is . . ." Susan paused looking down at her fingernail which she had bitten to a nub.

"You can tell me anything," Emily said reassuringly, cupping Susan's face in her hand.

Susan felt a waterfall of warmth and electricity shoot down her spine at her touch and her mind began to melt into a puddle within seconds.

"The truth is . . . I'd like to go back to your house now. It's so cold." Susan said quickly.

Emily started to laugh. "That's it? My heavens you *are* spending too much time with me Susan Gilbert. I've made you quite dramatic after all these years."

Emily stood up and gathered the large quilt, placing it back into the basket they brought it in. She offered her hand to Susan who took it and stood, wiping off her thick, plaid dress.

"Why didn't you marry George Gould when he asked?" Susan said abruptly

The question took Emily by surprise and she nearly dropped the basket.

"What a ridiculous question," Emily said, "are you feeling well?" She placed the back of her hand on Susan's forehead and cheek.

"I mean it. Why not marry him? He's kind and treats you well. He is obviously in love with you."

"Susan, I'm not in love with him."

Susan bit down on her lower lip. "And do you think one should not marry someone unless they are in love with him?"

Emily raised an eyebrow. "Well, I don't intend on ever marrying since the person I love can never marry me back."

Susan blushed and she looked down at her feet. Somehow, Emily still could disarm her with a simple look or phrase or touch, even after so many years together. It was one of the things she loved and feared so much about being with Emily. One second, she could be having a perfectly fluent, coherent conversation, and the next she was a bumbling idiot simply because of the way Emily looked at her.

"You didn't answer my question," Susan pressed on, gathering her wits.

"Do I think someone should marry someone they do *not* love?" Emily bit the side of her cheek and looked at Susan pondering the question.

Susan nodded.

"What difference does it make what I think?" Emily said turning around to walk back towards the house.

"Because your opinion matters to me," Susan replied.

Emily stopped briefly and looked over her shoulder at Susan. "Are you certain about that?"

Susan stopped walking and tilted her head slightly. There was a hint of bitterness to the way she said the last word that made Susan uncomfortable.

She knows. A part of her brain instantly said. *Don't be ridiculous of course she does not know. There is nothing to know technically, but even then, she still doesn't know.*

Susan's mind continued to race and they left the woods together, holding hands in silence.

December 1853

That Christmas was one of the busiest the Dickinson house had seen in years. Fannie and Louisa Norcross made their usual appearance, this time with their new beaus, along with Emily's aunt, Lavinia. George Gould was invited at the behest of Vinnie as he had no remaining family in the area. Austin was returning home after his recent graduation from Harvard Law School and he apparently had a big announcement to share. Susan, Harriet, and William were also invited. The house was bursting at the seams. Carlo marched room to room inspecting each new guest, smelling their shoes and pants while Lavinia's fat cat sat twitching its fluffy grey tail at the top of the steps.

The Christmas tree was one of the largest Emily had ever seen in the house and she, Vinnie, and Mrs. Dickinson worked for hours stringing up popcorn and stuffing cornucopias to make sure it looked grand for the occasion.

George was the first to arrive that evening for Christmas Eve supper and to no one's surprise, he immediately insisted on helping lay out the meal. Mrs. Dickinson, also to no one's surprise, whisked him out of the kitchen saying it was, "women's work," and that he should go enjoy a glass of scotch with Mr. Dickinson.

Emily looked at Vinnie and smirked while Vinnie stared at him as he left. Vinnie and George were practically inseparable since their picnic alone a few months ago and Emily could not be more pleased to see her sister finally happy.

She had a feeling this was going to be the best Christmas ever.

After about an hour of exchanging pleasantries, George suggested they all sing Christmas carols before supper. Vinnie excitedly sat at the piano and began playing, "Hark, the Herald Angel Sings", which everyone immediately began singing along with.

Emily scanned the room looking for Susan.

*Joyful all ye nations rise,
Join the Triumphs of the Skies;*

She smiled brightly when she found Susan leaning against the window sill alone. Emily tilted her head, signaling for Susan to come over to her. Susan's cheeks flushed and she looked around the room, still singing along with the crowd as she slowly started making her way behind Edward, Fannie, and Lavinia Norcross over towards Emily.

Emily inched slightly towards the back of the room and left half of her body hanging in the archway while the other half was already in the hallway. Susan entered the hall and Emily ducked the rest of her body out of the room. She grabbed Susan's hand and dragged her into the dining room where the plates were already set waiting for the Christmas goose to be served.

Emily peered out of the dining room, listening to the faint sounds of singing before pressing Susan against the wall and kissing her.

Susan kissed her back briefly and then, remembering where they were, pulled away.

"What in the world has gotten into you?" She said, smiling and tucking a strand of Emily's hair behind her ear.

"Holiday cheer?" Emily shrugged as she leaned in to kiss Susan again.

Susan dodged her and slid around to the other side of her, still holding her arm.

"You are being wild tonight," Susan said, looking around the corner to ensure their departure had gone unnoticed.

"Wild nights, wild nights," Emily said raising one eyebrow, moving closer toward Susan.

"And now you're quoting yourself. Are you drunk, Emily Dickinson?"

Emily started to laugh. "Perhaps I *am* a little drunk now that you mention it."

Susan looked over to the kitchen table where the wine stood, completely full.

"You're lying," Susan said, placing her hand on Emily's neck smirking.

"Okay fine, let's call it drunk on love then," Emily said playfully.

The song stopped and both girls froze for a moment before they heard the opening lines to, "Joy to the World", erupt from the other room.

Emily stepped closer to Susan, this time without the look of playfulness in her eyes.

She inched closer to her and whispered in Susan's ear, "I need you tonight."

Susan felt her entire body melt into her boots with the sensations of Emily's warm breath tickling her ear lobe. She wanted nothing more than to spend Christmas Eve night with Emily, in her bed, in her arms, wrapped entirely into her.

"How?" Susan whispered quietly.

"Leave your window unlocked. I'll sneak out."

"And walk all the way to my house in the cold? That's dangerous."

Emily shrugged. "What's life without a hint of danger? Especially to be with the woman you love?"

Emily stepped back and winked before turning and leaving Susan alone in the dining room. Susan felt her heart rising and falling in her dress and she lifted a hand to her forehead to see if she felt as hot outside as she did inside.

He rules the world with truth and grace
And makes the nations prove (and makes the nations prove)

Susan cleared her throat before returning to the other room where Emily joined in the singing. It took every ounce of strength she had not to stare at her throughout the remainder of the song.

After Vinnie insisted on playing a new song she recently learned called, "Good King Wenceslas", to which only she knew the words, Mr. Dickinson announced that it was time to be seated for supper.

Susan was seated across from Emily and next to Austin and Harriet. Being in such proximity to Austin and Emily at the same time gave Susan a feeling of suffocation and she tried very hard to look down at the food and not think about everything that was going on around her at this moment. She tried not to think about what her night with Emily would hopefully look like. She tried not to think about Harriet's glaring eyes next to her. She tried not to wonder if Harriet could read the thoughts she was having about Emily. She tried not to think about what happened in March in Boston with Austin.

She was about halfway through her portion of peas when Austin's loud voice beside her broke the silence. He rose, clanking his glass and adjusting his cravat.

"I have an announcement I'd like to make before you all," he said proudly, his chest puffed out in an unnatural manner.

Susan froze.

She looked to her right to Harriet and then to William. Harriet simply stared at her smiling a wide-toothed grin and William nodded his head firmly in her direction before they both continued to stare up at Austin as if the Ascension itself was taking place right there in the Dickinson dining room.

"Well, as you know, Susan and I have been courting for some time now," Austin continued.

Oh no. Susan looked up and Austin and cleared her throat, "Austin, what are you . . .?" She felt her heart begin to race faster and faster.

Austin ignored her. "Well, tonight, I am happy to announce that Susan Gilbert is soon to be Susan Gilbert Dickinson. We're engaged!"

Austin raised a glass triumphantly over his head. She saw his mouth moving but heard only burred sounds. She looked around the room and saw the white, clapping hands circling the table but she could not hear them. They seemed to all be moving in slow motion. Their hands, their faces, their voices. It was all blending together. Then she heard a loud, low ringing in her ears. She felt sweat begin to trickle down her forehead and back. The room started to spin and she gripped the table to steady herself.

Engaged. The word kept replaying over and over again in her ears as the clapping continued and the ringing got louder. Finally, the room stopped spinning and landed on a single pair of brown eyes seated directly across from her.

Amidst the sea of laughter, celebrating, and clapping, one person sat speechless with her mouth dropped open, and her eyes welled up with hidden tears.

Emily.

***

Emily felt her head begin to spin as the blood rushed away from it.

She hadn't felt this much pain and shock since learning of Newton's death. She looked over to Susan for reassurance. For some form of confirmation that this was a big joke or misunderstanding. But when she met Susan's eyes and saw how ghostly white her face had flushed, she knew the only joke was on her for believing Susan would never lie to her.

Emily began to focus on her breathing. She looked briefly down the table at Vinnie who was staring back at her, her mouth hanging open in shock and concern. Everyone else at the table was raising a glass and toasting the newly engaged couple. Emily turned to her mother who was giving her a reproaching look. Emily mustered a forced smile and raised her glass along with the crowd.

"To Susan Gilbert. My newest sister," Vinnie said through gritted teeth, her voice nearly choking on the words.

Her distraction had worked as the entire table turned to face her, giving Emily the moment she needed to compose herself.

Susan feigned a smile and looked up at Austin, yanking at his arm and begging him to be seated. She looked angry, shocked, and embarrassed.

Good. Emily thought. *She should be embarrassed.* That's how Emily certainly felt right now. Embarrassed and foolish and writhing with anger at her own ignorance.

Austin sat down next to Susan and placed his arm around her as she leaned in and whispered something to him. His face changed from a smile to a frown and he turned his attention back to the table.

"If you'll all excuse us for just a moment," Austin said politely, "my future bride has something she wishes to speak to me about in private."

Emily's spine shivered as they both stood up. Susan looked at Emily briefly and mouthed, "I'm sorry," before quickly leaving the dining room with Austin.

Emily stood abruptly. "I too must be excused. I'm afraid the wine isn't settling well with me this evening."

Mrs. Dickinson scowled but said nothing. Edward was more sympathetic.

"My dear, I told you not to overdo it with the port, did I not? Go and collect yourself, a cool rag on the forehead should help."

Emily nodded quickly and made her excuses to the table. As she left the dining room, she could see Austin and Susan standing on the porch, both shivering and speaking in hushed tones. Susan was almost yelling at him and Austin was bent over, looking shocked and hurt. Emily could not be bothered to eavesdrop, she thought she was going to be sick.

Instantly she raced upstairs and shut her bedroom door behind her. A few moments later there was a soft knock at the door.

"Go away," Emily said instinctively, assuming it was Susan.

"It's Vinnie," she heard from the other side of the door.

Emily paused a moment, biting her nail before opening the door for her sister.

"Oh, Emily," Vinnie said, reaching out her arms and wrapping them around Emily.

Emily began to softly cry into her neck before collapsing onto the bed.

***

"What the hell were you thinking?" Susan asked unable to control the anger behind her voice.

She looked back inside through the window to ensure their conversation was not being overheard. Austin stood dumbfounded, his hands hanging helplessly by his side.

"I don't understand, I thought you'd be happy."

"Happy? Austin, you just announced to your entire family – to Emily – to everyone that we are engaged."

"But . . . we are, aren't we?" He asked true confusion crossing his brow.

"No!" Susan yelled back.

She looked inside again. She saw Emily walking up the stairs and wanted nothing more than to run inside and follow her.

"But . . . I asked you back in March and . . ."

"And I never said yes! I said I needed time! Time to think, time to process, time to make this decision for myself."

"But when I talked to Harriet and William about it the other day, they said . . ." Austin paused before finishing the sentence, beginning to feel like he had been part of some large jest at his expense.

"What did they say?" Susan asked urgently.

"Harriet said that you talked about it with them and that you accepted but were too shy and nervous to approach me about it. They said all you needed was a grand gesture. Something to show you how serious I was about you."

Susan covered her mouth with her hand and dropped her head.

Harriet and William. Of course, they did this. Harriet would see her marry Austin if it was the last thing she did. Even if she knew it meant ruining their relationship, ruining Susan's happiness, even ruining Austin's happiness potentially. None of that mattered to Harriet. All that mattered was that Susan not be in the same position Harriet had previously been in. That she married a man who could provide for her – a man with money. Austin had been used. The entire idea made her angry, though not with him. He was a victim in all of this just as she was, just as Emily was.

She reached up and placed her hand on Austin's arm and he looked down at her sadly.

"Have I done something wrong here?" Austin asked, his voice full of confusion.

"No," Susan said letting out a sigh. "No, Austin, you didn't do anything wrong. But I fear my family has misinformed you. I still need time to make this decision. Will you please do that for me?"

"But Susan, I've just announced it to the family and . . ."

Susan looked up at him, her brown eyes filled with pleading and desperation. He did not want to feel like he coerced someone into marrying him. He wanted Susan to *want* to marry him. Besides, he had waited this long for her. If a little more time is what she needed to reach that conclusion, he would give it to her.

"Very well," he said softly.

April 1854

George Gould fidgeted nervously with his hat while he waited in the front room of the Dickinson Mansion. He stood briefly, looking out the frost-covered window into the front yard. The large tick-tock of the grandfather clock clicked in the hollow room.

Edward Dickinson was in Washington D.C. for the congressional term, Austin was away in Boston on business, and only Mrs. Dickinson, Emily and Vinnie now filled the large house.

After a few moments of silence, he heard the clacking of footsteps as they slowly marched down the front steps.

"I'm sorry George, she won't be coming down."

Emily had not been seen since Christmas Eve. Vinnie had reported to him that she was taking meals in her room now and would not leave for anything or anyone. George knew it had been a long shot, but he stopped by once a week to call on Emily regardless. One time he had peered up from outside and seen her standing by the window, just staring out at the cemetery. He waved up at her but when she looked down it was as if she were a ghost. She had looked right through him before turning around and shutting the curtains.

George frowned gripping his hat. "Has she done this before?"

Vinnie nodded. "Yes, twice now. Once when she found out about Mr. Newton dying and once when . . ." Vinnie hesitated for a moment. "When Susan moved away to Baltimore."

"Hmm"

"My sister deals with loss in unique ways," Vinnie said sadly.

George nodded. "Indeed. Although it does seem that Susan Gilbert holds a certain . . . power over her wouldn't you say?"

Vinnie opened her mouth to speak, but George cut her off.

"Vinnie, I assure you, I do not intend on disseminating any information to anyone. I have nothing but your family's best interest at heart. But I know a look of love when I see it." George paused. "Emily looks at Susan the way I once looked at her." He looked down and swallowed hard before continuing. "The same way I look at you now."

Vinnie's mouth dropped open momentarily and she felt a red blush crawling up her chest and into her cheeks. She couldn't believe what George was saying. He knew Emily loved Susan and he didn't care? And he loved her? It was all too much for her mind to process. Vinnie suddenly burst into laughter.

George stepped back, looking flushed and embarrassed.

"I've overstepped my mark, I see. My apologies, I did not mean to offend you."

"No! No, George, it is not that. I have loved you even when you loved my sister. I just can't believe you feel the same way."

George stepped closer to Vinnie and held out his hands timidly. She rested hers in his, feeling the sweat of his palms against her thin fingers.

Slowly George leaned forward and Vinnie closed her eyes before feeling the hot warmth of his lips. She smiled slightly when his five-o clock shadow began to tickle her and after a few brief seconds, George stepped back clearing his throat.

"If it wouldn't be too much trouble, would it be alright if I called on you more formally?"

Vinnie looked down, flushed at the touch of George's skin against hers as he delicately stroked the back of her fingers.

"It would be no trouble at all." Vinnie blushed.

***

Susan shook her head as she paced in the small kitchen. Austin was standing before her, his face pleading and his arms outstretched.

"But Susan, I simply do not understand what all of this fuss is about. It has been a full year since I asked you to be my wife, yet still, you insist on prolonging not only the engagement but the formal announcement of it."

Susan continued to pace, not responding.

"It should be in the Boston Gazette by now, and it should have been in the Springfield Republican back at Christmas when it was announced to the family."

"I told you at Christmas I needed time, Austin. I needed time to think about it before I gave you an answer. I never even said yes for Heaven's sake! And then you just made my mind up for me and announced it in front of everyone at Christmas."

"We've been through all of this a hundred times, Susan. I told you Harriet and William said you were just being shy. That you'd spoken about it with them and you'd said yes. I would have never made such a presumption. I would never make that decision for you."

"They lied," Susan snipped.

Austin looked down, his face worn and a look of hurt spreading across his chocolate eyes.

"Are you saying then that you do not want to marry me?" He asked, his voice cracking slightly.

Susan looked over at him and felt pity. His head hung low and his shoulders sagged from the weight of their conversation. She could see how much unhappiness she was causing him and it genuinely caused her pain. No part of her was repulsed by Austin's proposal and there was a large part of her that did actually love him. He had shown himself to be a loyal companion and correspondence over the last several years and his devotion to her and her family proved him to be more than worthy of her hand. But she could not ignore the nagging feeling in the pit of her stomach that told her that she would never be truly happy with him. That she would never be truly happy with anyone unless that person was Emily.

She walked over to him and placed her hands on his face, "I'm not saying that," she said kindly. "I just . . . I need some time to truly decide before we go announcing it to all of Massachusetts."

Austin sighed and looked down, grabbing her hands in his.

"Take all the time you need, Susan," he said gently, "I'll be waiting."

With that, he turned and left. Before she could finish inhaling, she was startled by her sister Harriet coming down the stairs.

"Couldn't help but overhear," Harriet said, her tone cold and menacing.

"I'm certain your ear was pressed flush with the door," Susan said rolling her eyes.

Harriet shook her head, "I will never understand you, Susan Gilbert. You are ungrateful and short-sighted. What do you think will happen here? You think you'll ever find someone who will provide for you as Austin can?"

Susan scoffed. "Perhaps I am waiting to marry the person I love."

"The person you love? Be serious, Susan. You will never marry Emily Dickinson."

Susan froze.

"Yes, that's right, I've seen you two lurking around in dark hallways, sneaking off into the woods. You're not fooling anyone but yourself if you think this school girl romance you have with each other will ever amount to anything."

Susan felt the weight of Harriet's words pressing down on her chest. She and Emily had been careless. She knew this was bound to happen. Her worst fear was coming true. Who else had seen them? What had they seen exactly? Susan but her lip and looked down, trying to hide the tears and panic that now rushed through her head.

"You're speaking nonsense," Susan said looking at her sister, a panicked expression covering her face.

She needed to keep up the ruse. She couldn't admit the truth of the accusations. She had no idea what the repercussions would be and she had no intention of finding out.

"Am I?" Harriet's face turned into stone and she walked towards Susan, grabbing her wrist firmly. "Very well then. Deny it. But let me make myself perfectly clear. You *will* marry Austin Dickinson. If you won't listen to me, then I'll find someone you will listen to."

July 1854

"Are you certain you won't come with us?" Vinnie pleaded with her sister as she tightened the bright yellow bonnet beneath her chin.

Emily slowly began making appearances outside of her room lately, and the warm sunshine provoked her to even venture as far as her front garden and the orchard outback, but she had not left the confines of the Mansion grounds since winter. The neighborhood children were beginning to gossip about her, but she didn't care. They would come by and toss rocks up at her window until she appeared and waved them off. Sometimes she would bake them cookies and lower them in a basket for the children to eat. That made them happy, which in turn made Emily happy. But no matter what, she did not want to leave the house grounds.

Beyond the border of this white fence, there was only pain. Pain and memories. Memories of her and Susan walking arm and arm down West Street. Memories of their intimate moments in the woods. Memories of picnics with Newton. Even memories of long, boring walks with George and Vinnie. She did not want to remember any of the things that had passed. She was safer here. She would stay here.

"I'm sure," Emily said hugging her sister.

Mr. Dickinson invited the entire family to come to tour Washington D.C. with him and spend a month down there. Austin, Mrs. Dickinson, and Vinnie all fluttered with excitement at the adventure. But Emily declined, stating she would look after the old Mansion with Carlo.

"My flowers need attending to," was her formal answer when the invitation came. At first, her parents and Austin strongly protested at the idea of her remaining home alone. It wasn't until George Gould promised to stop in and ensure she was well protected, that Emily convinced them to leave her.

The idea of being alone in the big house both excited and frightened Emily. She had never been completely alone before. Her days of locking herself in her room were nothing compared to the ghosts that were sure to come out in an empty house like theirs.

Mrs. Dickinson hugged her eldest daughter.

"Do take care not to set fire to the kitchen," she said before kissing her cheek coldly and walking out the front door.

Austin was already waiting for them by the carriage, checking his pocket watch endlessly and fidgeting with his cravat. She had only seen him a few times since Christmas but she could not help but notice how his shoulders seemed to slump more than they used to and how his normal smiles and smirks were replaced with furrowed brows and frown lines. She did not want her brother to be unhappy, even if he was stealing away the love of her life. It was not his fault he was born a man, and she a woman.

Emily waved as the carriage finally pulled away. As she watched the large, black wheels spinning slowly down the dirt road, she felt a strike of inspiration. Immediately she ran upstairs and slammed her door shut. She needed to write this down. She needed to keep writing all of these things down. The more she wrote, the less time she had to think about how she still felt about Susan Gilbert. She began to scribble furiously.

Because I could not stop for Death –
He kindly stopped for me –

The Carriage held but just Ourselves –
And Immortality.
***

The sudden knock at the door made Susan jump from her needlepoint. She set the needle and thread down on the table beside her and walked over to the front door. Harriet came down the stairs behind her, brushing back her hair.

"Are we expecting someone?" Susan asked.

Harriet instructed her to open the door, ignoring her inquiry and when she did, the face staring back at her was enough to make Susan physically gasp with shock.

There, standing plain as day, was her Aunt Sophia.

Susan looked the old woman up and down. She now carried a cane, which seemed to offer more support than style and her long, grey tresses were pulled back tight across her wrinkled brow. She wore a long, black mourning dress with a large garnet broach. For the most part, she looked as if she had not aged a day, though it had been nearly a decade since they last saw one another.

"Don't just stand there, girl. Aren't you going to invite me in? Or have you lost your manners along with your senses?"

Susan stuttered for a moment and Harriet pushed passed her, opening the door wide.

"Aunt Sophia, please come in," Harriet said, ignoring Susan.

Susan stood dumbfounded as the old woman pushed past her. William's stable boy was unloading a large trunk from the back of the carriage and William took off his hat and gave Susan somewhat of a sympathetic look as he walked past her into the front room.

"Can I get you some tea?" Harriet asked politely.

"No," Sophia snapped coldly. "But Susan can. She should begin practicing her wifely duties more frequently now that her wedding is imminent."

Susan spoke for the first time. "I think you misunderstand; I have not said yes to Austin's proposal."

Sophia sat down, banging her cane on the wood floor. "I misunderstand nothing. Your sister has called me here to ensure that the decision is made efficiently and publicly. Where is the young man now?"

"He is away, in Washington," Susan said quickly.

She had never been so happy that Austin was nowhere near Amherst and she felt an instinctive need to protect him from the clutches of her aunt's claws.

"Ah, no matter. Just gives me more time to whip things into shape here." Her aunt thrust the cane down once more into the ground with a loud thud. "Now, let me make this perfectly clear to you, Susan."

Susan shivered slightly at the woman's sudden aggressiveness.

"You will marry the Dickinson *boy*. Or . . ." Sophia paused looking at Harriet briefly before continuing. "You will never see the Dickinson *girl* again."

"What . . .?" Susan began.

"It was not so long ago that your sister, Mattie, lost her way in this world. She was younger than you and it was a scummy little black smith boy that caused her to stray. I had hopes that you had a steady head on your shoulders; that you knew the obligation you have as a woman, as a Gilbert. But from the reports I have been hearing, it seems you are no wiser than your sister, Mattie. Like her, someone has caused that strong head to be filled with daydreams, butterflies, and silliness. We sorted your sister out and we shall do the same to you – in the same manner if need be."

Sophia paused again to adjust herself in the seat.

"Before your uncle died, God rest his soul, I promised him that I would ensure the success of this family. And I intend to do just that. As I said, you will marry the Dickinson boy or you shall be shipped off to Michigan to live with your sister, Mattie, and her family. You will never return to Amherst, not even to visit your sister, Harriet, and what's more, you will never see the Dickinson family ever again – including this Emily character."

Her words dripped like poison as she spoke Emily's name and Susan bit down on her lip hard to keep quiet.

"Now," Sophia continued. "I think I will take that cup of tea."

Susan nodded silently and escaped down the stairs to the kitchen. She put the kettle over the fire and began wringing her hands and pacing. She looked up at the wooden beams running overhead and began to feel like the room was growing smaller. She knew things about her and Emily which meant her sister must have told her. How much did they know though? Enough to know Emily was in some way hindering her marriage to Austin. Did William know? Who would they tell? No one, most likely, considering the negative impact it would have on the family. Would her sister really let her be shipped off to Michigan? The idea of being so far away from Emily made her sick to her stomach and she bent over the table, clutching at her chest, trying to breathe.

People made all of her decisions for so long that she no longer knew what was her own choice and what was simply compliance. Her parents forced her to live with her aunt and uncle. Her aunt forced her to move back to Amherst. Her sister forced her to move to Baltimore. Now the entire family was forcing her to marry Austin Dickinson.

It was all too much for Susan to stand. She could see her entire life playing before her eyes, right down to a wedding in Aunt Sophia's living room back in New York. She slammed her hands down on the table and inhaled, deeply focusing on steadying her breathing. Before she could tell her feet not to, she flew out the kitchen door without even bothering to remove the kettle from the fire. She didn't care if it steamed for hours or burned the house down, she needed to get out of there. She needed to get somewhere safe.

She ran. She ran and ran and did not stop or look up until she saw an ivory picket fence and a safe large, white house standing in front of her. Without pausing, she threw open the gate and raced to the front door. Furiously she began to bang on the massive door until finally, it opened. There, staring back at her was the familiar face of Emily Dickinson.

Instinctively, Susan flung herself into Emily's arms. And without thinking, Emily caught her.

"Susan," Emily said shocked, "what are you doing here?"

Susan stepped back and caught her breath.

"I didn't know where else to go."

Emily pushed Susan away to arm's length, slowly regaining her strength and composure.

"What's happened?"

"My aunt is here... Sophia."

"Your aunt, from New York? What in the name of all that is holy has made her come here?"

Susan shook her head and tried to catch her breath. "She says she's come to make me see reason about marrying your brother. Emily, please listen to me, I swear I didn't know he was going to do that at Christmas. I never thought..."

"What did you think Susan? That you would marry my brother and what? Just never tell me about it?"

Susan looked down, a tear beginning to form now. "I never said I'd marry him. He assumed . . . I mean Harriet. Please, Emily, there is so much to explain. Please let me inside?"

Emily looked around. She had never seen Susan looking so frantic, so desperate. Her rich, chocolate eyes that usually bounced with joy and life were now hollow and sunken in. Her skin was pale and worn and her hair was haphazardly pulled back behind her ears, loose curls flying freely from her run across town. Her light blue dress was covered up to the hem in mud and her hands were shaking. A bead of sweat dripped down her temple and her eyebrows were furrowed in desperation. She could not look at the woman she loved in such a state and possibly turn her away. Silently, Emily nodded and ushered Susan inside.

Once inside, Susan looked around sheepishly. She had not been to the house since Christmas. The windows were now flown open, white curtains blowing in the warm, summer breeze. It was a transformation to be sure and it made Susan realize just how long she and Emily had gone without speaking.

As soon as Emily shut the door behind her, Susan began speaking, divulging everything to Emily. She told her about the visit to Boston to see Austin last March. About how he proposed to her at the Revere Hotel. How he invited her back to his room but she declined and he paid for her to have her own room instead. How she had not said yes to his proposal and how instead she said she needed time. How she had not told anyone, not even Harriet, because she wanted to speak to Emily first. How Austin reached out to Harriet and William and how they lied and told Austin she said yes. And about how she and Austin had been fighting ever since his announcement at Christmas.

"That explains the sad shoulders," Emily said quietly as Susan finished her story.

"Sad shoulders?"

"Nothing," Emily replied, "so, what do you intend to do?"

"I don't know."

"You should have told me, Susan. You made me feel like a fool in front of everyone. In front of my family."

Susan looked down. "I know. I just . . . I didn't even know what to say."

Emily paused looking around at the empty house. She could understand how Susan felt. She felt the same way after George proposed to her. It was jarring, having so many expectations placed on you and not knowing what to do to meet them. Caring for someone, but not caring for them in that way. Loving someone but not being in love with them. The truth was Emily and Susan were two sides of the same coin. Both fighting for their own happiness and independence, but both consumed the expectations of others. Both longing for freedom, but both fearing to go beyond the safety of what they already knew. Emily could see that now. She felt a familiar warmth begin to grow inside her chest as she looked at Susan.

"Would you like to stay for supper?" She asked.

Susan looked up and smiled slightly. "Yes, I would."

Emily nodded and the two women went down to the kitchen to begin preparing the meal in silence. They worked quietly, peeling potatoes and carrots, braising a chicken, and roasting it over the fire. There was a peace to being there, alone in the silence with Emily, and Susan felt at ease for the first time in almost a year.

It was only the sound of a knock on the front door that broke their reverie.

Emily wiped her hands on her apron and looked skeptically up the stairs.

"Stay here," she said protectively placing a hand on Susan's arm before making her way up the stairs.

Emily peered out of the front window and sighed with relief when she saw who it was.

"George," she said, swinging the door wide open.

George removed his hat and smiled his big, toothy grin. He had not laid eyes on Emily since Christmas and it felt good to see her standing there before him. She looked thinner than usual and paler than she normally did in the warmer months, but other than that she was well enough for his satisfaction.

"Good afternoon, just came to see if you needed anything?"

Emily laughed. "My family only left this morning, you know."

George nodded. "Just so, I was in the neighborhood and figured I would pop in."

"Well, do come in then," she said, ushering him inside. "Susan is just downstairs and we are preparing supper. Would you like to join us?"

George looked flustered for a moment and began to back away. "Oh, Miss Gilbert is here? My apologies, I did not know."

Emily shook her head and reached out, grabbing him by the arm and tugging at him. "Don't be obtuse, George. Come and stay."

Reluctantly, George agreed and came inside.

"You can come up now, Susan. It's only George."

A few seconds later, the kitchen door opened slowly and Susan emerged looking like a frightened cat coming out from under a bed.

George bowed politely as she approached. "Lovely to see you, Miss Gilbert."

Susan nodded her head. "And you, Mr. Gould."

Emily rolled her eyes. "Let's not stand on airs here. We have all known each other for long enough now. George will be joining us for supper, Susan."

Susan hid a look of disappointment. She had been looking forward to dining alone with Emily, but she understood her desire to place some form of the boundary between them, even if it did take the shape of George Gould.

"George, I'm surprised you didn't go to Washington with the rest of the family. Not to . . . have a private word with my father." Emily winked.

George's face turned red at the insinuation. He had been visiting Vinnie more and more often and it was no shock that Emily had seen it all unfold from the sanctity of her bedroom window.

"There is plenty of time for that," George replied coolly, causing Emily to raise an eyebrow, impressed at the new confidence George was displaying.

The three of them made their way down to the kitchen where George insisted on helping them prepare the rest of the meal and Emily, unlike her mother, let him. Once everything was prepared, they all brought the food up together on trays. George lit the dining room candles and Emily drew the curtains around the house. George took Edward's usual seat at the head of the long, rectangular table and the two women were seated on either side of him.

They all smiled and held hands as George said grace. As he began carving into the chicken, there was another knock at the door.

Silently, they all exchanged glances. Susan's face went ashen at the realization of who must be at the door. Emily looked pleadingly at George.

There was another knock.

Slowly, George pushed the chair back and stood, walking steadily over to the front door. He looked over his shoulder where Susan and Emily sat with desperate looks. Emily placed a finger over her mouth and shook her head motioning toward George. George nodded, seeming to understand the unspoken request and opened the door just enough for his face to be seen and nothing more.

Standing on the other side of the door were Harriet and William.

"May I help you?" He said formally.

"Mr. Gould," William said shocked, "apologies, we were not expecting you to be here. We are looking for our sister, Susan. Have you seen her?"

George paused a moment and shifted his weight.

"No," he said blankly, "I have not."

Harriet's voice chimed in next. "Nonsense. We have searched all over town, there is simply nowhere else she would be. I demand you turn her over to us at once."

Susan's face turned paler and she sank slightly in her chair. Emily could see from her chest that she was holding her breath.

George's chest puffed out slightly and he pulled his shoulders back.

"As I have said, she is not here. I have been placed in charge of this house, and those inside it, while the Dickinson's are away and I am afraid that I must insist you leave this premises at once."

With that, George stepped back and slowly closed the door with both Cutler's standing awestruck on the other side.

Emily's jaw dropped. Susan did not breathe again until George watched them out the window as they left. Emily leaped up from her seat at the table and ran over to George throwing her arms around his tall shoulders.

"George! I can't believe you just lied to Harriet!"

George smiled, awkwardly leaning over and hugging her small frame.

Susan stood and came over to him extending her hand and shaking his.

"Thank you," she said, looking sincerely into his eyes for the first time.

She could see now what Emily saw in him all along. She could see what Vinnie saw in him now. He was a good man, George Gould, and she would forever be grateful to him for this night.

"Pay it no mind," George said, his voice beaming with bravery and pride. "Now, how about that supper?"

***

The next morning Susan awoke to the sunlight beaming in through the unfamiliar room. She had slept at the Dickinson house many times in the past, but every time she shared Emily's bed under the guise of platonic friendship. Last night Emily insisted she stay over, but she led her to Vinnie's room instead of her own. Susan did not push the issue and was just happy to even be under the same roof.

George also insisted on staying, considering how insistent Harriet and William were before supper and he slept on the stiff sofa downstairs, even though Emily offered him Austin's room. He claimed he did not want to dirty any linens that Emily would need to wash.

By the time Susan came downstairs, George was already gone, leaving behind a note promising to check in on them often. Emily sat in the breakfast room, sipping a cup of tea and reading the morning paper.

Susan smiled at how masculine and natural Emily looked, her leg crossed over her thigh as she sipped her tea with one hand, reading the paper in the other.

"Good morning," Susan said quietly.

"Morning," Emily replied, not breaking her concentration from the paper or lowering it to look at Susan.

"I expect I should be going now. Thank you for . . . last night."

"I've been thinking," Emily said setting down the paper and leaning back in the chair, placing her feet up on the table next to her teacup. "Perhaps it would be best if you didn't return to your family just yet."

The chair continued to teeter under Emily's weight as she rocked. Susan crossed her arms and raised an eyebrow.

"Perhaps . . . it would be best if you stayed here. At least for the time being."

Emily tilted her head to one side and picked up her teacup and made a loud slurp before tipping the chair back down onto all fours.

"You would have me . . . stay here?" Susan began. "With you? Just you?"

"You'll stay in Vinnie's room, of course. And we won't be able to venture far beyond the gates, not with your family lurking about. But you'll be safe here. When Austin returns, we'll get this Aunt Sophia mess sorted out. He'll take care of it. Trust me."

Susan nodded silently, biting her lip. She wanted nothing more than to stay here with Emily forever. To live with her, tend to their gardens together, read books, exchange poetry, and grow old in each other's arms. But Susan knew that is not what Emily was proposing now. She knew the only thing Emily was extending to her now was out of pity and courtesy.

"I'd love to," Susan said softly.

Emily nodded and returned to the newspaper. With that, it was all settled.

June 1854

Emily was not surprised that she caved so easily and let Susan move in with her while her family was away. She had never been able to say no to Susan, even when they were little girls. She was, however, surprised by how quickly she adjusted to the new living arrangements, and how happy she was having Susan there with her after only a week and a half.

She expected to be in agony being so close to the woman who was soon to be her sister-in-law, but instead, the entire arrangement just felt natural. Emily would wake early and make enough tea for both of them. She would read the newspaper alone until Susan came down, then they would take turns reading the various sections. They ate little more than scones or biscuits for breakfast and occasionally Emily would make fresh eggs that George would bring by and he would join them for early afternoon games or gardening in the back orchard.

George reported to them that Susan's aunt was still in town and attending weekly Meeting at the church. Harriet and William created a narrative that Susan was not feeling well and taken to her room for her health, thus explaining her prolonged absence from society.

Emily, whose presence had long gone unnoticed from Church, chuckled at the scandal it must be creating in such a small town. No one would have ever imagined that the two missing girls were hulled up in the Mansion and were. . . what were she and Susan now anyways? Friends? Sisters? Lovers?

There had been nothing intimate between them since Susan's moving in, Emily had made sure of that, but as the days passed, the air in the house seemed to feel smaller, tighter. As if the spaces between them were shrinking, pulling them in and closer towards one another.

One day, she and Susan were in the library each reading their respective books. Emily caught herself looking at Susan, in the way she used to look at her. She watched as her pale chest rose and fell across the room. She watched as her long fingers had turned the pages, the vein on the back of her hand rolling back and forth as she made the repetitive motion. She watched as a bead of sweat from the summer heat trickled down between Susan's breasts.

After realizing what was going on in her mind, Emily jumped up, run outside and drew a full bucket of water from the well before promptly dumping it over her head.

Susan ran outside to the front door and hollered after her. "What are you doing?"

Emily stared back at her, the ends of her hair dripping wet in front of her eyes. "Just cooling off!"

Since then, Emily tried repeatedly to ignore Susan's presence. To consider her the sister she was soon to be. But each day it grew harder and harder.

Emily wiped her brow, bit down into her biscuit and sipped her tea loudly. She looked up at the clock. Susan was late for breakfast and the room was already filled to the brim with the early heat of summer. June was typically a cool, refreshing month in Amherst, but this morning she could barely breathe from the heat.

A few moments later Emily checked the large grandfather clock again.

It's nearly ten, she thought.

Then, Emily heard the familiar creak of the steps and saw Susan come around the corner, her head hung low. Emily immediately began to laugh uncontrollably at the sight. There, in front of God and everyone, Susan stood in her chemise and stays in the breakfast room.

"I need to launder my dress!" Susan shouted over Emily's howls. "I've worn it every day for the last week and a half."

Emily steadied herself from laughter and noticed that now Susan too was smiling.

"Fair enough," Emily said, taking another large sip of her tea. "But why didn't you ask me earlier? You know we wear the same size."

"Well, it's not like this is anything you haven't seen before," Susan said back, her voice more flirtatious than she originally intended.

She watched as crimson spread from Emily's chest to her face, all laughter now coming to a standstill. Emily took another large bite of biscuit before standing up in silence.

"Follow me," she said, walking past Susan and up the stairs.

Susan obeyed and the two of them made their way up to Emily's room. Susan paused at the doorway, almost afraid to enter the sanctuary without an express invitation. When Emily noticed her looming at the doorway, she tilted her head motioning for Susan to come inside.

Susan looked around the room. Not much had changed since she was last here in winter. The chest of drawers was exactly where she had last seen it, nestled safely against the side of the western wall. The small, squared writing desk still faced the window that overlooked the cemetery, though now a large stack of different sized papers were spread messily on top of it. The small, wooden framed bed still jutted out into the center of the room from the eastern wall.

Susan's eyes lingered on the bed for a moment as she allowed herself to remember the moments the two of them had stolen beneath the same sheets just months prior. Winter was always a good excuse for the two of them curl up in bed next to one another. It wasn't unusual for two women to share such a small space in order to conserve heat and Emily and Susan certainly took advantage of the societal norm more than once in the past.

Susan smiled, remembering the events of their previous winters together as she made her way slowly over to the writing desk. As she did, she found herself stealing a lingering look at Emily who was now bent over rifling through the bottom of her chest of drawers.

"What are these?" Susan asked, picking up the stacks of papers from Emily's desk.

They were pages, envelopes, and scraps of paper, all sewn together with thread. Each stack contained approximately 10-20 pages.

"My poems," Emily said in a matter-of-fact manner.

Susan delicately set them back down on the desk. "You've been writing a lot."

"I have a lot to write about," Emily said bluntly.

She bent down further, reaching deeper into the large chest of drawers and finally fishing out a baby blue dress with eyelet lacing over the top.

"Here," she said holding it up to Susan. "Take this one."

Susan walked over and took the dress, holding it up to herself in the long, full-length mirror.

Emily came around and stood behind Susan helping her hold up the dress.

"Try it on."

Susan felt a shudder run down her spine as Emily's breath reached the back of her neck, but she held in the reaction, aware that Emily could see her face in the mirror.

"Shouldn't I have privacy?" Susan asked into the mirror.

Emily smirked slightly. "Like you said, it's nothing I haven't seen before."

Susan's breath hitched in her chest and she looked down, trying to hide the smile that spread across her face. Emily turned around and placed her hands over her eyes.

"Okay, Susan Gilbert, be dressed in privacy," she exclaimed in a dramatic tone,

Susan smiled now. That was exactly something the old Emily would do. Before she ruined everything. Before everyone ruined everything.

Susan slid the blue dress up over her knees and shoulders. The light blue complimented Susan's dark hair even more so than it did on Emily's auburn-tinted locks.

"I'll need help buttoning it up," Susan remarked.

Emily spun around and gulped slightly at the image of Susan standing in her dress. The sudden realization of their proximity and that they were entirely alone in the house for the first time in their adult lives came flooding into Emily's mind as she stepped toward Susan.

Susan shivered as Emily's warm hands began slowly and carefully fastening each button from the bottom of her spine up towards her shoulders.

"Are you cold?" Emily asked, her breath tickling the back of Susan's neck.

Susan cleared her throat. "No."

"You have goosebumps."

Susan looked down, hiding her face from the mirror. "Must have been a reaction."

"Reaction to what?" Emily asked, continuing to button.

She leaned in closer this time and her breath was so warm on the back of Susan's neck, that it made her entire body feel like it was going to combust right there in the dress.

Susan looked up in the mirror, her eyes locking with Emily's for the first time in what felt like ages. Emily paused as she reached the bottom of Susan's shoulders. Slowly, she reached her hand up to the top of the blue dress and began to trace the lace lining along the top of Susan's shoulders. Susan closed her eyes and titled her head, her heart racing furiously inside her chest.

Emily watched Susan's reaction in the mirror as she continued to trace her fingers around the front of Susan's neck and along her collar bone. Susan's lips parted slightly and she let out a slight gasp. Emily leaned closer now, gently placing her lips on the back of Susan's exposed neck. Susan slowly turned around to face Emily.

She was so close now their breath was interchanging and she could smell the faint remains of lavender and bergamot lingering in the small space between them. Emily began to lean in, but then stopped, afraid to take that final step; afraid to cross that final, thin line they had drawn in the sand.

Susan too contemplated pulling away, in hopes of preserving some shred of future they may have as friends, but it was as if two opposite ends of a magnet had been placed next to one another and she felt herself being drawn in closer to Emily's waiting lips.

She grabbed the back of Emily's neck and pulled her face closer towards her, pausing for a second just before their lips touched.

"Are you sure?" Susan managed to choke out, her breath pouring into Emily's parted mouth.
Emily nodded and Susan finished closing the space between them, her lips landing firmly on Emily's.

Within seconds a frenzy took over them. Emily pulled at the buttons she had just delicately fastened until she felt two of them pop and fall onto the floor. Susan tugged the dress down the remainder of the way and spun Emily around so she could unbutton hers. They had made love many times before, but this time felt different. There was a desperation in both of their hands, a quick need to fulfill some deep seeded need they had both been denying for months.

Before long they fell into Emily's bed, both grasping desperately at one another. Once their undergarments were both off, Emily placed her hands between Susan's legs and instantly they parted for her. Susan let out a loud moan as Emily's hand made its way up her inner thigh to the place only Emily had been before.

"Please," Susan begged.

Emily leaned in, knowing exactly what it was Susan wanted.

***

The next morning Susan rolled over to the sun beaming in through the window and light piercing her eyes. She drew the thin bedsheet around her chest and sat up. Emily sat hunched over her writing desk, furiously scribbling and scratching at the paper, a quilt draped around her otherwise naked body.

Susan propped herself up on her shoulder and watched as Emily continued to write. Her hand moved so furiously; it was a wonder the words would even be legible once she got done putting them down.

After a few moments, Emily looked up from her fury and felt a new set of eyes resting on her.

"Good morning," she said, smiling.

Susan rolled over onto her back and stretched.

"I don't remember your bed being so small."

"That's because usually, you're sneaking out the window by now."

Susan giggled slightly. "That's not true. I've spent plenty of nights in this bed."

"Certainly, when we were children. But I don't think we were doing the same . . . activities back then."

Emily whipped around in her seat, displaying a playful grin. Susan sat up, her dark curls now loose and free around the tips of her shoulders.

"Hold on," Emily said, "don't move."

She stared at Susan for a moment and turned around continuing to scribble.

"So that's your plan then? Just keep me locked in your tower to use as your muse. Use me at night for your devilish delights?" Susan said laying back again, swaying a bare foot out over the edge of the bed.

"I seem to recall that I was not the only one *delighting* last night," Emily said continuing to write, a smirk growing from the visible corner of her mouth.

Susan smiled and rolled over curling up in the sheets so she could watch as Emily wrote.

"You really are talented with your hands, Miss Dickinson."

Emily's head perked up at the innuendo and she smiled broadly before finishing the poem she had been working on.

"I could say the same thing about you – Mrs. Dickinson."

Susan cringed. "Please, don't call me that."

Emily came back to bed and sat beside her. Susan reached out her hand and kissed Emily's fingers one by one.

"And what shall I call you now then? Sister?"

Susan winced again. "Can you not still call me Susan? Or even Sue as you once did?"

"I cannot," Emily said, resting her hand on Susan's face. "It seems you've outgrown that name too now."

"These past six months have been agony without you, I hope you know." Susan said leaning her head into Emily's hand.

"I know," Emily said, "but the truth is, married or not, you will always be mine, first and foremost. And I will always be yours."

Susan kissed Emily's hand and looked down. "I wish I could just marry you."

"Do you mean that?"

Susan nodded. "I do."

"Then, what's stopping us? Come away with me Susan! We can go out west or . . ."

Emily could not even finish the sentence herself. She, the girl who was too afraid to leave the front yard currently, living a life as a pioneer in the wild west. The two of them fighting off Indians and dysentery. The idea ridiculous and they both knew it.

Susan frowned. "If I don't marry Austin, my family will ship me off to Michigan and I'll never see you again."

Emily sighed. "But if you do marry him, what's to say he won't take you away from me anyways?"

"He won't," Susan assured her. "I made a promise, remember? To never be farther than the length of this yard away from you."

Emily laughed slightly remembering the day she had made that silly promise. It was not even a year ago, but somehow it felt like ages had passed between them.

A part of them both felt as if they were finally saying goodbye to the life they had been living for so long. The life they had both been too afraid to enjoy fully. And yet, in many ways, it felt like only the beginning. The beginning of something new and terrifying. Something deeper and more meaningful than what they had ever experienced before. They lay in bed for most of that morning, going between kissing, making love, weeping, laughing, and reminiscing, imagining what would happen when Emily's family returned from Washington - when Austin returned from Washington.

Eventually, they both decided it was time to get dressed and eat something of substance. Susan wore another one of Emily's gowns, this one light pink with frills at the top of the sleeves. Emily donned a simple, white morning dress with a large collar that folded down flat against her collarbone. It had no room for undergarments of any kind and simply went straight down to the floor. It was so white that Emily almost glowed.

"That's not a dress," Susan said observing the plain ensemble. "You look like a specter."

"It is a morning dress!" Emily protested.

Susan rolled her eyes. "It's a frock," she retorted.

"Dress," Emily sniped back playfully. "And besides, who needs a corset when you plan on taking it off of me later anyways?" Emily said, bumping into Susan gently.

As they made their way downstairs, there was a knock at the door. Emily swung it open to find George Gould, hat in hand and his usual optimistic smile plastered across his face.

"Good day, ladies. I've come to pay a visit and - "

"George!" Emily exclaimed. "George, you are just the person we wanted to see."

"I am?" Inquired George.

"He is?" Asked Susan.

Emily nodded rapidly, peering out the front door. The sun had not set yet and from her estimation, they had about two hours or so before it finally dipped down permanently. Emily darted back into her father's library and returned with a large leather-bound book tucked beneath her arm.

"Come with me," Emily said wildly, "we haven't got much time!"

Emily shot out of the front door and made a right turn towards the woods. The familiar path taken by Emily and Susan for so many years was now worn down with use.

Susan and George exchanged a confused glance but followed anyways. Carlo followed as well, his long fur flowing in the wind as they all ran. Emily led them frantically along the river which was still roaring from the late spring thaw. Finally, she paused at the place – their place – by the river, under the maple tree.

It was the place where they first kissed as teenagers. The place where they literally ran into each other when Susan moved back from New York. The place they shared their first, true adult kiss. The place where Susan told Emily about William's gambling debts. The place they first said I love you to one another. The place where they first made love. This was a sacred place for Emily and Susan. A place only they knew.

Emily held out her hand and Susan looked at Emily and then at George before cautiously taking it. Then she removed the large book from under her arm and handed it to George.

He looked down at the cover for the first time. A gold inscription with the words, "Holy Bible," was engrained into its worn cover.

"George," Emily said decidedly, "marry us."

***

Later that night, Emily fell asleep with Susan in her arms, listening to the steady, rhythmic beating of her heart. She dreamt of them running through tall wheat fields across the prairies out west. She dreamt of them collecting shells and holding hands as they walked along the endless, crashing shoreline of New England. She dreamt of the countless travels they would have together to exotic places like Paris, Rome and Madrid. She dreamt of them growing old together, raising a family together, and falling asleep together just like this every night.

She did not know what would happen when Austin returned, or what their future held. But now, if only for tonight, she dreamt.

Epilogue

November 1855

Edward Dickinson burst through the front door of the Mansion.

"Children! Mrs. Dickinson!" He shouted.

Immediately the three women came running into the room.

"What is it?" Mrs. Dickinson asked.

"I've done it! I've bought back the old Dickinson Homestead! It went on the market just this week and I bought it. We're going home!"

A few days later, when the carriage pulled up to the dense, unsightly house, Emily cringed. She hated every part of it. The bulkiness of its stature, the way it sat so close to Main Street, how far away it was from her beloved cemetery. There was no orchard in the backyard, no mighty oak tree growing in the front. The worst part was that it was farther away from where Susan lived, even though it was technically on the same street. There would be no more sneaking off into the woods to see one another in this new house. This big yellow house was not her home. It never would be.

Reluctantly, Emily climbed the long stairs and found a room with a fireplace in it, claiming it to be her own before Vinnie could proffer an opinion. It was the window she loved. It overlooked a large collection of trees and a space where a new house was being built.

"Perfect. Neighbors." Emily sighed looking down at Carlo.

The last thing she wanted was to be so close to strangers that she could practically see through their window. She reached down and patted Carlo on the head. Her most loyal companion, he now had several grey whiskers and his gait was a little slower, but still, he stayed by her side.

"Emily?" A familiar voice echoed from downstairs.

It was Austin. Emily walked down the stairs and saw Austin and Susan standing at the bottom of the steps.

"Good morrow, Oliver," Emily said reaching up to mess with Austin's hair.

He leaned back thwarting her advances but smiled. Susan and Austin had been engaged for over two years now, and still, there was no wedding date in sight. Emily knew Susan was just prolonging the inevitable, but still, Emily made it a point to wear the white dress she had worn in the woods with Susan last summer nearly every time she saw her. She knew Susan hated it, but it was her way of showing Susan that in her mind, it didn't matter who she married. She belonged to Emily and Emily belonged to her. It would be that way forever now. They had made sure of that before George Gould, Carlo, the bees, and the butterflies.

"Susan has something she'd like to show you," Austin said motioning towards the door.

They walked out onto the large front porch of the new house and down the steps, making their way in the general direction of the construction next door. Emily wrapped the green shawl from Susan tighter around her neck. It was worn out now from so much use, but still, she refused to wear any other.

"Do you see that house right there?" Susan began.

Emily nodded. "The Italian style eye sore? Who could miss it? Why?"

Susan smiled. "It's ours. Me and Austin's. Your father is having it built for us as a wedding present."

Emily's jaw dropped. "Wait, you mean . . .?"

"I told you I'd never live far from you, Emily Dickinson. And I intend on keeping that promise."

Emily slid her arms around Susan's waist, inhaling the warm scent of her perfume. She clung to her for as long as she could until Austin exited the large house and looked on at them briefly before returning to the warmth of the indoors.

He never lingered when they were alone together, a courtesy that made both of them grateful.

Emily marched over to where the brown weeds and garden were overgrown between the two patches of land and began marching back and forth repeatedly, mechanically stomping her feet like a soldier.

"What on Earth are you doing?" Susan shouted smiling, smoke billowing from her mouth as she exhaled.

"Making us a new path!" Emily replied. "We have to have a way to go see each other whenever we want."

"It's not exactly wide enough to be a path, is it?" Susan hollered as Emily marched on.

Emily shook her head. "Sure, it is! In fact, it's just wide enough for two who love."

Photographs

"The Mansion" on North Pleasant Street.
The house is no longer standing.

South Hadley Female Seminary in Holyoke.
Now known as Mt. Holyoke College

Emily Elizabeth Dickinson

Susan Gilbert Dickinson

William Austin Dickinson

Lavinia "Vinnie" Dickinson

Edward Dickinson

Emily Norcross Dickinson

George Gould

A Newfoundland dog, the same breed as Carlo.

About the Author

Kacey is a licensed attorney living in Boston, Massachusetts. She is the owner and founder of Gender Traitor, a small business dedicated to helping individuals "live life label free." In her spare time, she can be found volunteering at Minute Man National Park, hiking, riding her bike, traveling, or visiting beautiful historic homes, just like Emily's.

GenderTraitorShop.com

Made in United States
North Haven, CT
14 November 2022